THE ADVENTURES OF DANIEL BOOM A.K.A. LOUD BOY

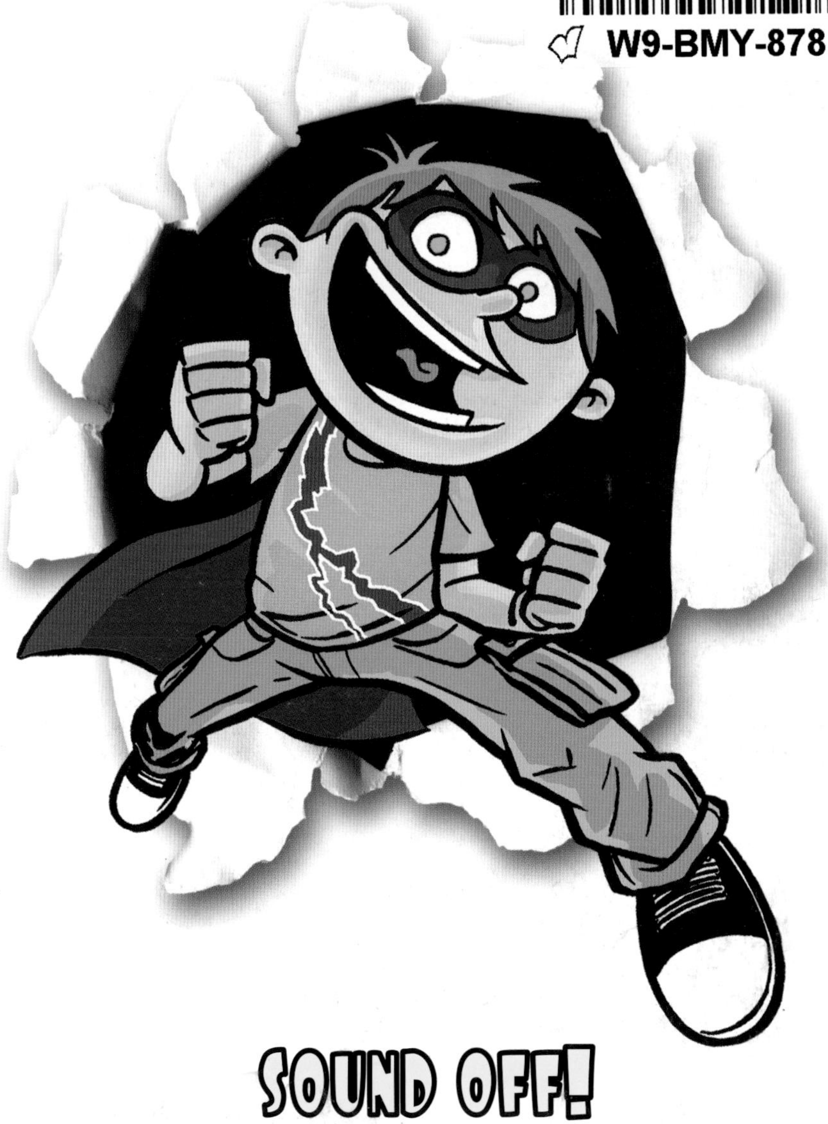

SOUND OFF!

WRITTEN BY D. J. STEINBERG

ILLUSTRATED BY BRIAN SMITH

GROSSET & DUNLAP

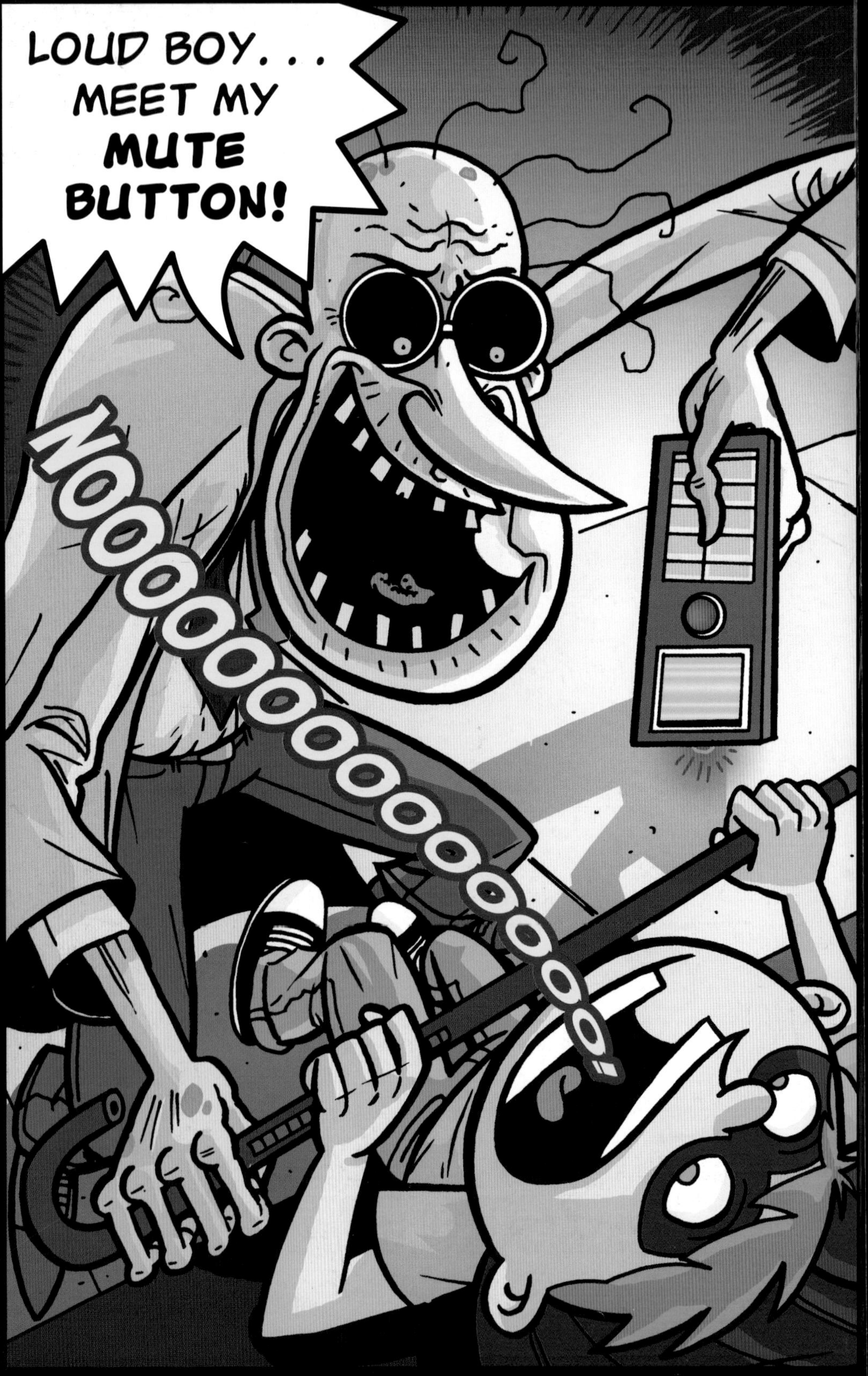
LOUD BOY. . . MEET MY **MUTE BUTTON!**
NOOOOOOOOOOOOOOO!

Will Old Fogey silence Loud Boy forever?

Have we heard the last

from our high-decibel hero?

Will Loud Boy be—EXCUSE ME?

What's that?

You don't KNOW who LOUD BOY is?

Okay, cut! Hit the rewind button.

Let's go back, WAY back to the beginning . . .

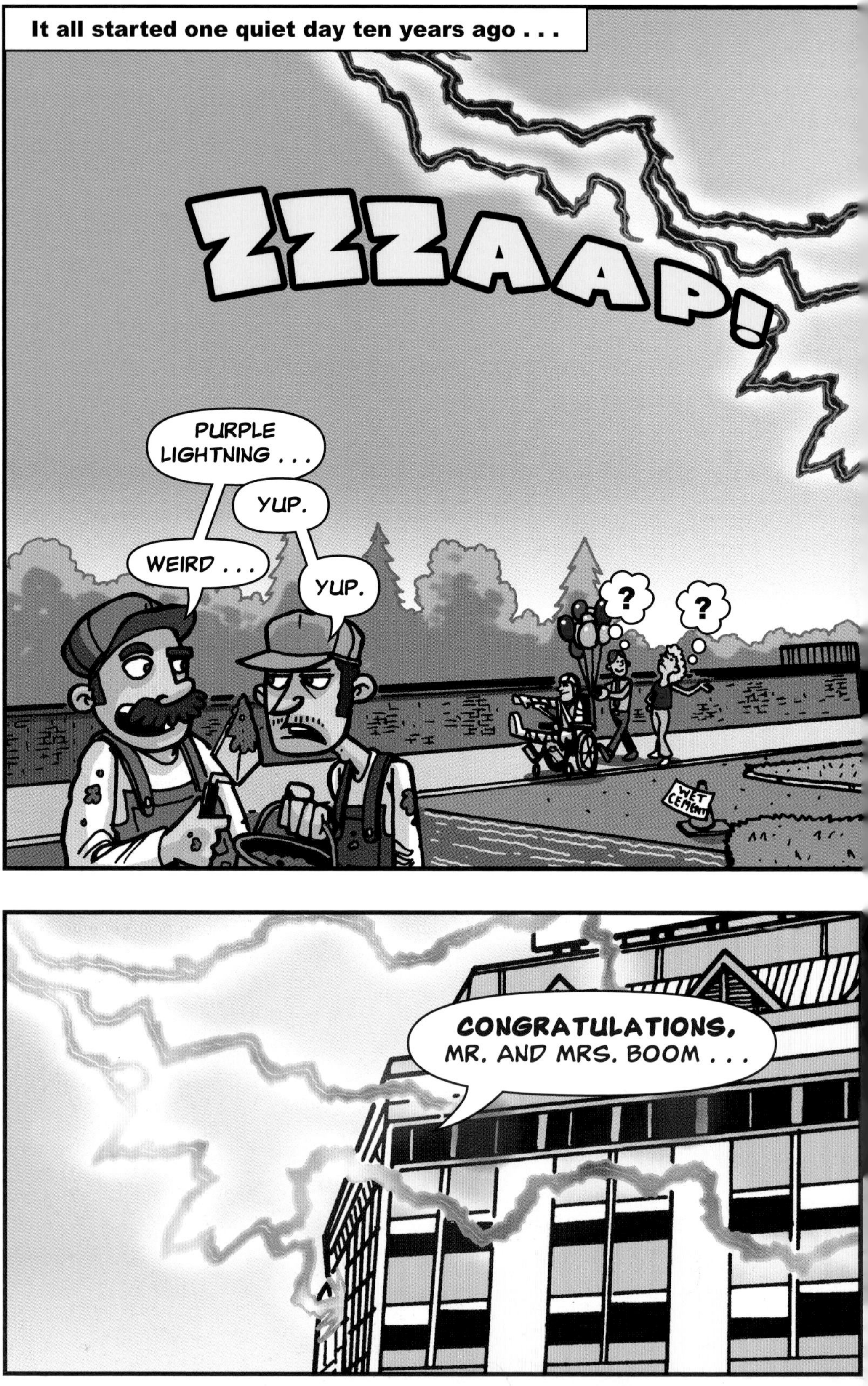
It all started one quiet day ten years ago . . .
ZZZAAAP!
PURPLE LIGHTNING . . .
YUP.
WEIRD . . .
YUP.
?
?
WET CEMENT
CONGRATULATIONS, MR. AND MRS. BOOM . . .

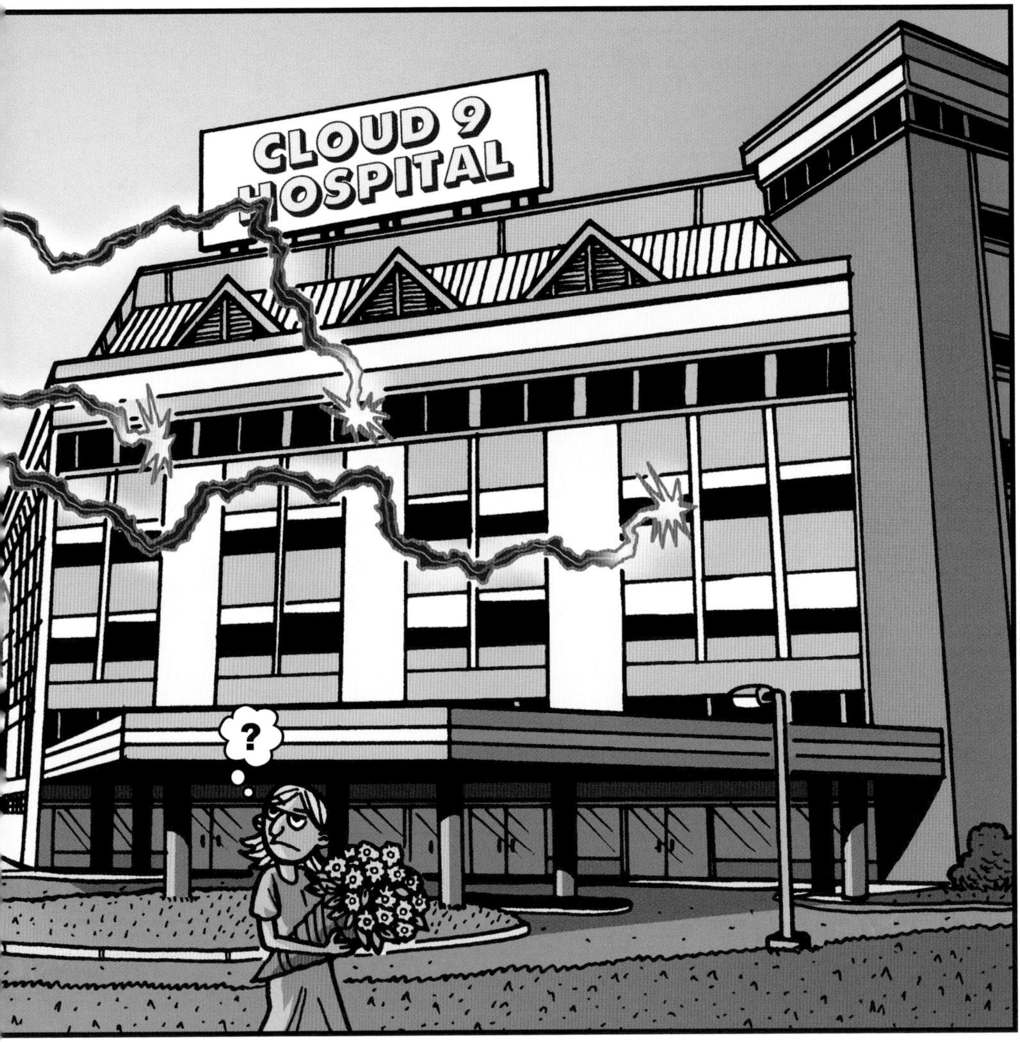

CLOUD 9 HOSPITAL
?

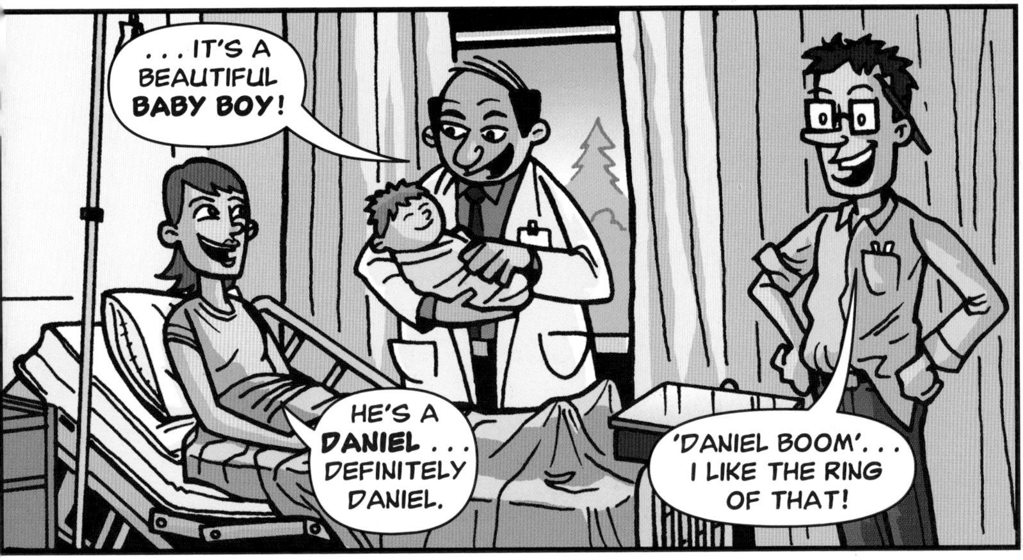

. . . IT'S A BEAUTIFUL BABY BOY!
HE'S A DANIEL . . . DEFINITELY DANIEL.
'DANIEL BOOM'. . . I LIKE THE RING OF THAT!

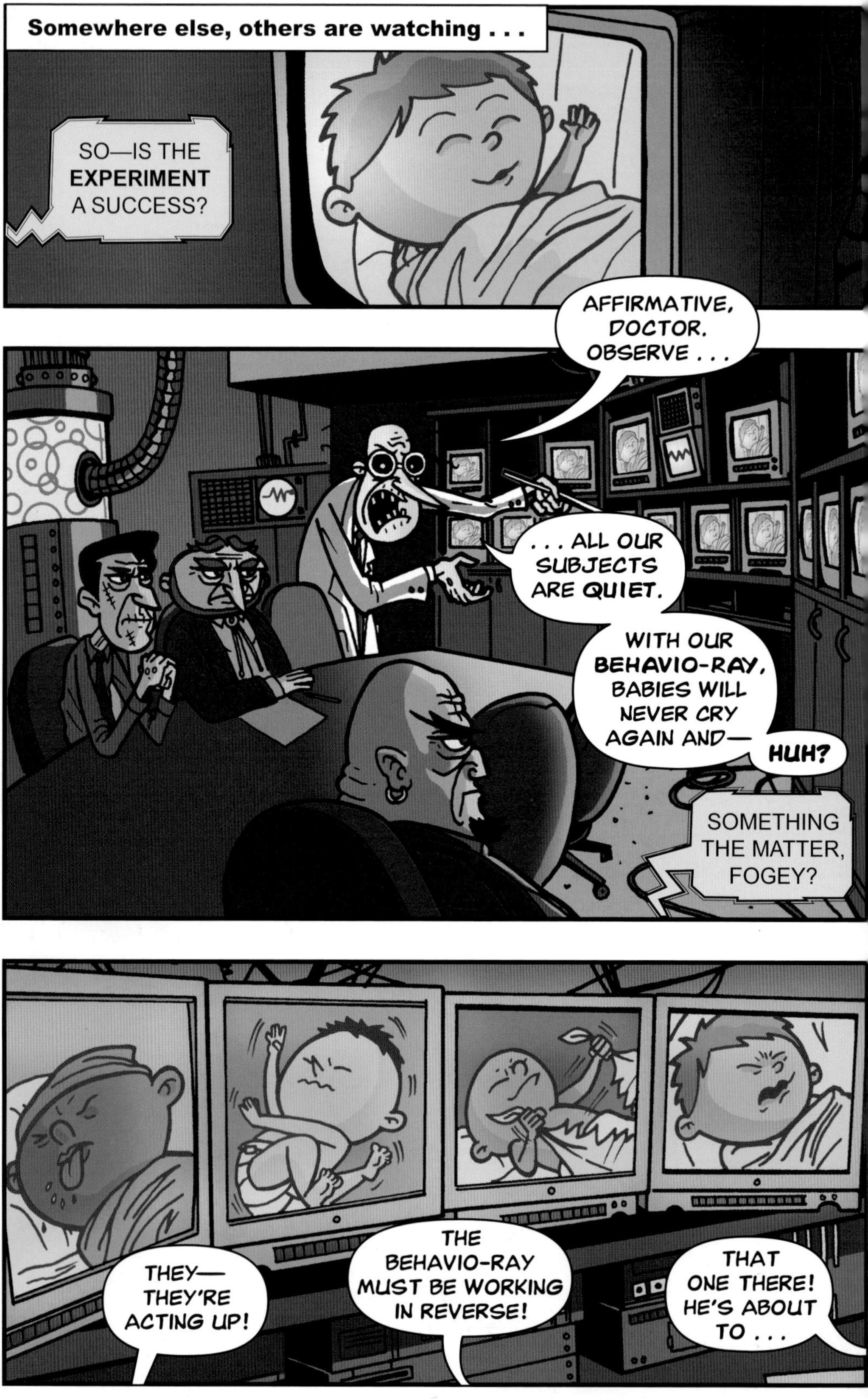
Somewhere else, others are watching . . .
SO—IS THE EXPERIMENT A SUCCESS?
AFFIRMATIVE, DOCTOR. OBSERVE . . .
. . . ALL OUR SUBJECTS ARE QUIET.
WITH OUR BEHAVIO-RAY, BABIES WILL NEVER CRY AGAIN AND—
HUH?
SOMETHING THE MATTER, FOGEY?
THEY— THEY'RE ACTING UP!
THE BEHAVIO-RAY MUST BE WORKING IN REVERSE!
THAT ONE THERE! HE'S ABOUT TO . . .

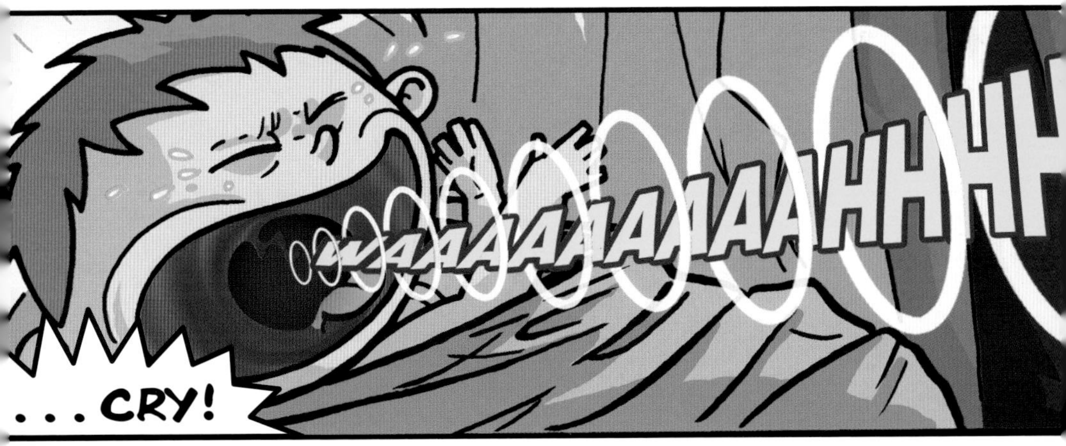
WAAAAAAAAAAAHHH
. . . CRY!

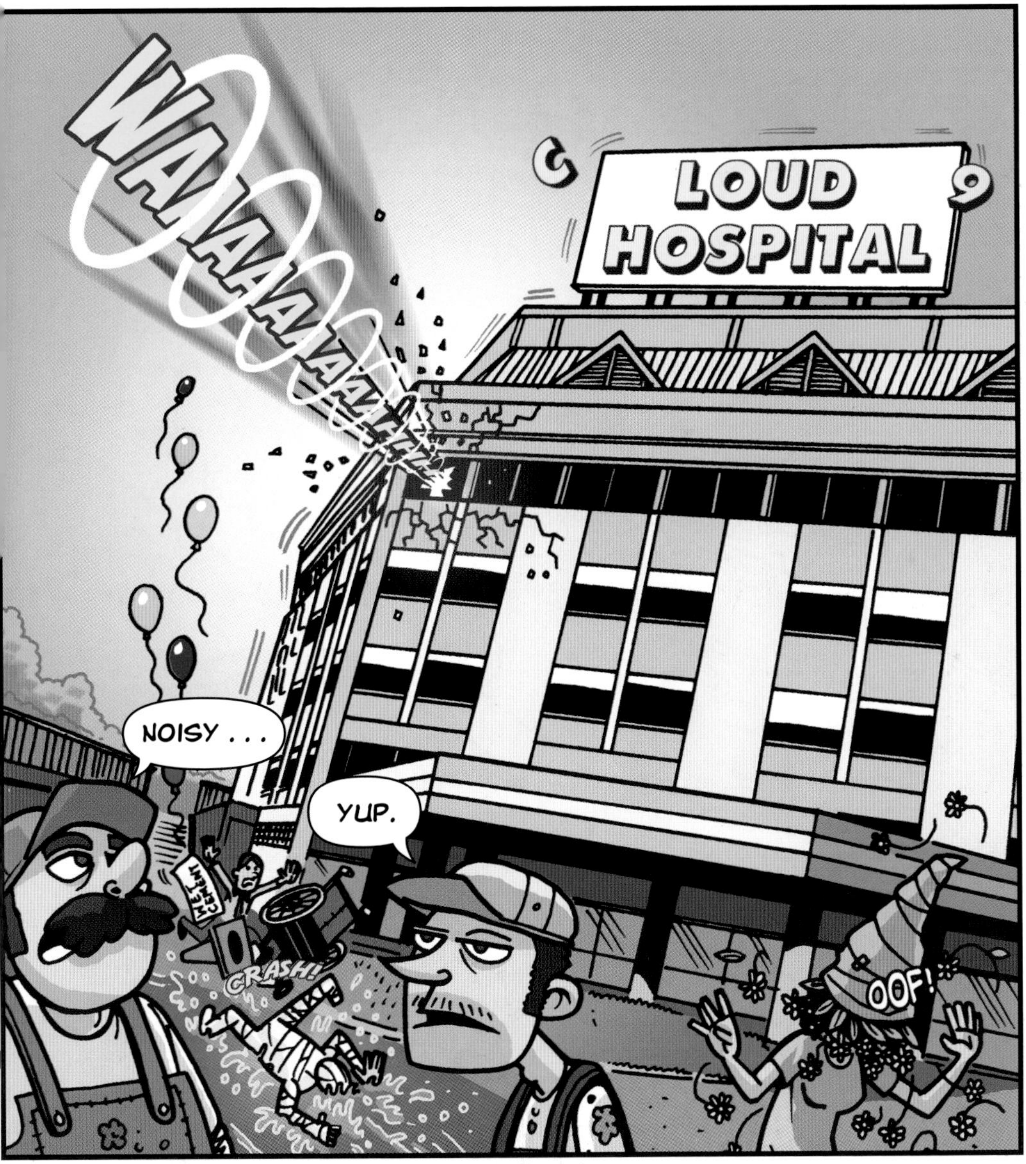
WAAAAAAAAH
LOUD HOSPITAL
NOISY . . .
YUP.
WET CEMENT
CRASH!
OOF!

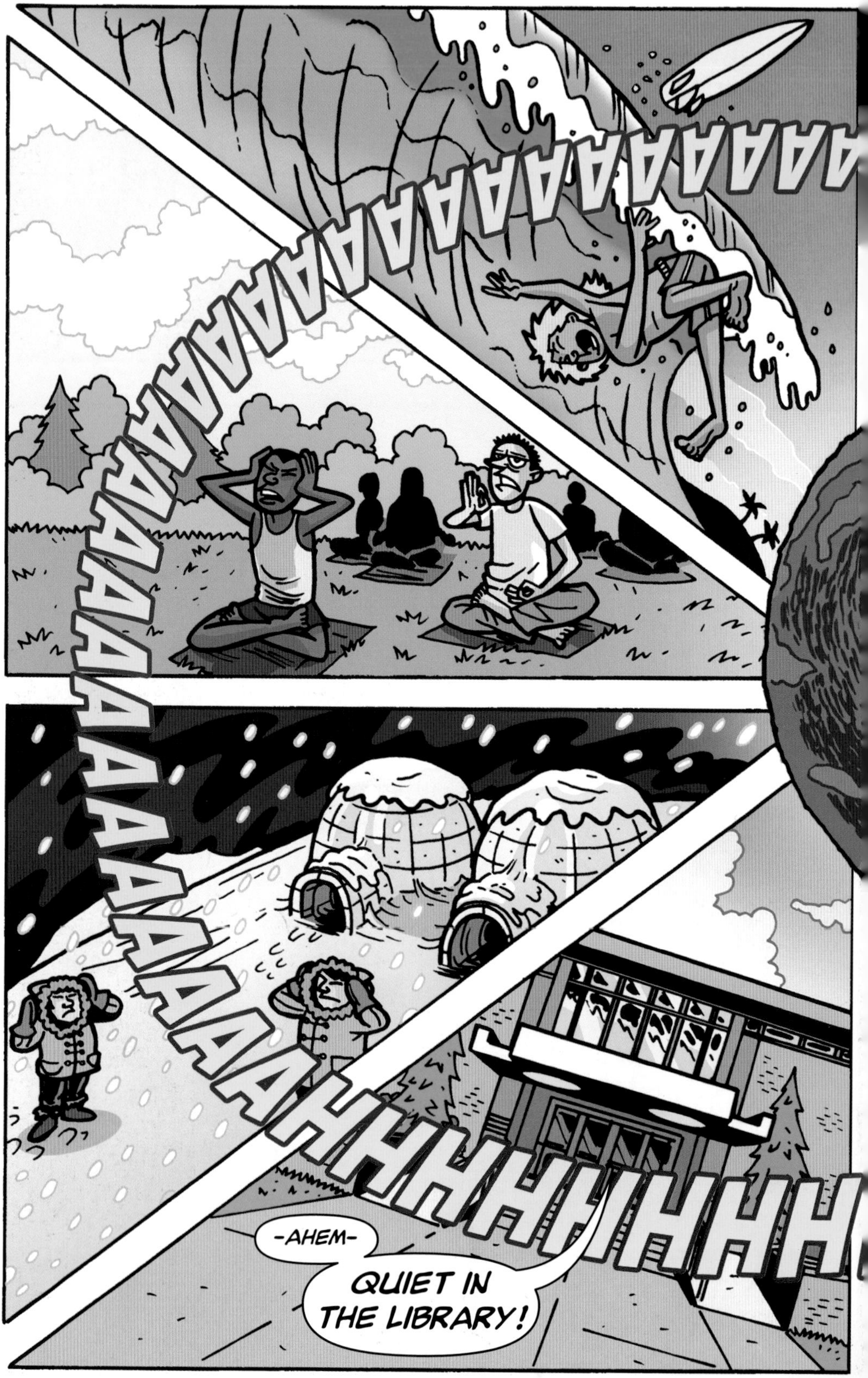
AAAAAAAAAAAAAAAAAAAAAAAAAAAAAAAAAAAAAAAHHHHHHHHHHH!
-AHEM-
QUIET IN THE LIBRARY!

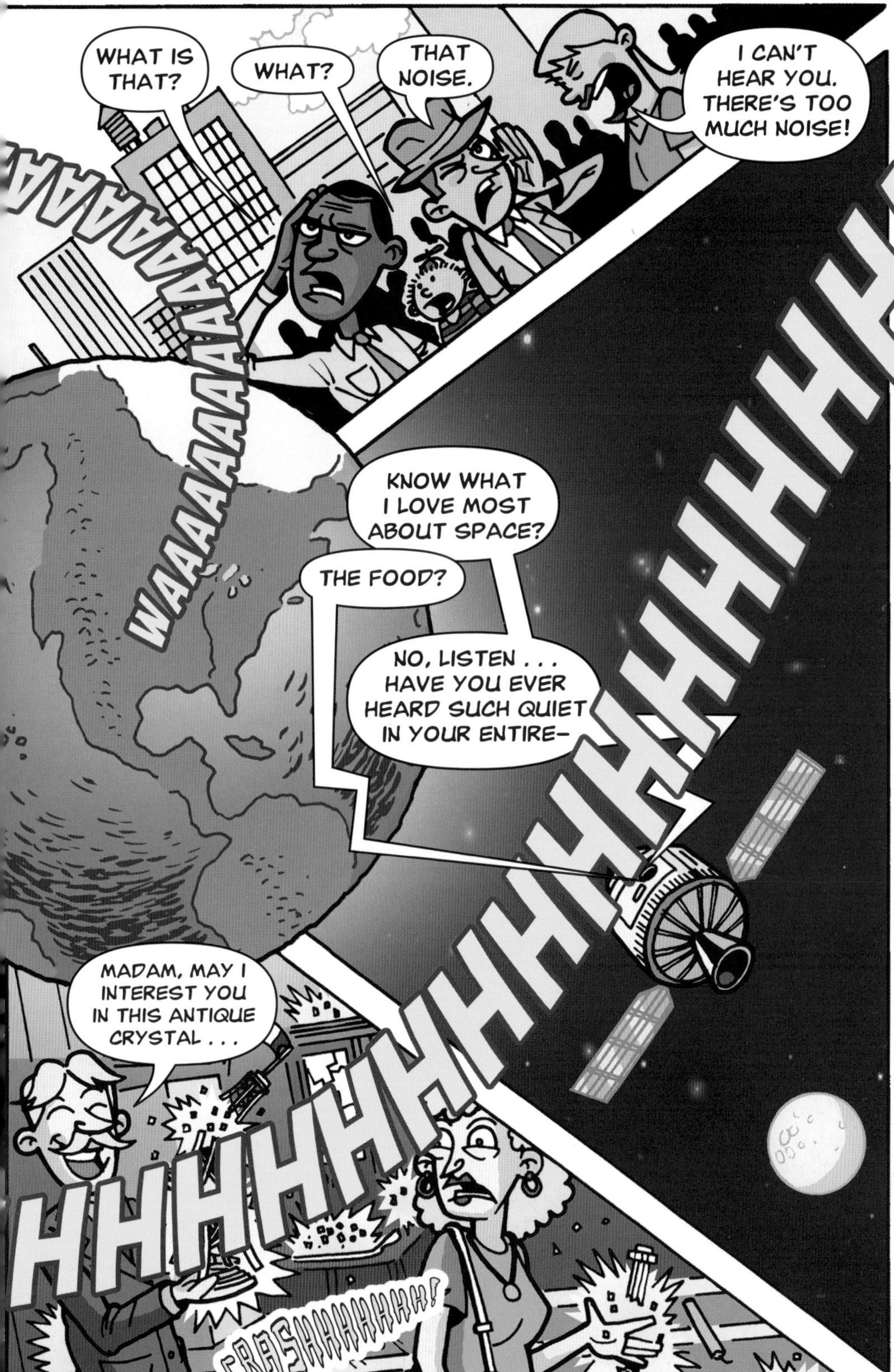
WHAT IS THAT?
WHAT?
THAT NOISE.
I CAN'T HEAR YOU. THERE'S TOO MUCH NOISE!
WAAAAAAAAAAAAAAA
KNOW WHAT I LOVE MOST ABOUT SPACE?
THE FOOD?
NO, LISTEN . . . HAVE YOU EVER HEARD SUCH QUIET IN YOUR ENTIRE–
HHHHHHHHHHHHHHHHHHHH
MADAM, MAY I INTEREST YOU IN THIS ANTIQUE CRYSTAL . . .
CRASHHHHHHHH!

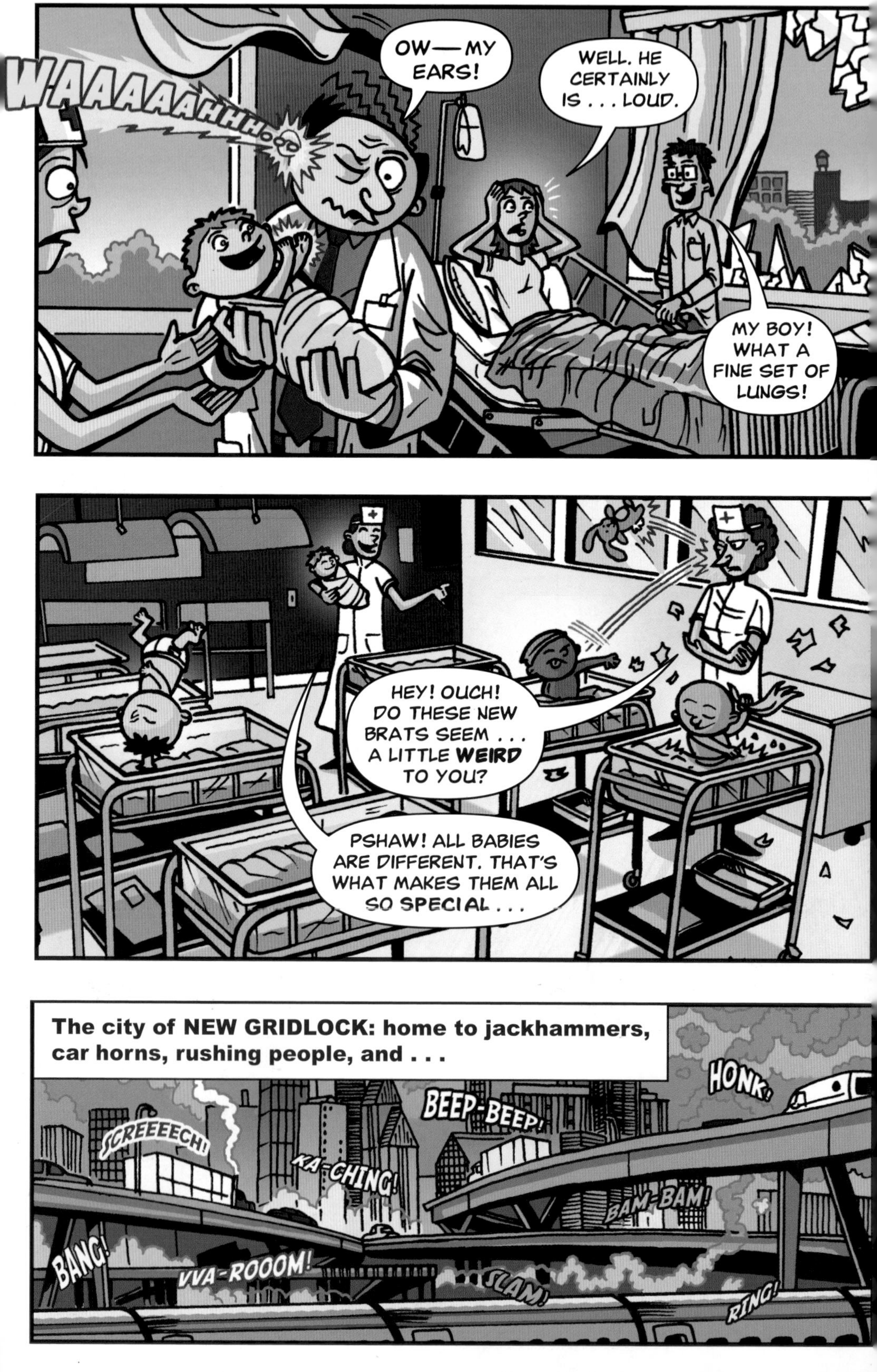
WAAAAAAHHHH
OW—MY EARS!
WELL. HE CERTAINLY IS . . . LOUD.
MY BOY! WHAT A FINE SET OF LUNGS!
HEY! OUCH! DO THESE NEW BRATS SEEM . . . A LITTLE WEIRD TO YOU?
PSHAW! ALL BABIES ARE DIFFERENT. THAT'S WHAT MAKES THEM ALL SO SPECIAL . . .
The city of NEW GRIDLOCK: home to jackhammers, car horns, rushing people, and . . .
HONK!
BEEP-BEEP!
SCREEEECH!
KA-CHING!
BAM-BAM!
BANG!
VVA-ROOOM!
SLAM!
RING!

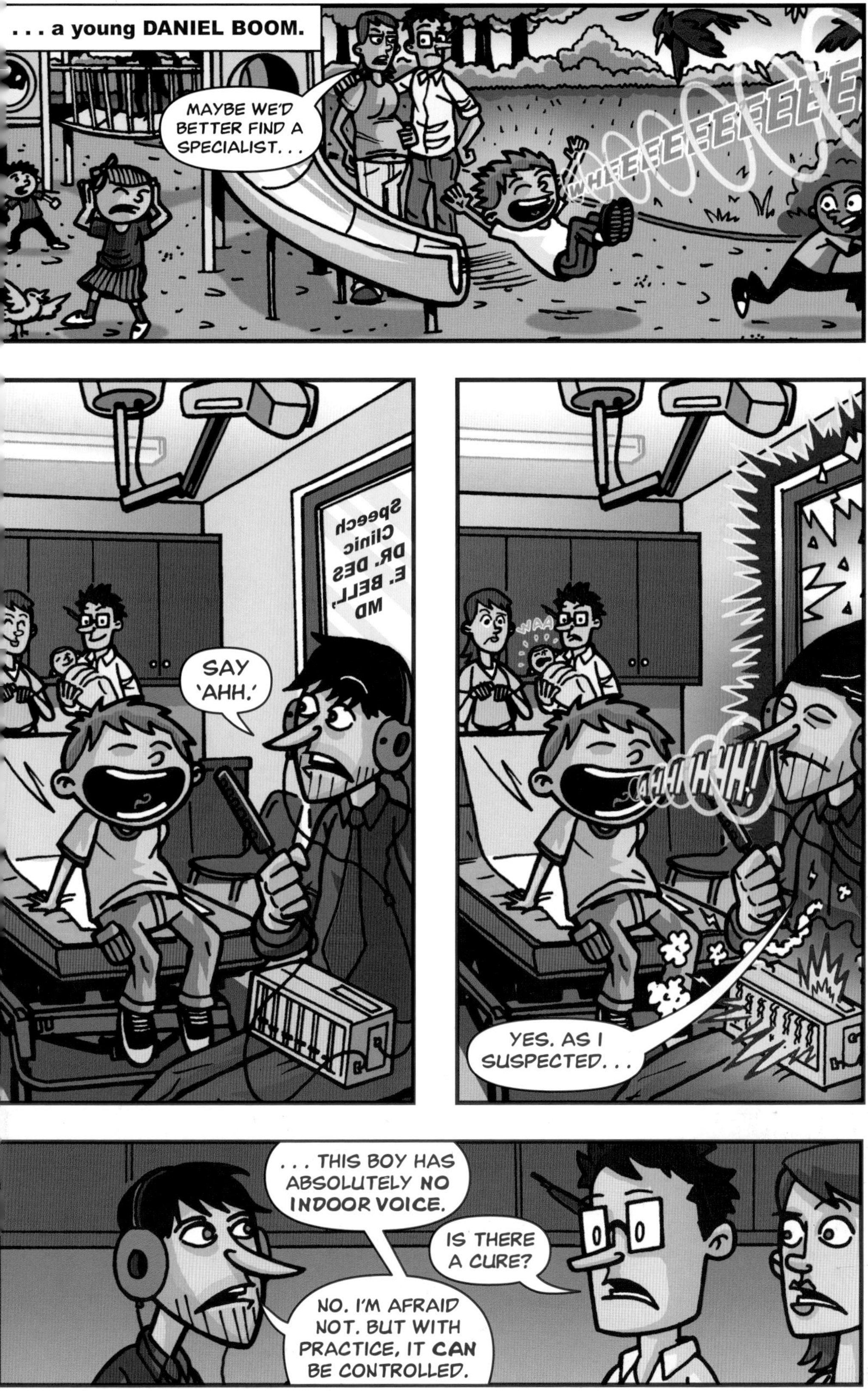
. . . a young DANIEL BOOM.
MAYBE WE'D BETTER FIND A SPECIALIST. . .
WHEEEEEEEEEE
Speech Clinic DR. DES E. BELL, MD
SAY 'AHH.'
WAA
AHHHHHH!
YES. AS I SUSPECTED. . .
. . . THIS BOY HAS ABSOLUTELY NO INDOOR VOICE.
IS THERE A CURE?
NO. I'M AFRAID NOT. BUT WITH PRACTICE, IT CAN BE CONTROLLED.

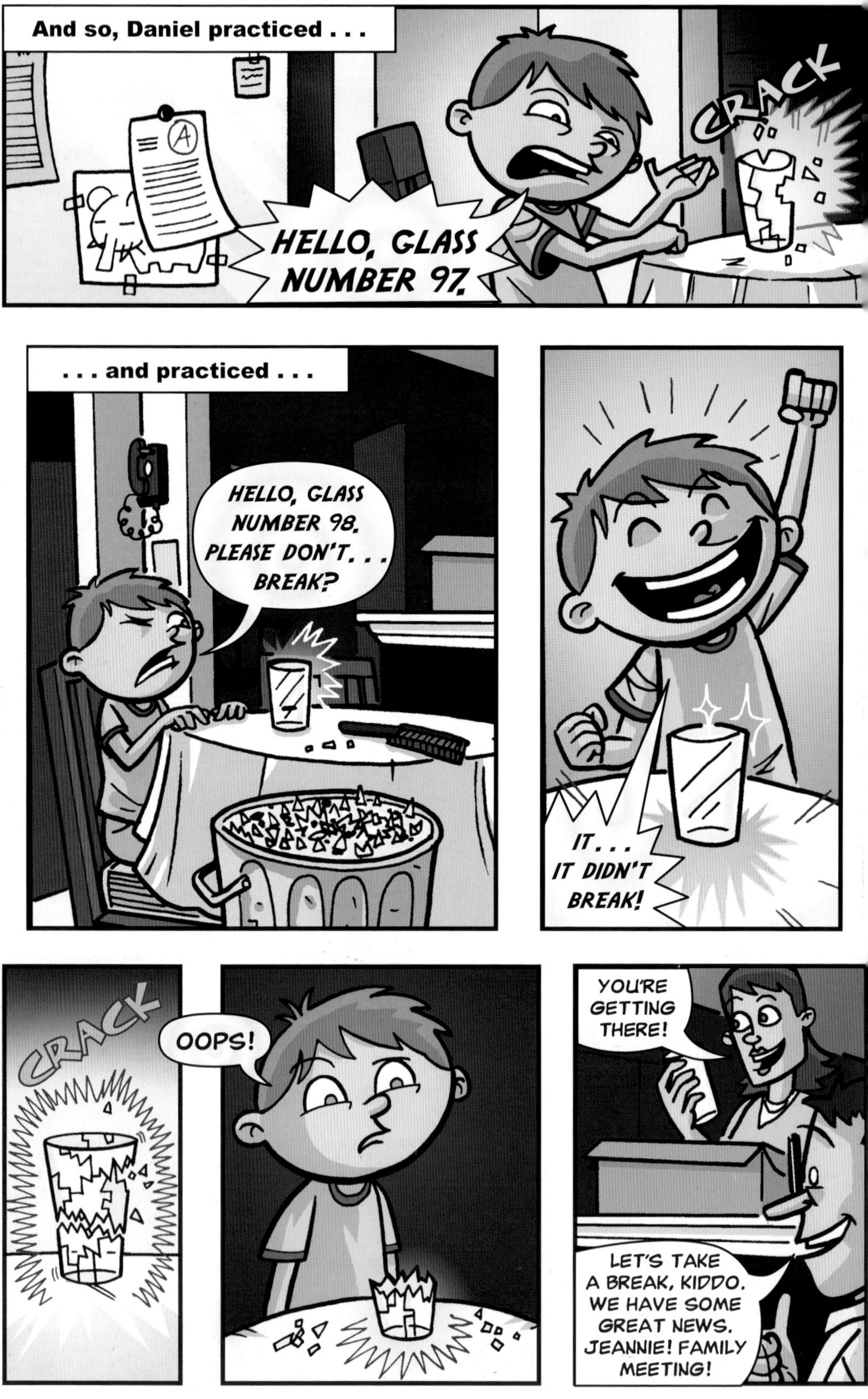
And so, Daniel practiced . . .
CRACK
HELLO, GLASS NUMBER 97.
. . . and practiced . . .
HELLO, GLASS NUMBER 98. PLEASE DON'T. . . BREAK?
IT. . . IT DIDN'T BREAK!
CRACK
OOPS!
YOU'RE GETTING THERE!
LET'S TAKE A BREAK, KIDDO. WE HAVE SOME GREAT NEWS. JEANNIE! FAMILY MEETING!

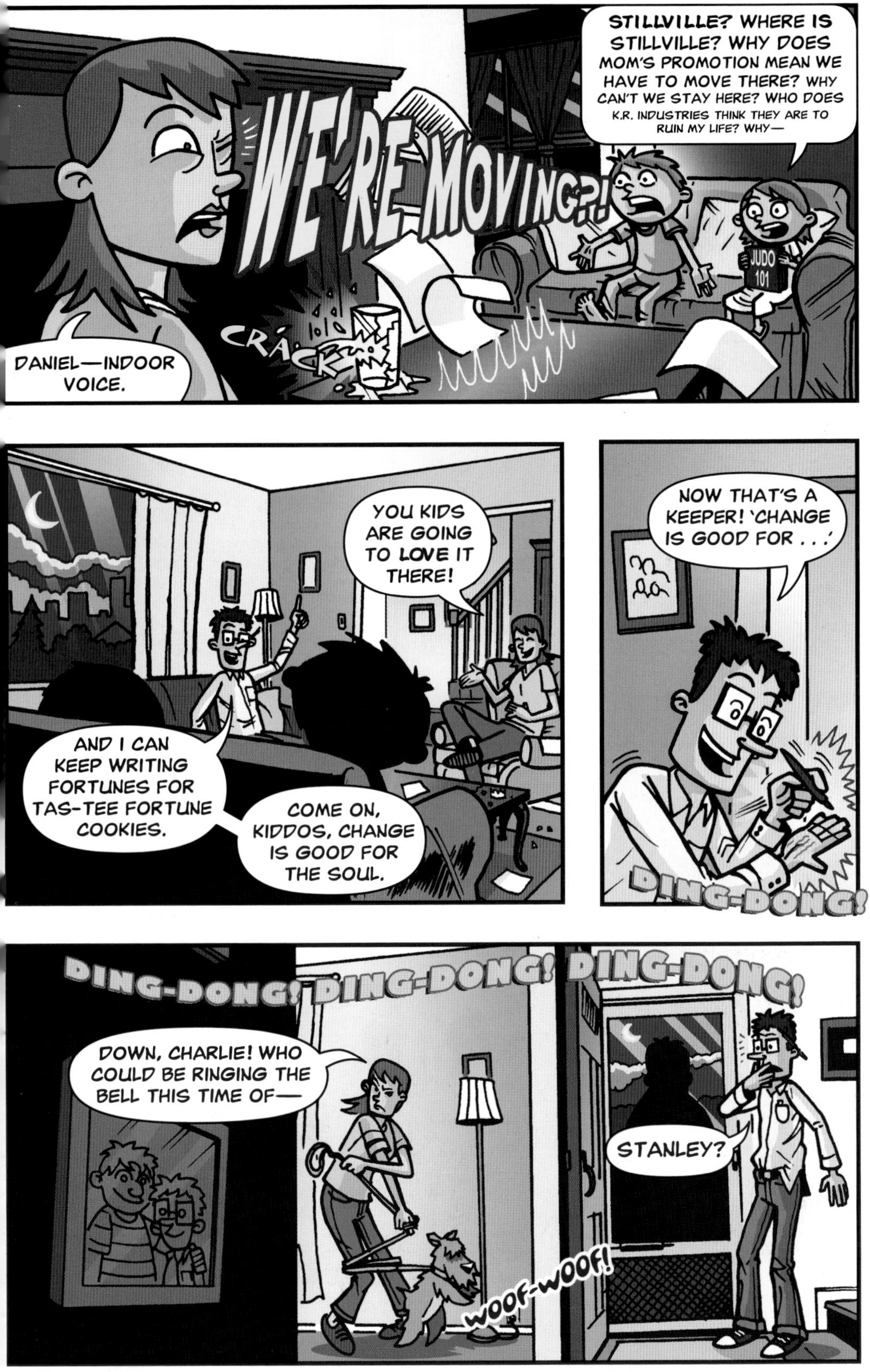
WE'RE MOVING?!
STILLVILLE? WHERE IS STILLVILLE? WHY DOES MOM'S PROMOTION MEAN WE HAVE TO MOVE THERE? WHY CAN'T WE STAY HERE? WHO DOES K.R. INDUSTRIES THINK THEY ARE TO RUIN MY LIFE? WHY—
JUDO 101
DANIEL—INDOOR VOICE.
CRACK
YOU KIDS ARE GOING TO LOVE IT THERE!
AND I CAN KEEP WRITING FORTUNES FOR TAS-TEE FORTUNE COOKIES.
COME ON, KIDDOS, CHANGE IS GOOD FOR THE SOUL.
NOW THAT'S A KEEPER! 'CHANGE IS GOOD FOR . . .'
DING-DONG!
DING-DONG! DING-DONG! DING-DONG!
DOWN, CHARLIE! WHO COULD BE RINGING THE BELL THIS TIME OF—
STANLEY?
WOOF-WOOF!

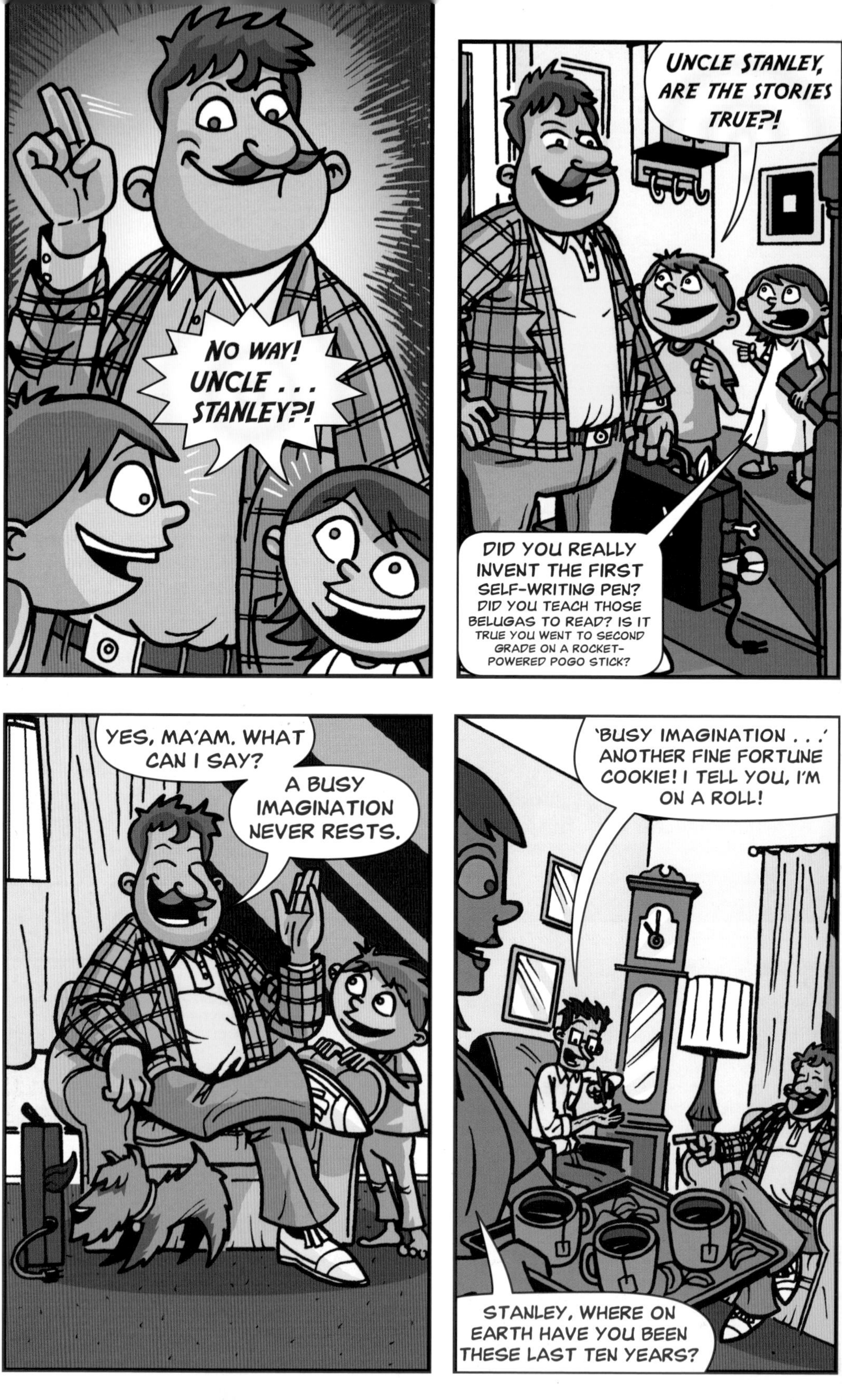
NO WAY! UNCLE . . . STANLEY?!
UNCLE STANLEY, ARE THE STORIES TRUE?!
DID YOU REALLY INVENT THE FIRST SELF-WRITING PEN? DID YOU TEACH THOSE BELUGAS TO READ? IS IT TRUE YOU WENT TO SECOND GRADE ON A ROCKET-POWERED POGO STICK?
YES, MA'AM. WHAT CAN I SAY?
A BUSY IMAGINATION NEVER RESTS.
'BUSY IMAGINATION . . .' ANOTHER FINE FORTUNE COOKIE! I TELL YOU, I'M ON A ROLL!
STANLEY, WHERE ON EARTH HAVE YOU BEEN THESE LAST TEN YEARS?

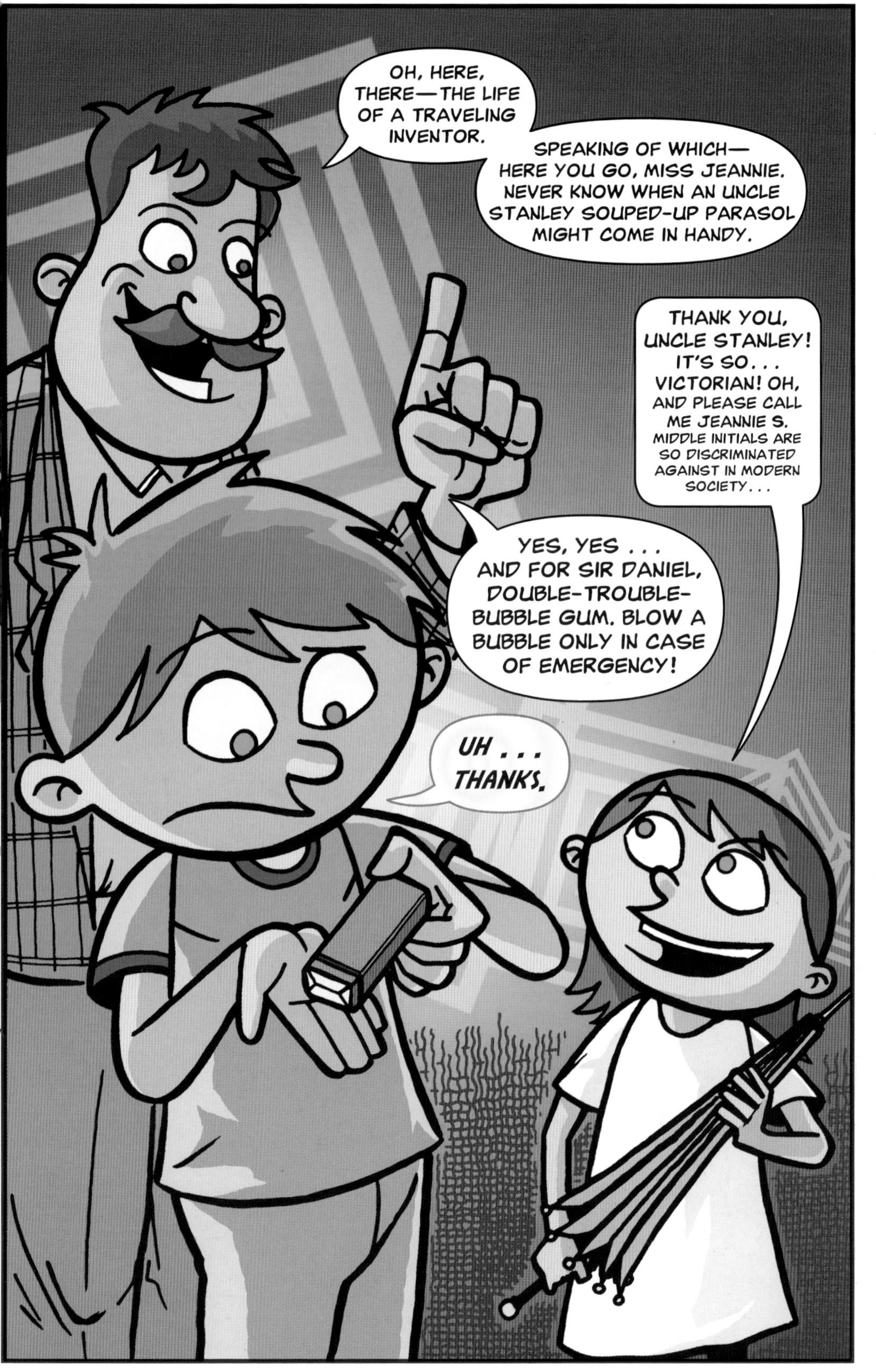
OH, HERE, THERE—THE LIFE OF A TRAVELING INVENTOR.
SPEAKING OF WHICH—HERE YOU GO, MISS JEANNIE. NEVER KNOW WHEN AN UNCLE STANLEY SOUPED-UP PARASOL MIGHT COME IN HANDY.
THANK YOU, UNCLE STANLEY! IT'S SO . . . VICTORIAN! OH, AND PLEASE CALL ME JEANNIE S. MIDDLE INITIALS ARE SO DISCRIMINATED AGAINST IN MODERN SOCIETY . . .
YES, YES . . . AND FOR SIR DANIEL, DOUBLE-TROUBLE-BUBBLE GUM. BLOW A BUBBLE ONLY IN CASE OF EMERGENCY!
UH . . . THANKS.

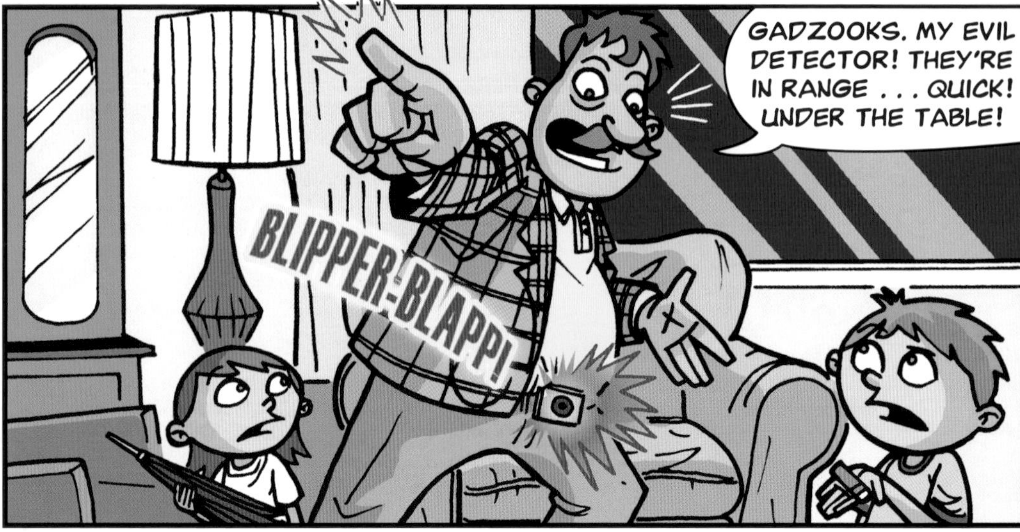
GADZOOKS. MY EVIL DETECTOR! THEY'RE IN RANGE . . . QUICK! UNDER THE TABLE!
BLIPPER-BLAPP!

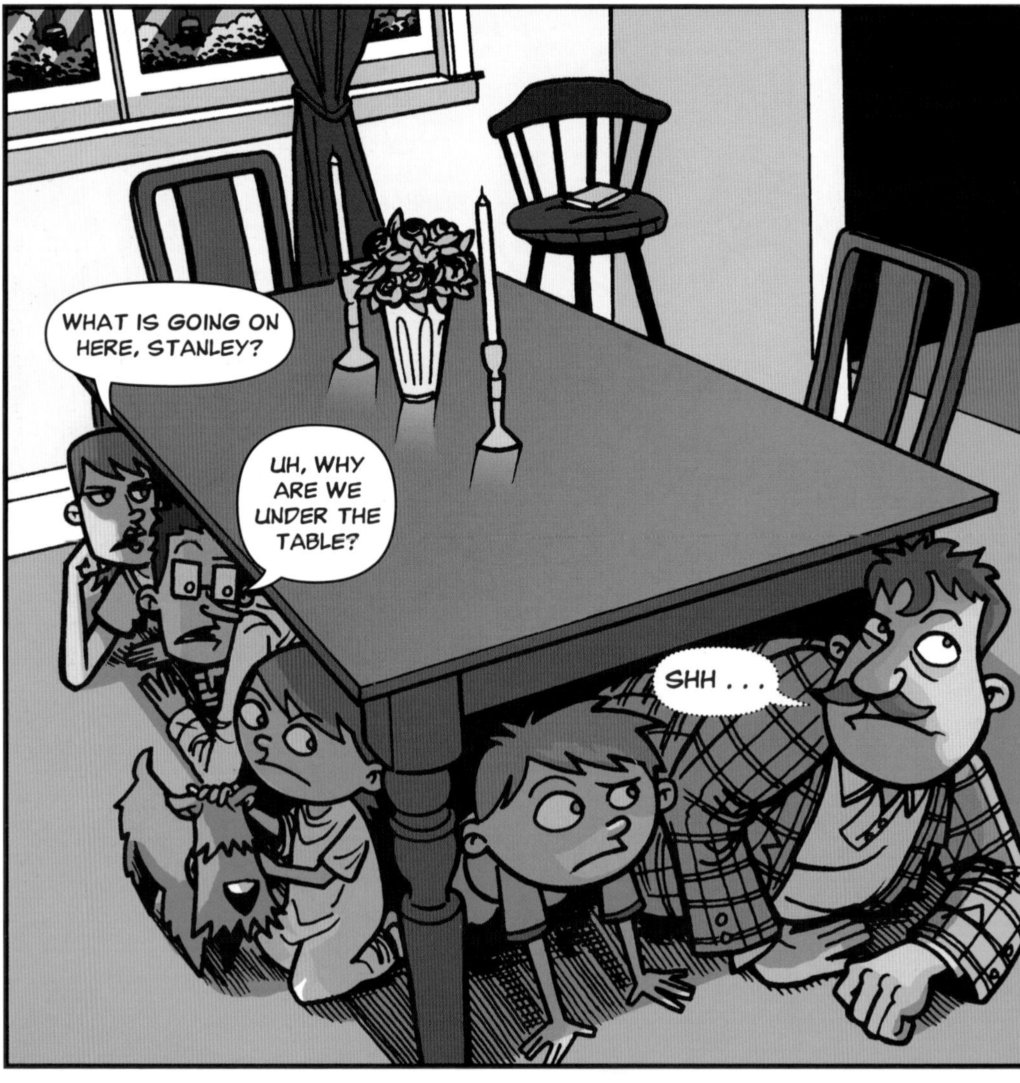
WHAT IS GOING ON HERE, STANLEY?
UH, WHY ARE WE UNDER THE TABLE?
SHH . . .

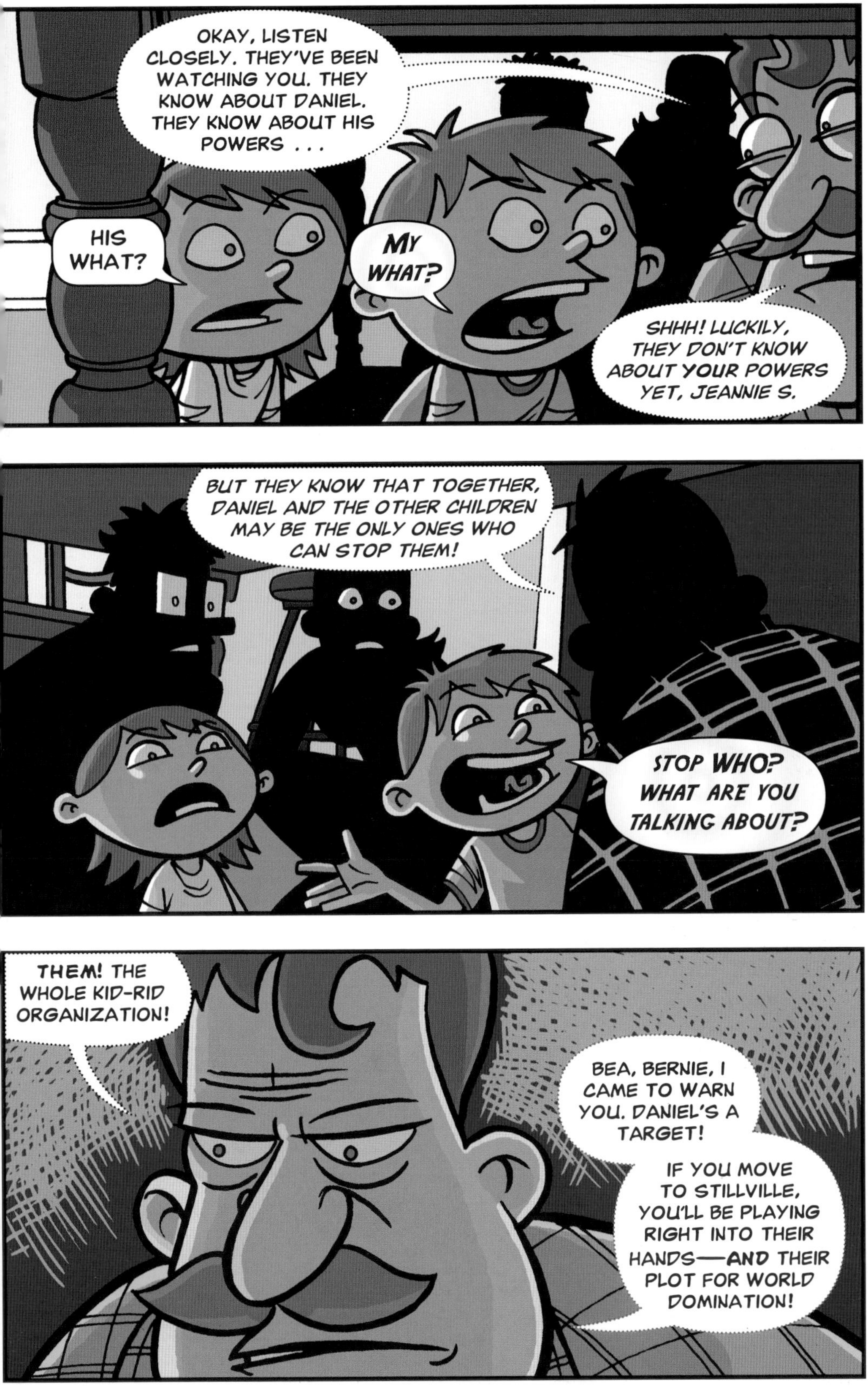
OKAY, LISTEN CLOSELY. THEY'VE BEEN WATCHING YOU. THEY KNOW ABOUT DANIEL. THEY KNOW ABOUT HIS POWERS . . .
HIS WHAT?
MY WHAT?
SHHH! LUCKILY, THEY DON'T KNOW ABOUT YOUR POWERS YET, JEANNIE S.
BUT THEY KNOW THAT TOGETHER, DANIEL AND THE OTHER CHILDREN MAY BE THE ONLY ONES WHO CAN STOP THEM!
STOP WHO? WHAT ARE YOU TALKING ABOUT?
THEM! THE WHOLE KID-RID ORGANIZATION!
BEA, BERNIE, I CAME TO WARN YOU. DANIEL'S A TARGET!
IF YOU MOVE TO STILLVILLE, YOU'LL BE PLAYING RIGHT INTO THEIR HANDS—AND THEIR PLOT FOR WORLD DOMINATION!

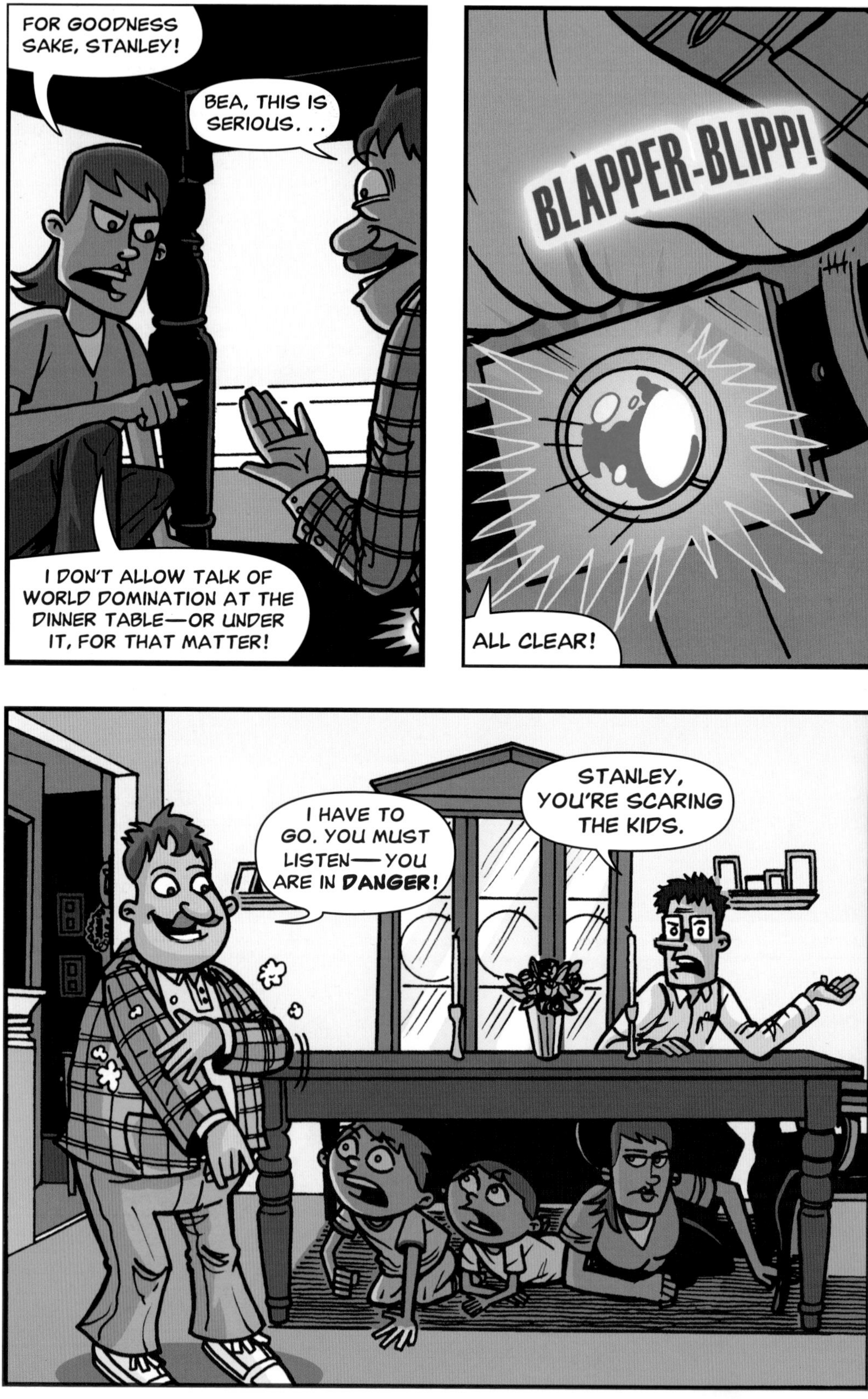
FOR GOODNESS SAKE, STANLEY!
BEA, THIS IS SERIOUS. . .
I DON'T ALLOW TALK OF WORLD DOMINATION AT THE DINNER TABLE—OR UNDER IT, FOR THAT MATTER!
BLAPPER-BLIPP!
ALL CLEAR!
I HAVE TO GO. YOU MUST LISTEN—YOU ARE IN DANGER!
STANLEY, YOU'RE SCARING THE KIDS.

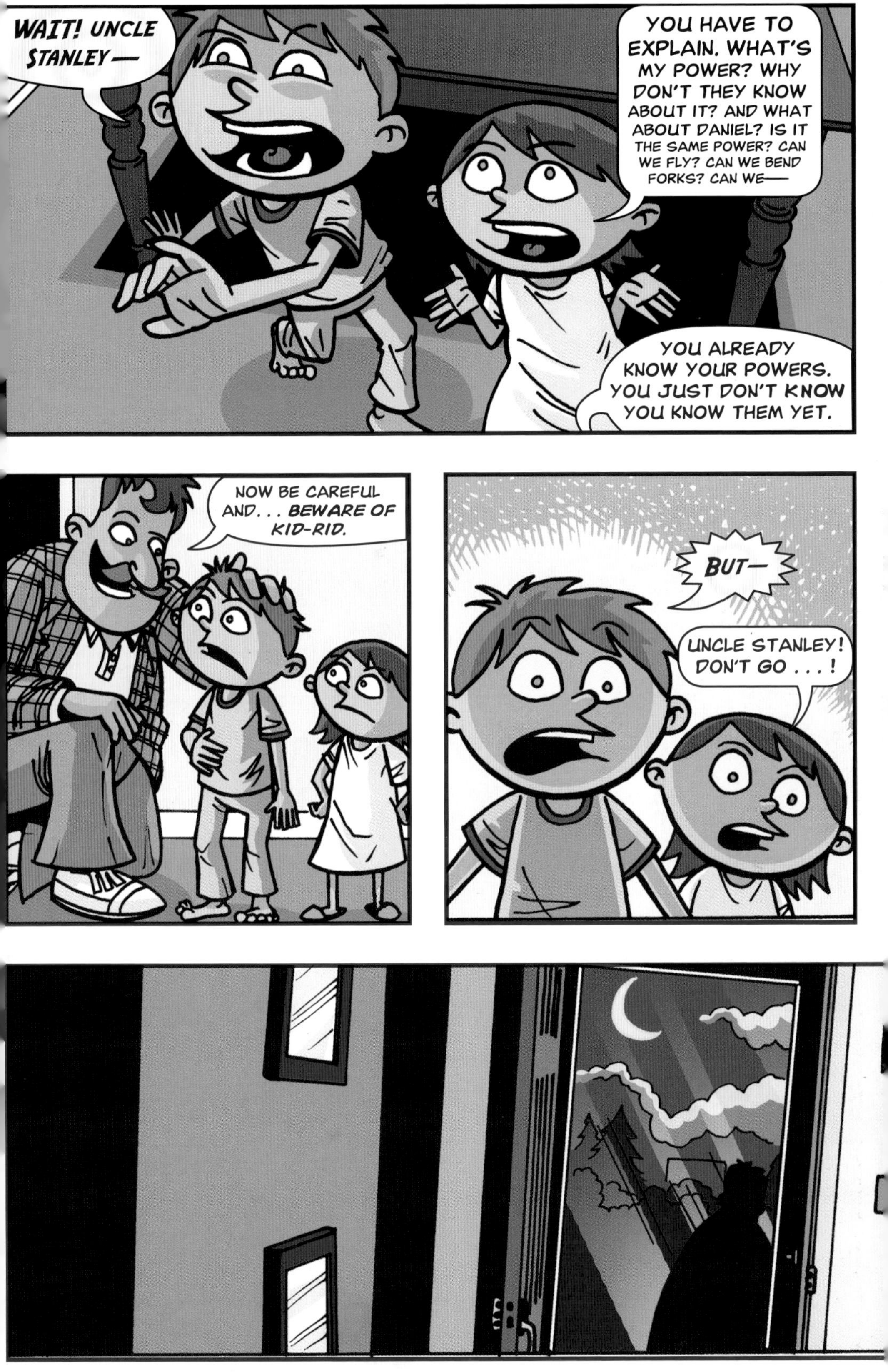
WAIT! UNCLE STANLEY—
YOU HAVE TO EXPLAIN. WHAT'S MY POWER? WHY DON'T THEY KNOW ABOUT IT? AND WHAT ABOUT DANIEL? IS IT THE SAME POWER? CAN WE FLY? CAN WE BEND FORKS? CAN WE—
YOU ALREADY KNOW YOUR POWERS. YOU JUST DON'T KNOW YOU KNOW THEM YET.
NOW BE CAREFUL AND. . . BEWARE OF KID-RID.
BUT—
UNCLE STANLEY! DON'T GO . . . !

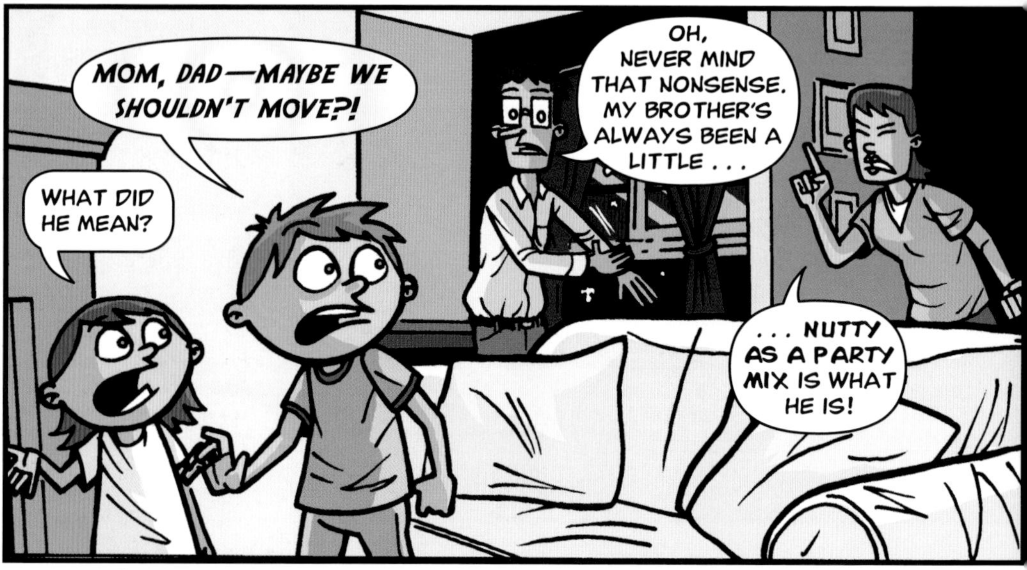
MOM, DAD—MAYBE WE SHOULDN'T MOVE?!
WHAT DID HE MEAN?
OH, NEVER MIND THAT NONSENSE. MY BROTHER'S ALWAYS BEEN A LITTLE . . .
. . . NUTTY AS A PARTY MIX IS WHAT HE IS!

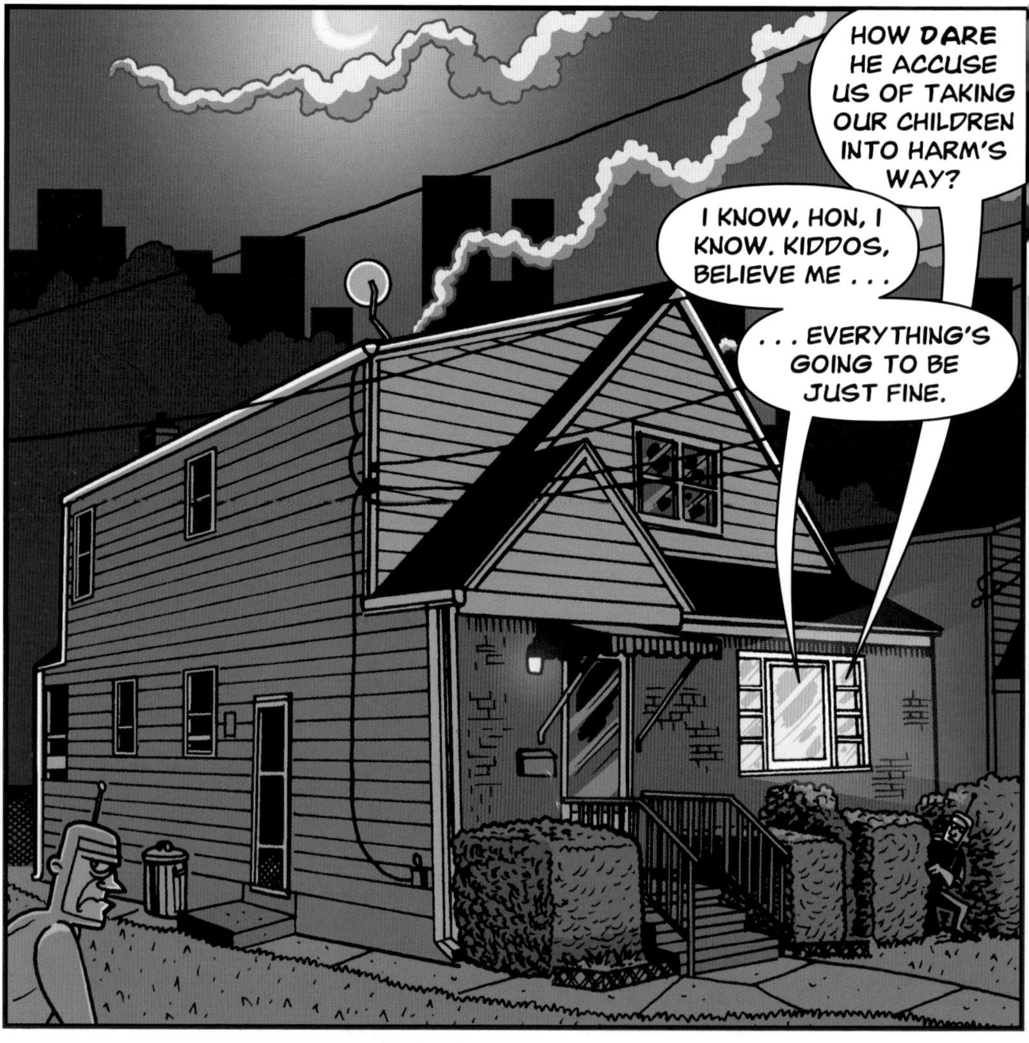
HOW DARE HE ACCUSE US OF TAKING OUR CHILDREN INTO HARM'S WAY?
I KNOW, HON, I KNOW. KIDDOS, BELIEVE ME . . .
. . . EVERYTHING'S GOING TO BE JUST FINE.

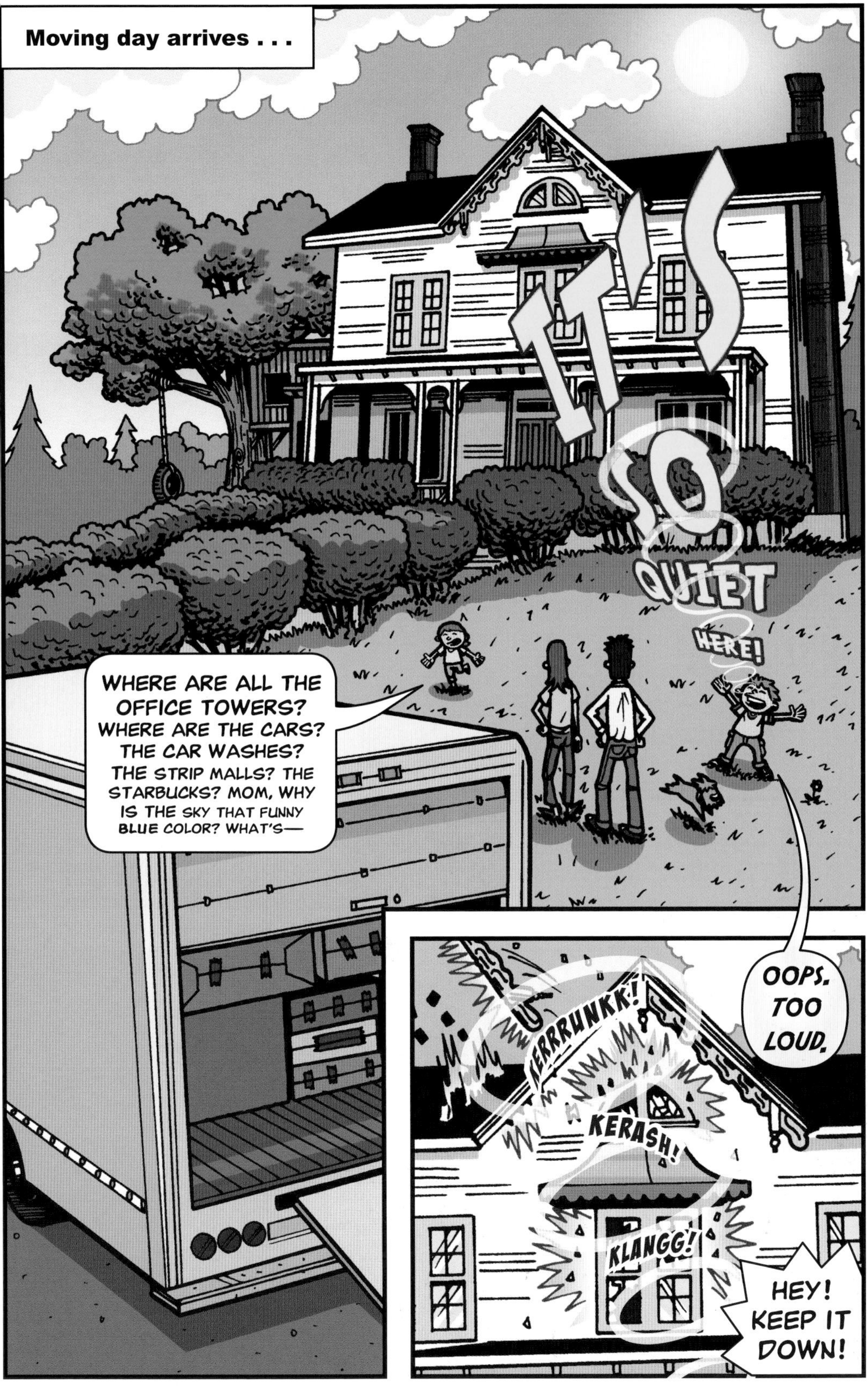
Moving day arrives . . .
IT'S SO QUIET HERE!
WHERE ARE ALL THE OFFICE TOWERS? WHERE ARE THE CARS? THE CAR WASHES? THE STRIP MALLS? THE STARBUCKS? MOM, WHY IS THE SKY THAT FUNNY BLUE COLOR? WHAT'S—
OOPS. TOO LOUD.
KERRRUNKK!
KERASH!
KLANGG!
HEY! KEEP IT DOWN!

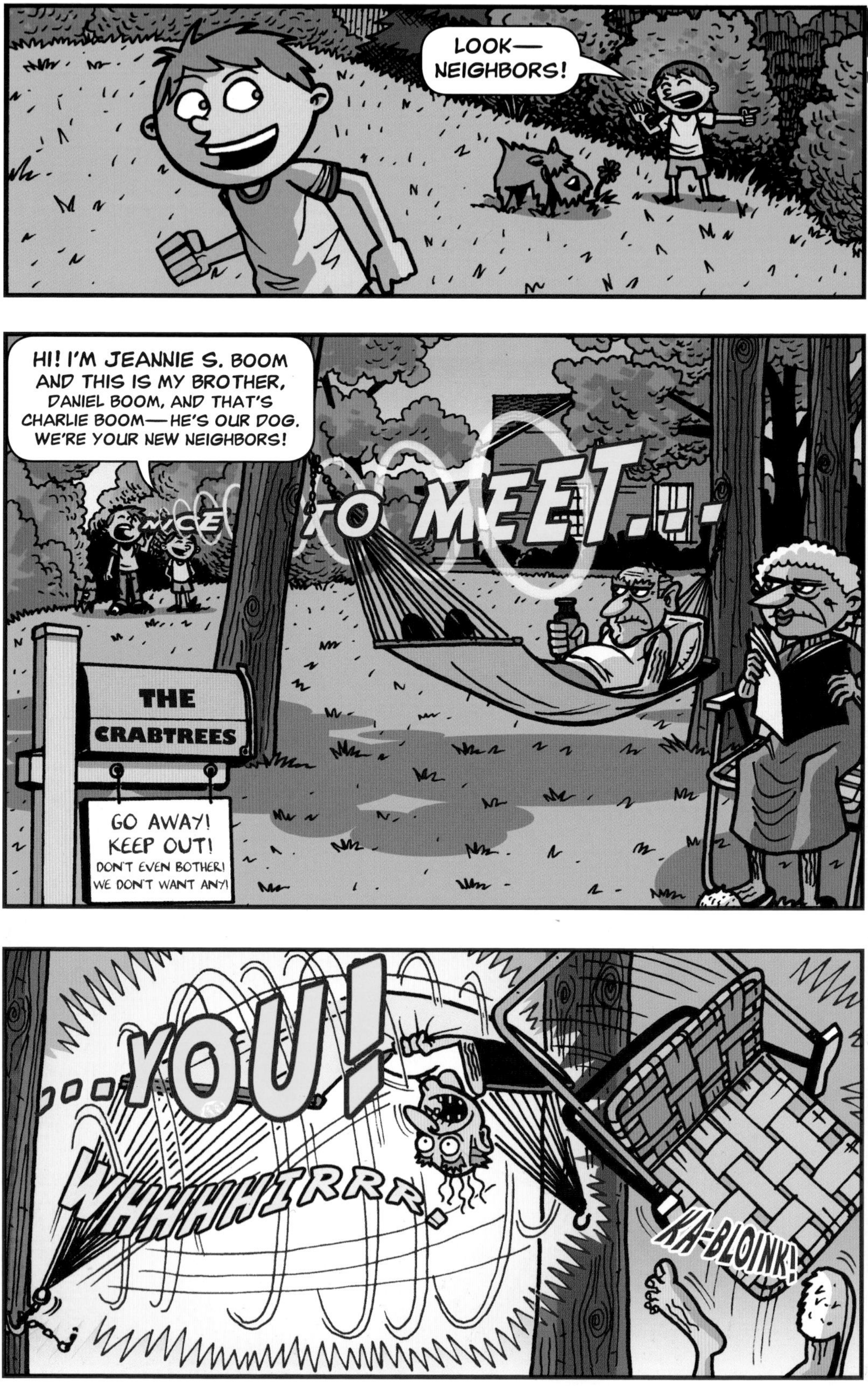
LOOK—
NEIGHBORS!
HI! I'M JEANNIE S. BOOM AND THIS IS MY BROTHER, DANIEL BOOM, AND THAT'S CHARLIE BOOM—HE'S OUR DOG. WE'RE YOUR NEW NEIGHBORS!
NICE TO MEET...
THE CRABTREES
GO AWAY!
KEEP OUT!
DON'T EVEN BOTHER!
WE DON'T WANT ANY!
...YOU!
WHHHHIRRRR.
KA-BLOINK!

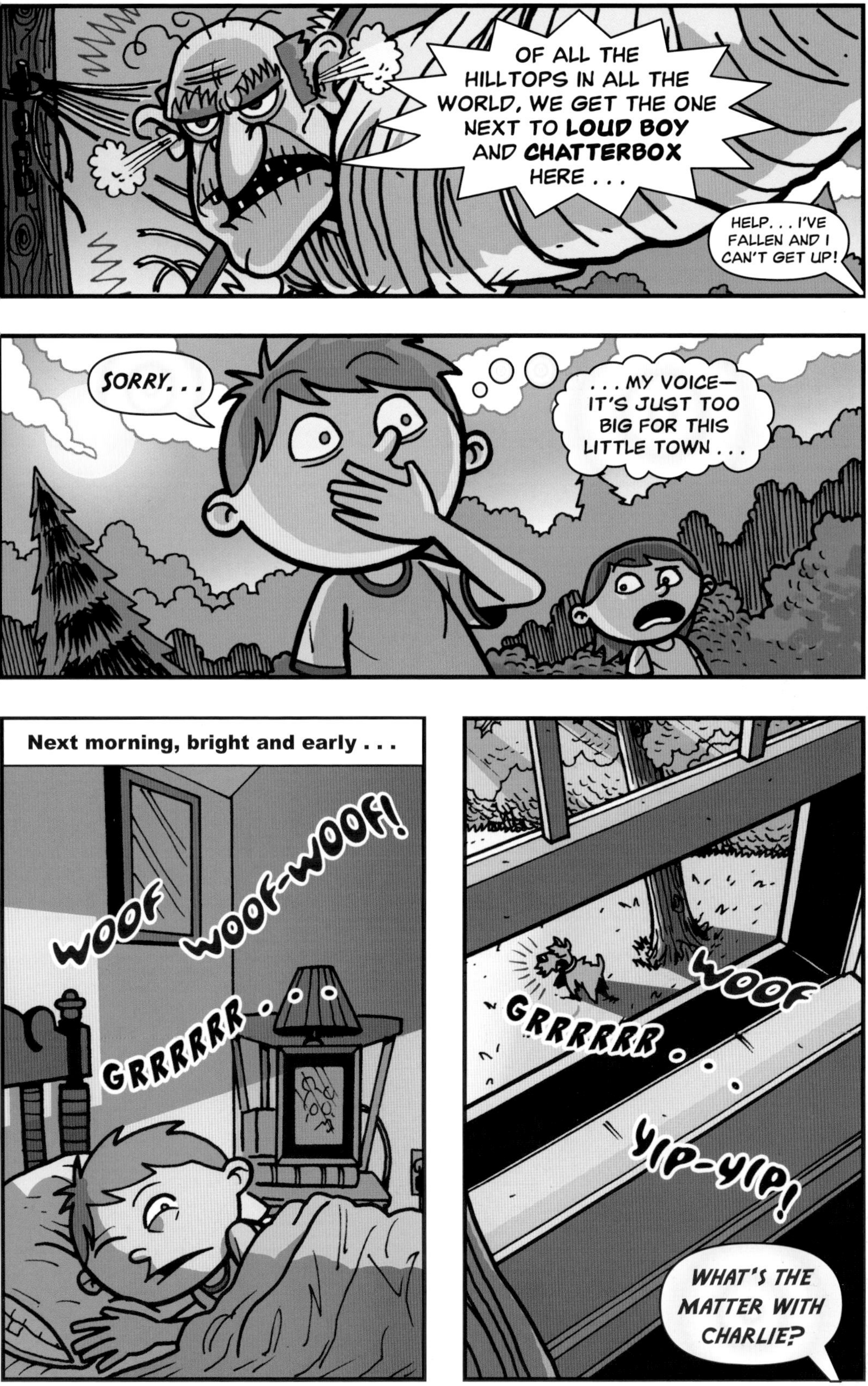
OF ALL THE HILLTOPS IN ALL THE WORLD, WE GET THE ONE NEXT TO LOUD BOY AND CHATTERBOX HERE . . .
HELP. . . I'VE FALLEN AND I CAN'T GET UP!
SORRY. . .
. . . MY VOICE— IT'S JUST TOO BIG FOR THIS LITTLE TOWN . . .
Next morning, bright and early . . .
WOOF
WOOF-WOOF!
GRRRRRR . . .
GRRRRRRR . . .
WOOF
YIP-YIP!
WHAT'S THE MATTER WITH CHARLIE?

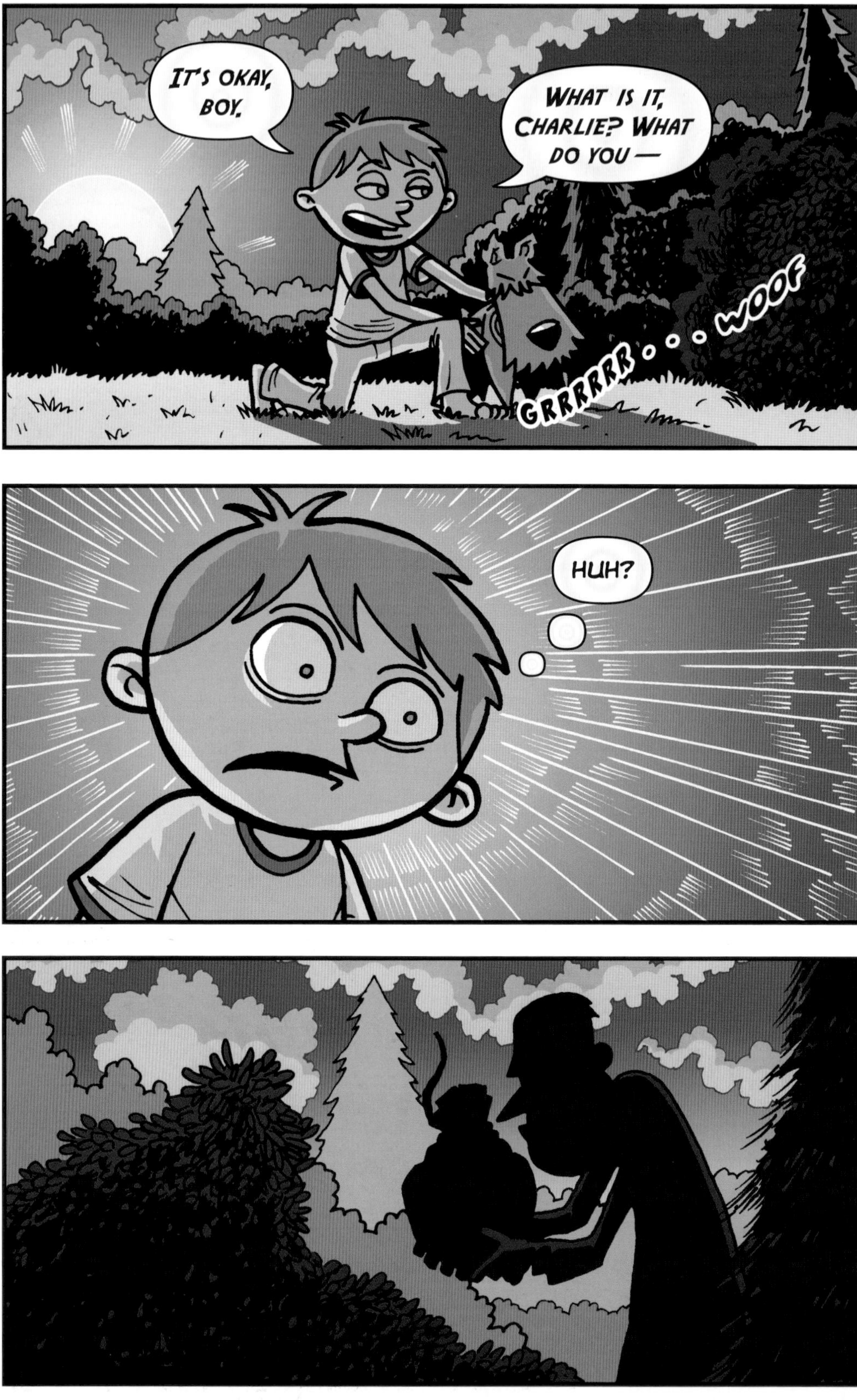
IT'S OKAY, BOY.
WHAT IS IT, CHARLIE? WHAT DO YOU—
GRRRRRR . . . WOOF
HUH?

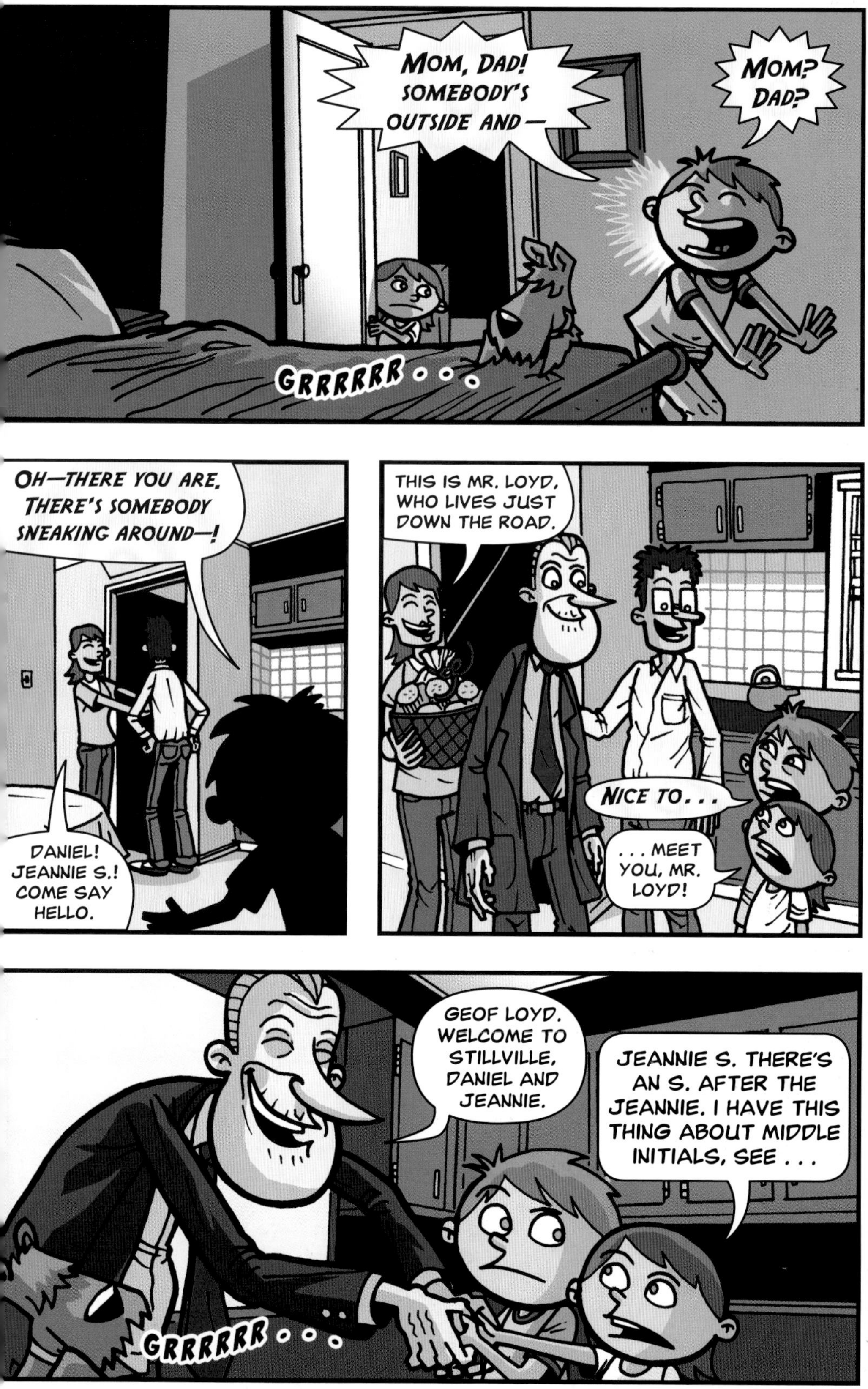
MOM, DAD! SOMEBODY'S OUTSIDE AND—
MOM? DAD?
GRRRRRR . . .
OH—THERE YOU ARE. THERE'S SOMEBODY SNEAKING AROUND—!
DANIEL! JEANNIE S.! COME SAY HELLO.
THIS IS MR. LOYD, WHO LIVES JUST DOWN THE ROAD.
NICE TO . . .
. . . MEET YOU, MR. LOYD!
GEOF LOYD. WELCOME TO STILLVILLE, DANIEL AND JEANNIE.
JEANNIE S. THERE'S AN S. AFTER THE JEANNIE. I HAVE THIS THING ABOUT MIDDLE INITIALS, SEE . . .
GRRRRRR . . .

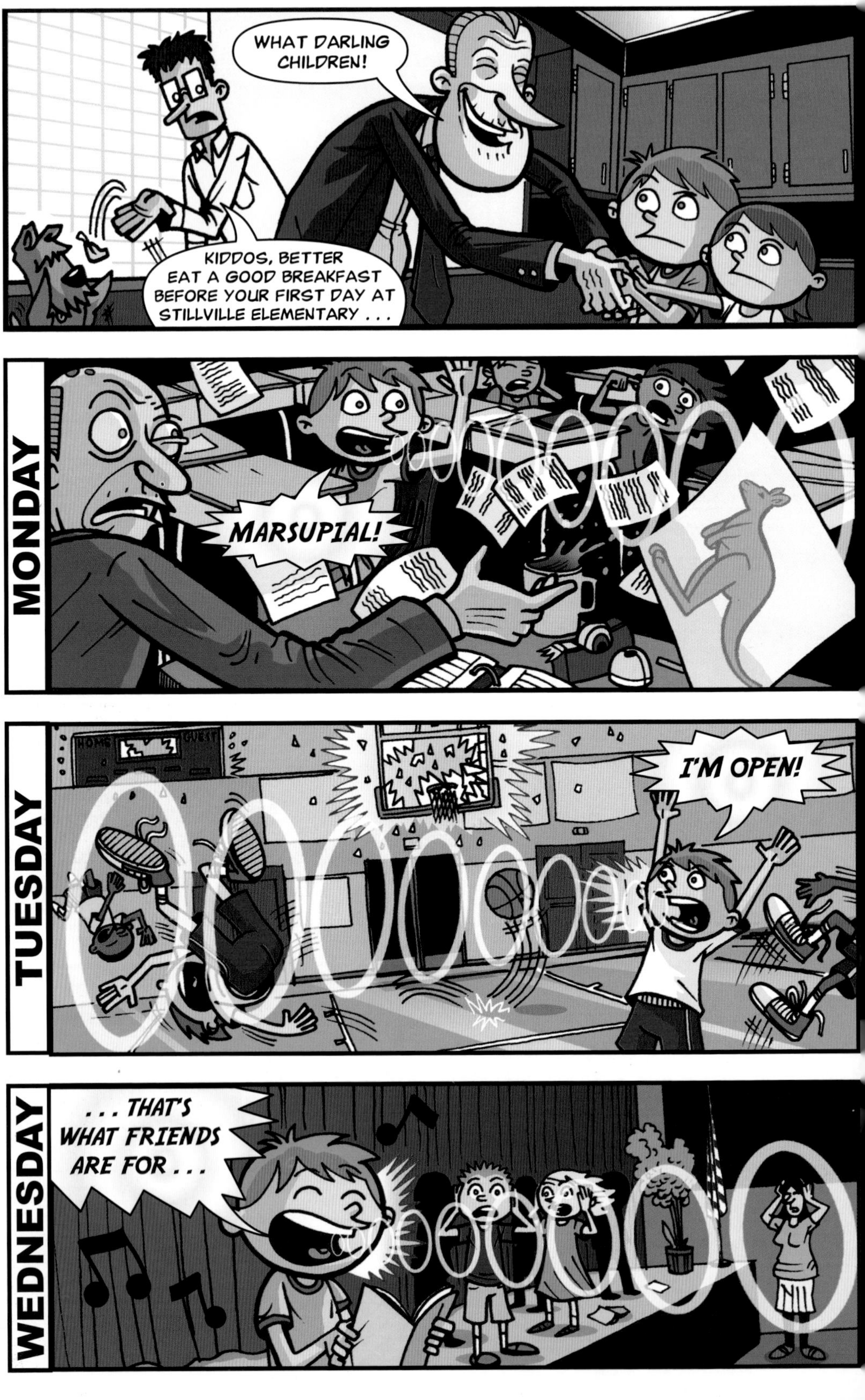
WHAT DARLING CHILDREN!
KIDDOS, BETTER EAT A GOOD BREAKFAST BEFORE YOUR FIRST DAY AT STILLVILLE ELEMENTARY . . .
MONDAY
MARSUPIAL!
TUESDAY
HOME
GUEST
I'M OPEN!
WEDNESDAY
. . . THAT'S WHAT FRIENDS ARE FOR . . .

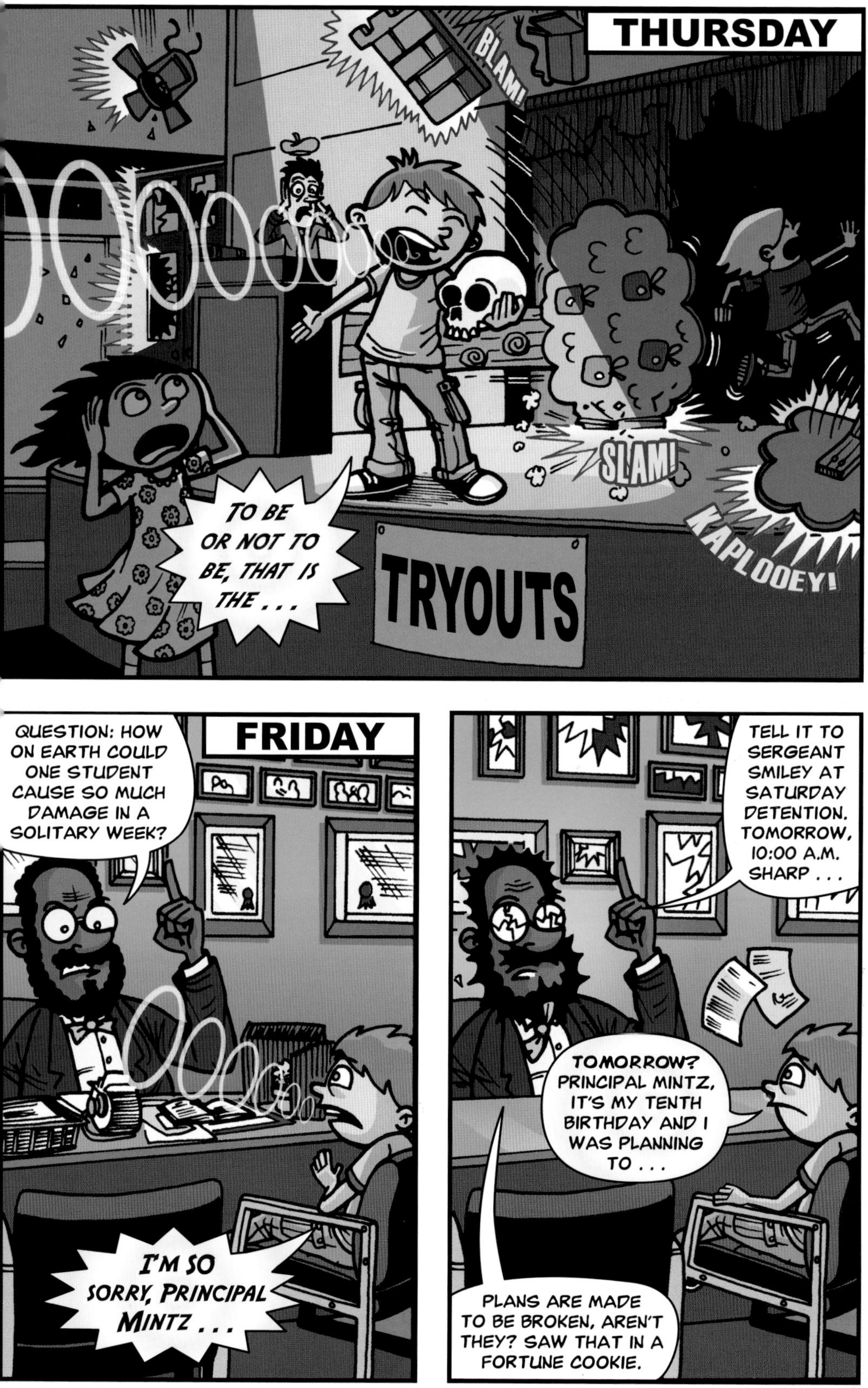
THURSDAY
BLAM!
TO BE OR NOT TO BE, THAT IS THE . . .
TRYOUTS
SLAM!
KAPLOOEY!
FRIDAY
QUESTION: HOW ON EARTH COULD ONE STUDENT CAUSE SO MUCH DAMAGE IN A SOLITARY WEEK?
I'M SO SORRY, PRINCIPAL MINTZ . . .
TELL IT TO SERGEANT SMILEY AT SATURDAY DETENTION. TOMORROW, 10:00 A.M. SHARP . . .
TOMORROW? PRINCIPAL MINTZ, IT'S MY TENTH BIRTHDAY AND I WAS PLANNING TO . . .
PLANS ARE MADE TO BE BROKEN, AREN'T THEY? SAW THAT IN A FORTUNE COOKIE.

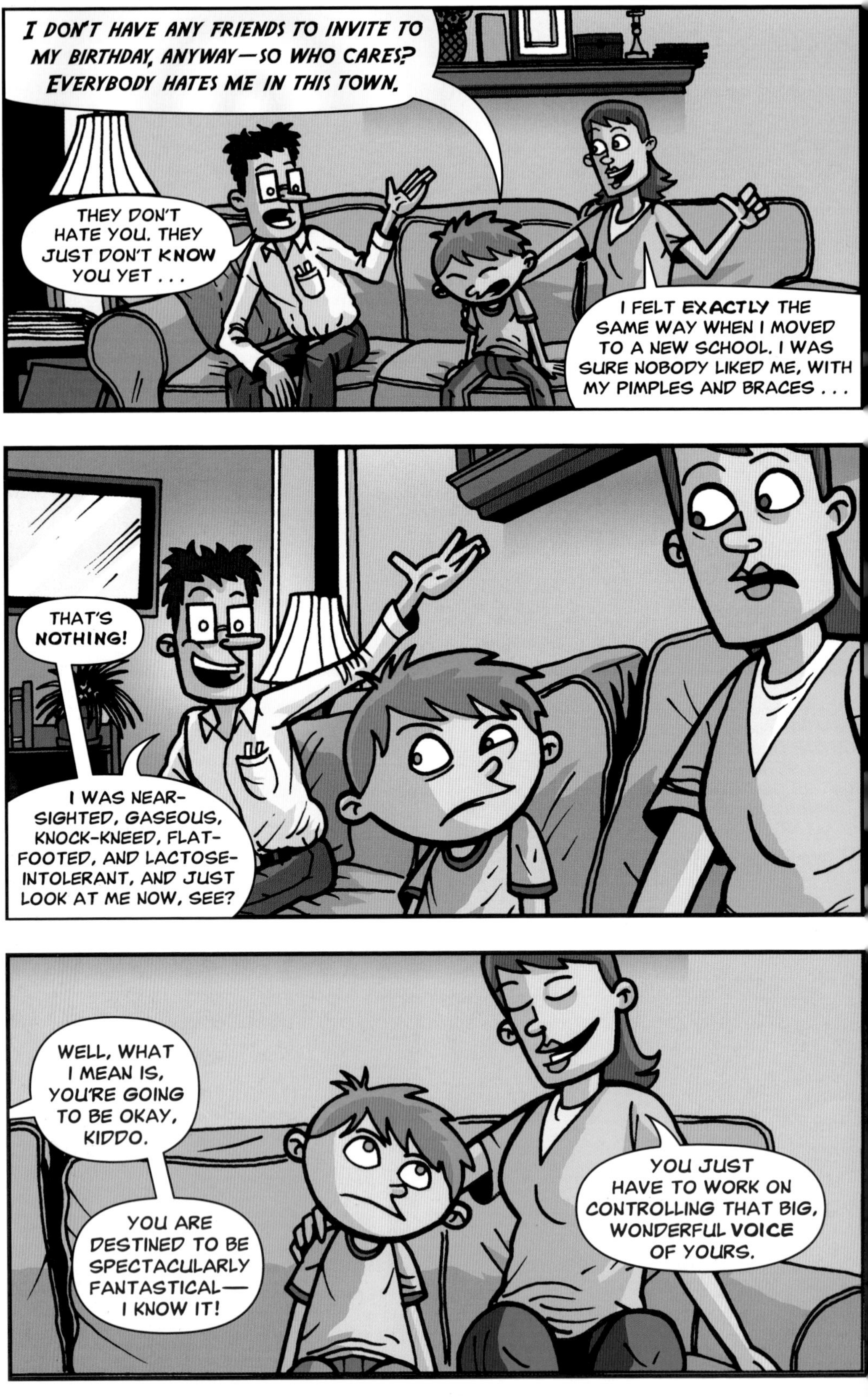
I DON'T HAVE ANY FRIENDS TO INVITE TO MY BIRTHDAY, ANYWAY—SO WHO CARES? EVERYBODY HATES ME IN THIS TOWN.
THEY DON'T HATE YOU. THEY JUST DON'T KNOW YOU YET . . .
I FELT EXACTLY THE SAME WAY WHEN I MOVED TO A NEW SCHOOL. I WAS SURE NOBODY LIKED ME, WITH MY PIMPLES AND BRACES . . .
THAT'S NOTHING!
I WAS NEAR-SIGHTED, GASEOUS, KNOCK-KNEED, FLAT-FOOTED, AND LACTOSE-INTOLERANT, AND JUST LOOK AT ME NOW, SEE?
WELL, WHAT I MEAN IS, YOU'RE GOING TO BE OKAY, KIDDO.
YOU ARE DESTINED TO BE SPECTACULARLY FANTASTICAL—I KNOW IT!
YOU JUST HAVE TO WORK ON CONTROLLING THAT BIG, WONDERFUL VOICE OF YOURS.

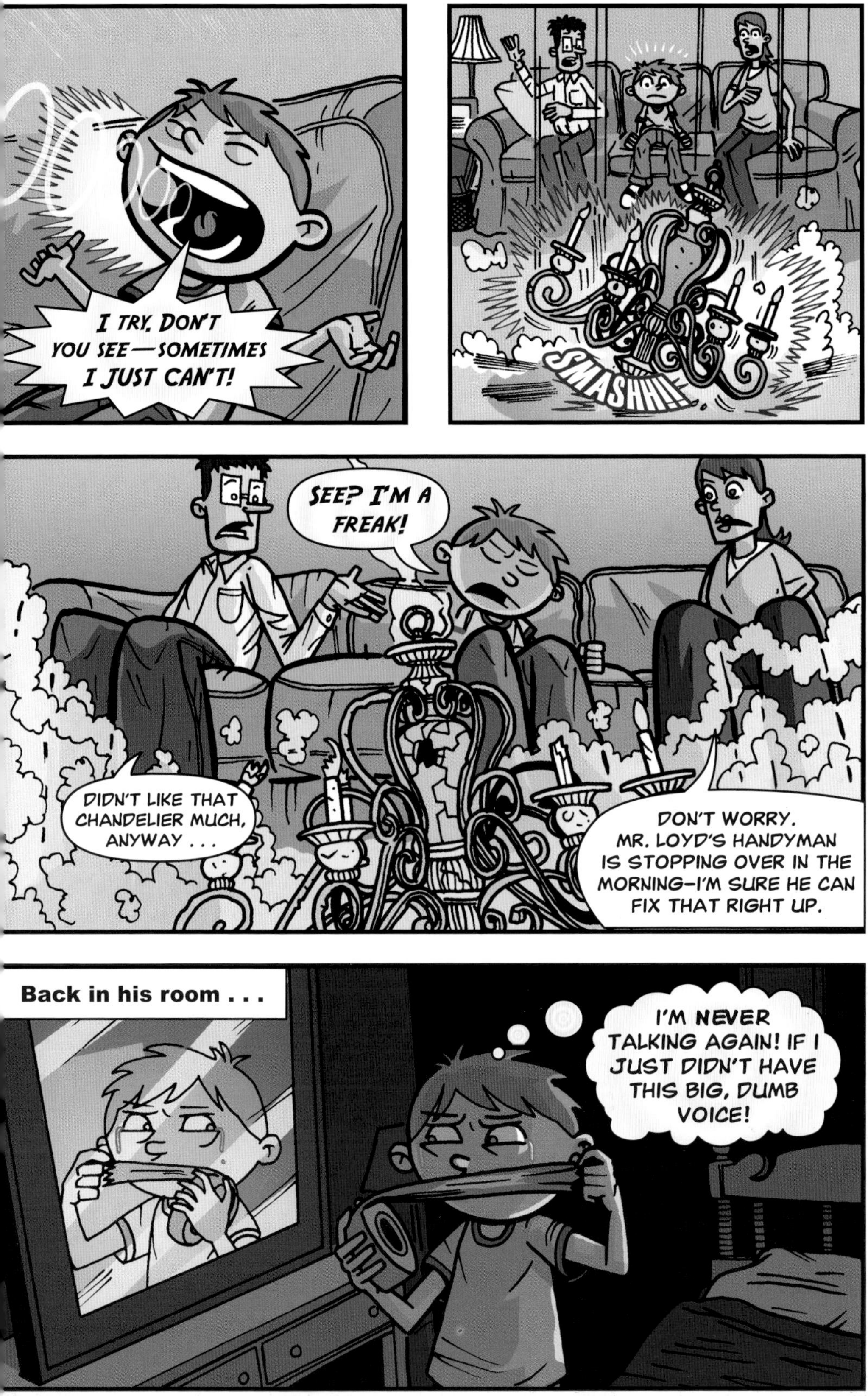
I TRY. DON'T YOU SEE—SOMETIMES I JUST CAN'T!
SMASHH!!
SEE? I'M A FREAK!
DIDN'T LIKE THAT CHANDELIER MUCH, ANYWAY . . .
DON'T WORRY. MR. LOYD'S HANDYMAN IS STOPPING OVER IN THE MORNING–I'M SURE HE CAN FIX THAT RIGHT UP.
Back in his room . . .
I'M NEVER TALKING AGAIN! IF I JUST DIDN'T HAVE THIS BIG, DUMB VOICE!

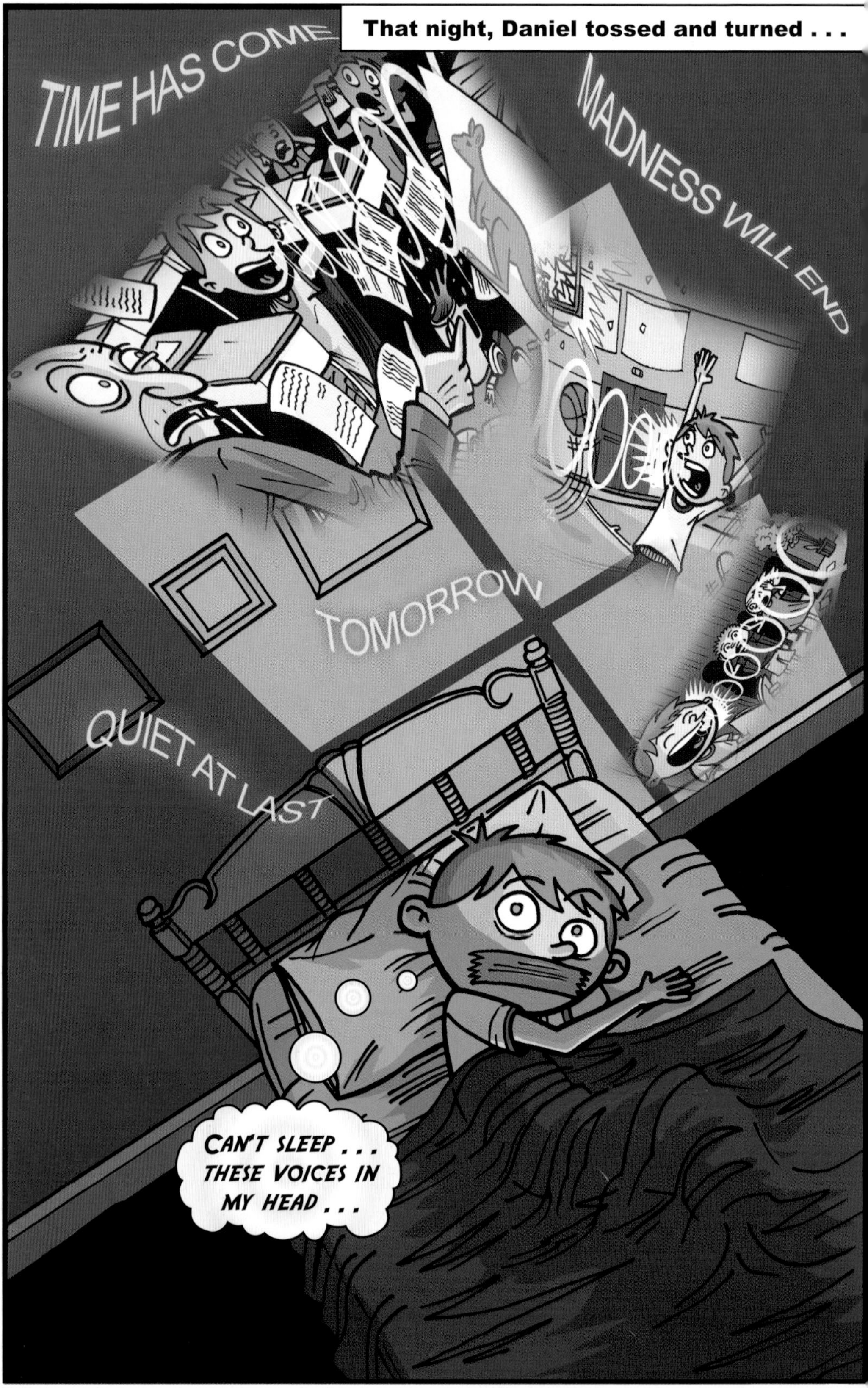
That night, Daniel tossed and turned . . .
TIME HAS COME
MADNESS WILL END
TOMORROW
QUIET AT LAST
CAN'T SLEEP . . . THESE VOICES IN MY HEAD . . .

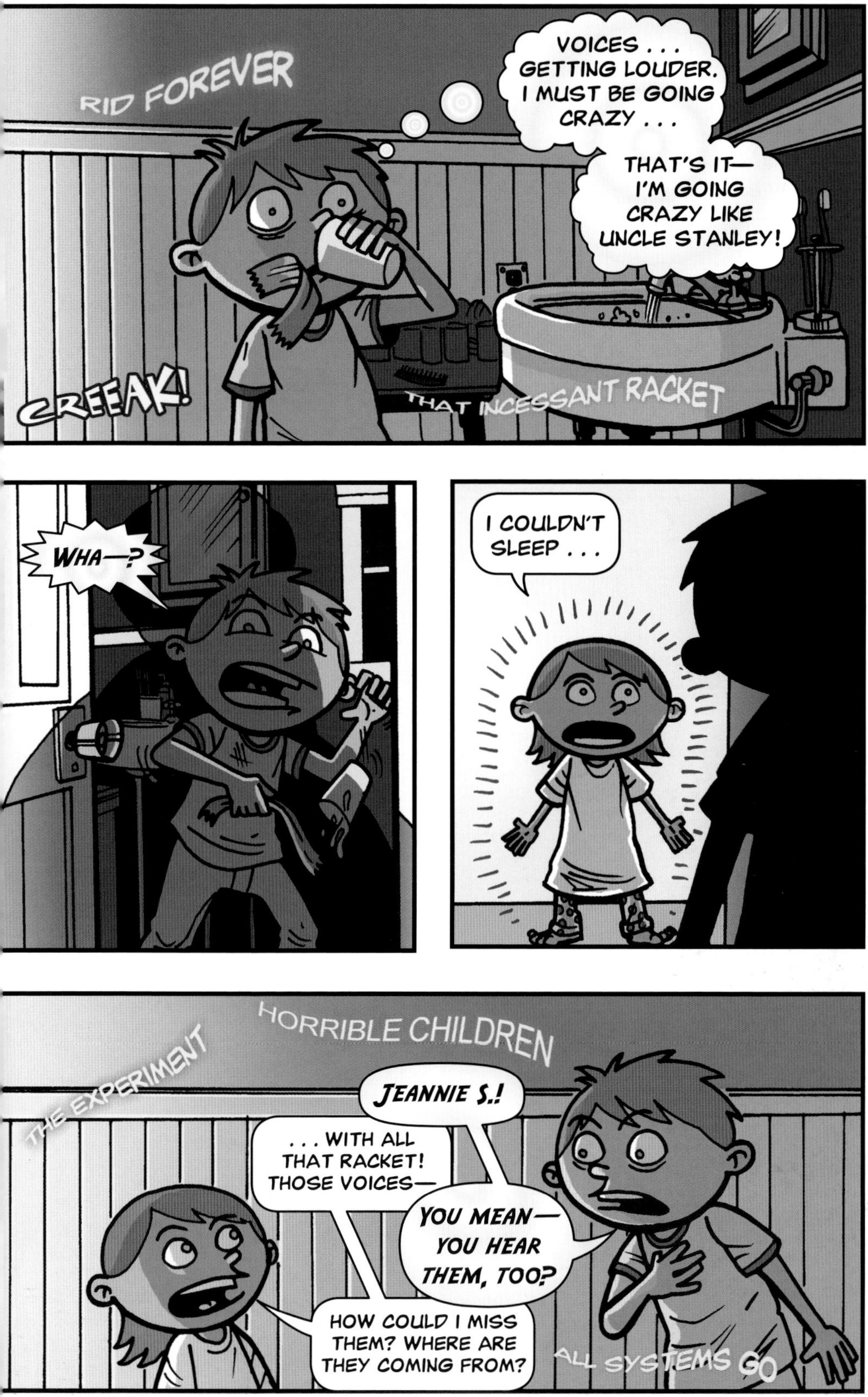
RID FOREVER
VOICES . . . GETTING LOUDER. I MUST BE GOING CRAZY . . .
THAT'S IT— I'M GOING CRAZY LIKE UNCLE STANLEY!
CREEAK!
THAT INCESSANT RACKET
WHA—?
I COULDN'T SLEEP . . .
HORRIBLE CHILDREN
THE EXPERIMENT
JEANNIE S.!
. . . WITH ALL THAT RACKET! THOSE VOICES—
YOU MEAN— YOU HEAR THEM, TOO?
HOW COULD I MISS THEM? WHERE ARE THEY COMING FROM?
ALL SYSTEMS GO

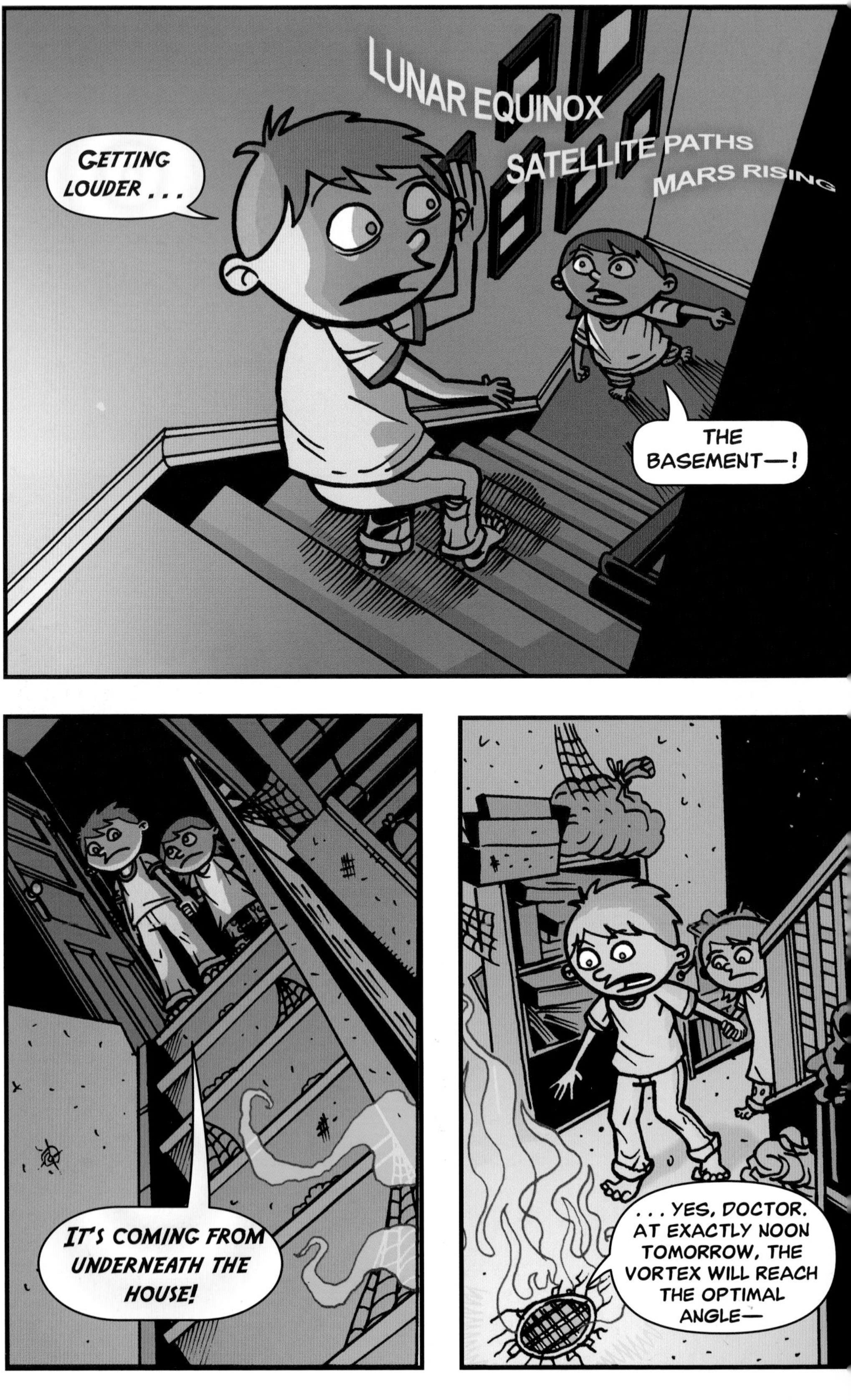
LUNAR EQUINOX
SATELLITE PATHS
MARS RISING
GETTING LOUDER . . .
THE BASEMENT—!
IT'S COMING FROM UNDERNEATH THE HOUSE!
. . . YES, DOCTOR. AT EXACTLY NOON TOMORROW, THE VORTEX WILL REACH THE OPTIMAL ANGLE—

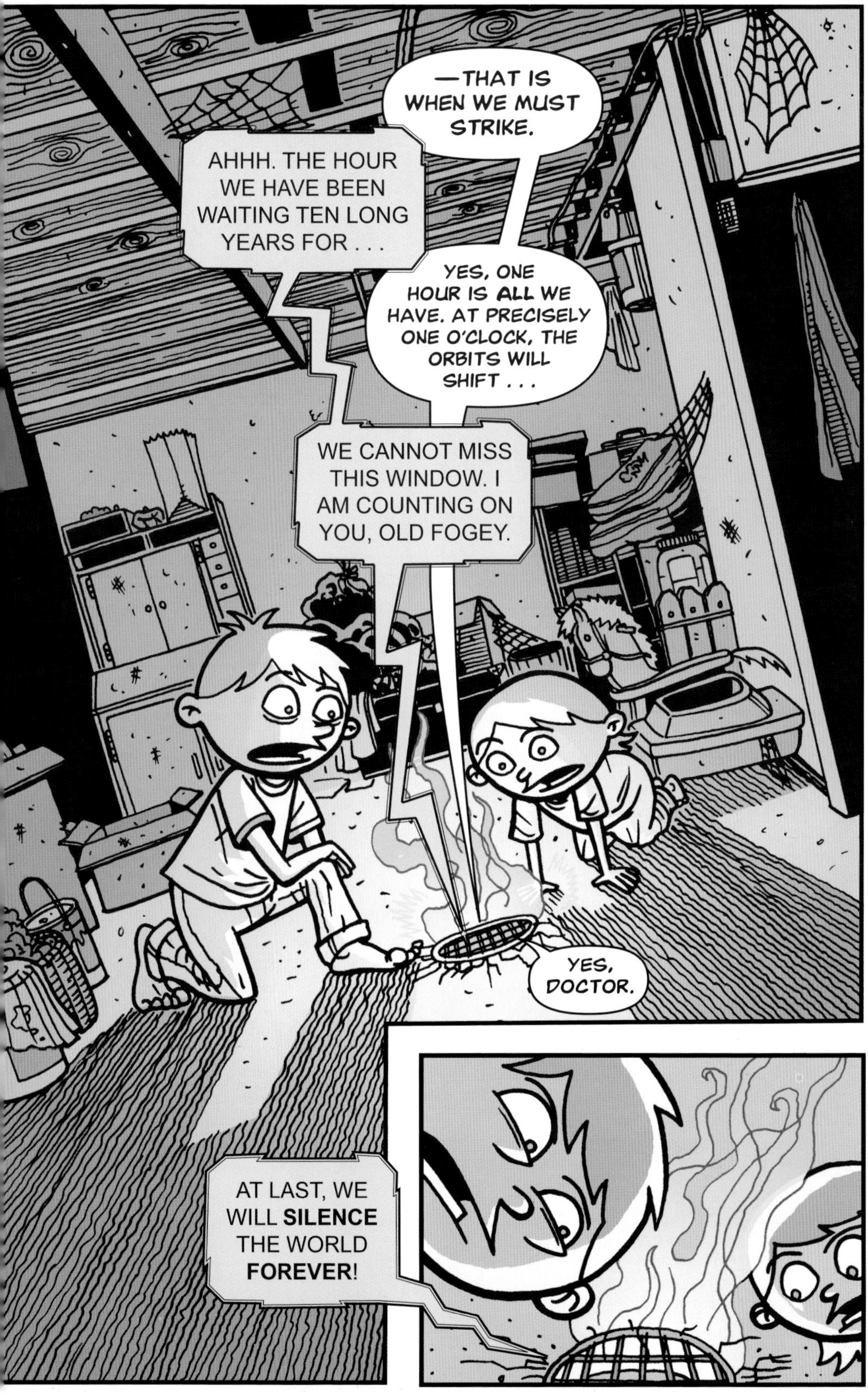
AHHH. THE HOUR WE HAVE BEEN WAITING TEN LONG YEARS FOR . . .
—THAT IS WHEN WE MUST STRIKE.
YES, ONE HOUR IS **ALL** WE HAVE. AT PRECISELY ONE O'CLOCK, THE ORBITS WILL SHIFT . . .
WE CANNOT MISS THIS WINDOW. I AM COUNTING ON YOU, OLD FOGEY.
YES, DOCTOR.
AT LAST, WE WILL **SILENCE** THE WORLD **FOREVER**!

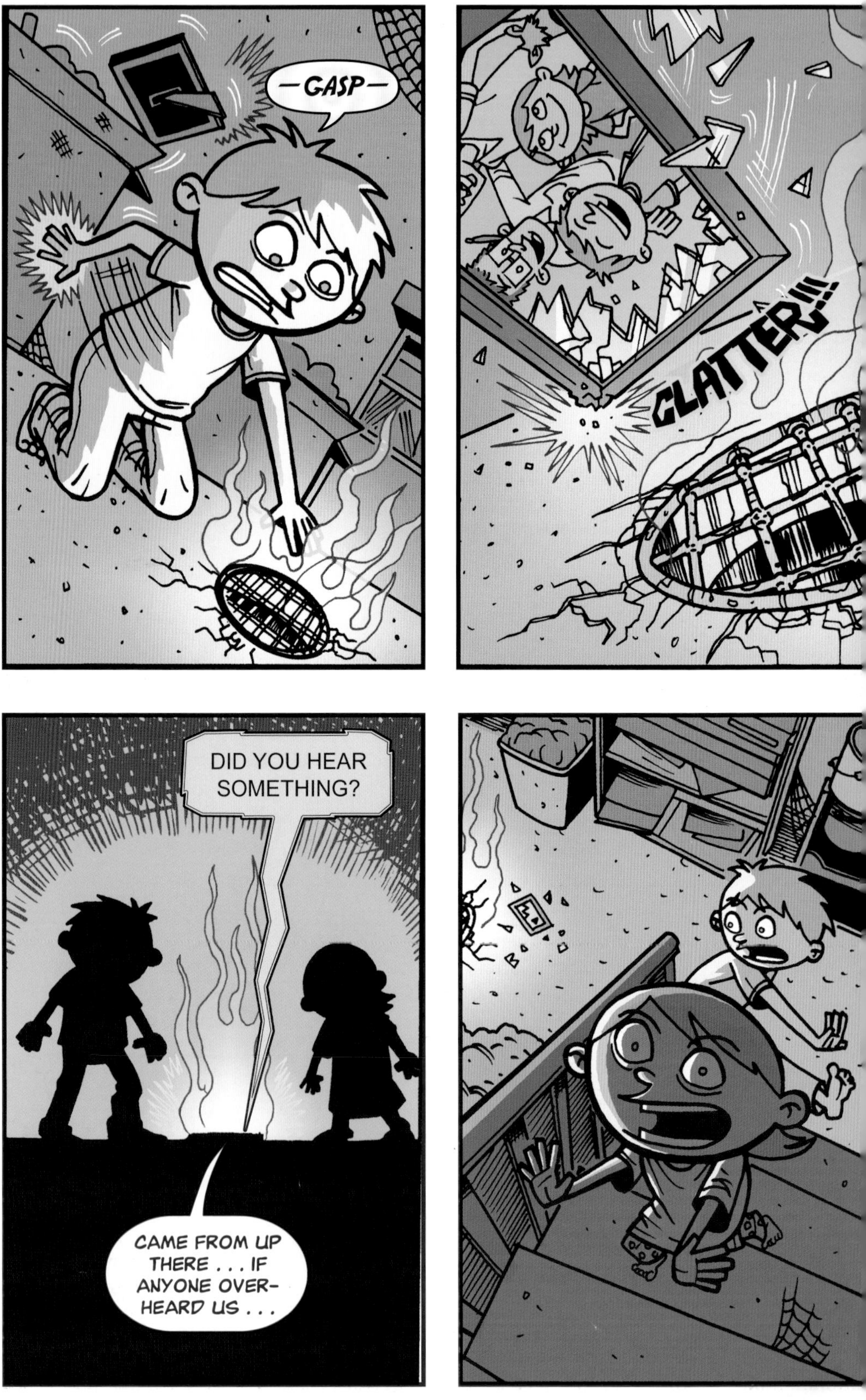
—GASP—
CLATTER!!!
DID YOU HEAR SOMETHING?
CAME FROM UP THERE . . . IF ANYONE OVER-HEARD US . . .

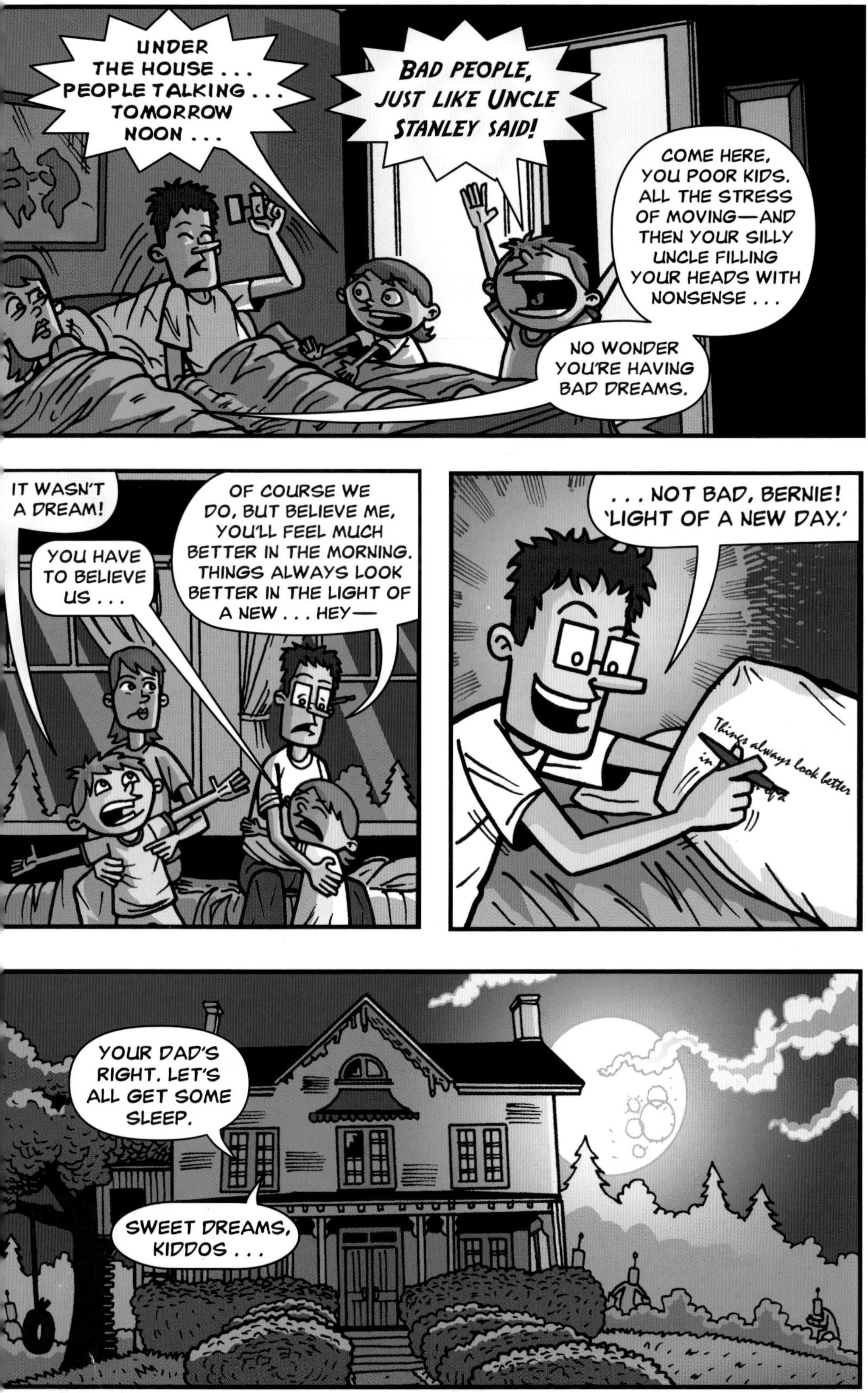
UNDER THE HOUSE . . . PEOPLE TALKING . . . TOMORROW NOON . . .
BAD PEOPLE, JUST LIKE UNCLE STANLEY SAID!
COME HERE, YOU POOR KIDS. ALL THE STRESS OF MOVING—AND THEN YOUR SILLY UNCLE FILLING YOUR HEADS WITH NONSENSE . . .
NO WONDER YOU'RE HAVING BAD DREAMS.
IT WASN'T A DREAM!
YOU HAVE TO BELIEVE US . . .
OF COURSE WE DO, BUT BELIEVE ME, YOU'LL FEEL MUCH BETTER IN THE MORNING. THINGS ALWAYS LOOK BETTER IN THE LIGHT OF A NEW . . . HEY—
. . . NOT BAD, BERNIE! 'LIGHT OF A NEW DAY.'
Things always look better
YOUR DAD'S RIGHT. LET'S ALL GET SOME SLEEP.
SWEET DREAMS, KIDDOS . . .

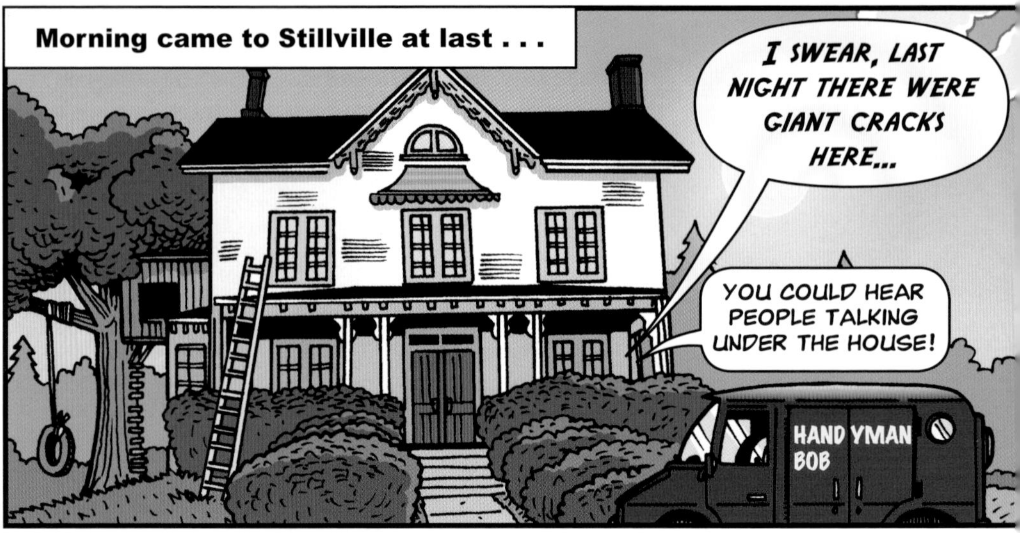
Morning came to Stillville at last . . .
I SWEAR, LAST NIGHT THERE WERE GIANT CRACKS HERE...
YOU COULD HEAR PEOPLE TALKING UNDER THE HOUSE!
HANDYMAN BOB

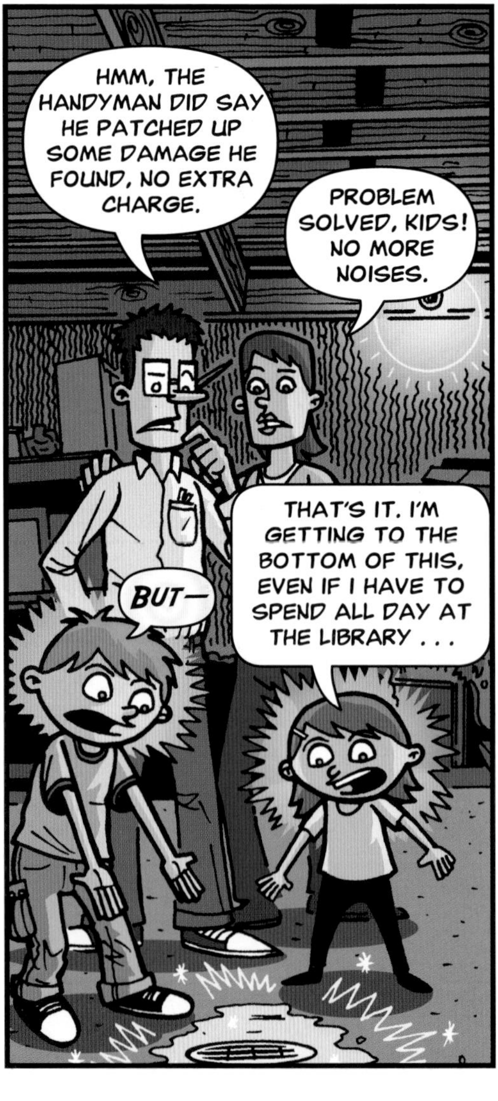
HMM, THE HANDYMAN DID SAY HE PATCHED UP SOME DAMAGE HE FOUND, NO EXTRA CHARGE.
PROBLEM SOLVED, KIDS! NO MORE NOISES.
BUT—
THAT'S IT. I'M GETTING TO THE BOTTOM OF THIS, EVEN IF I HAVE TO SPEND ALL DAY AT THE LIBRARY . . .

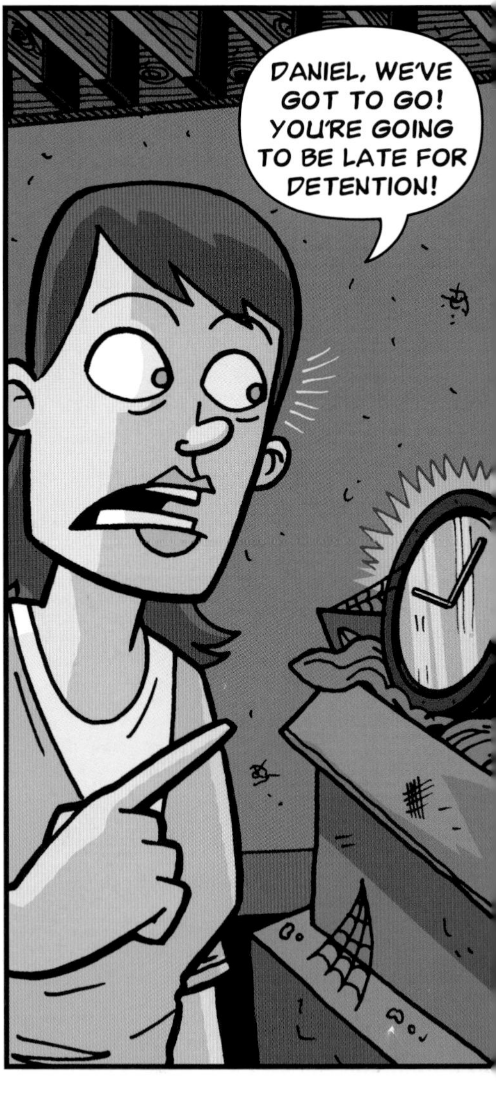
DANIEL, WE'VE GOT TO GO! YOU'RE GOING TO BE LATE FOR DETENTION!

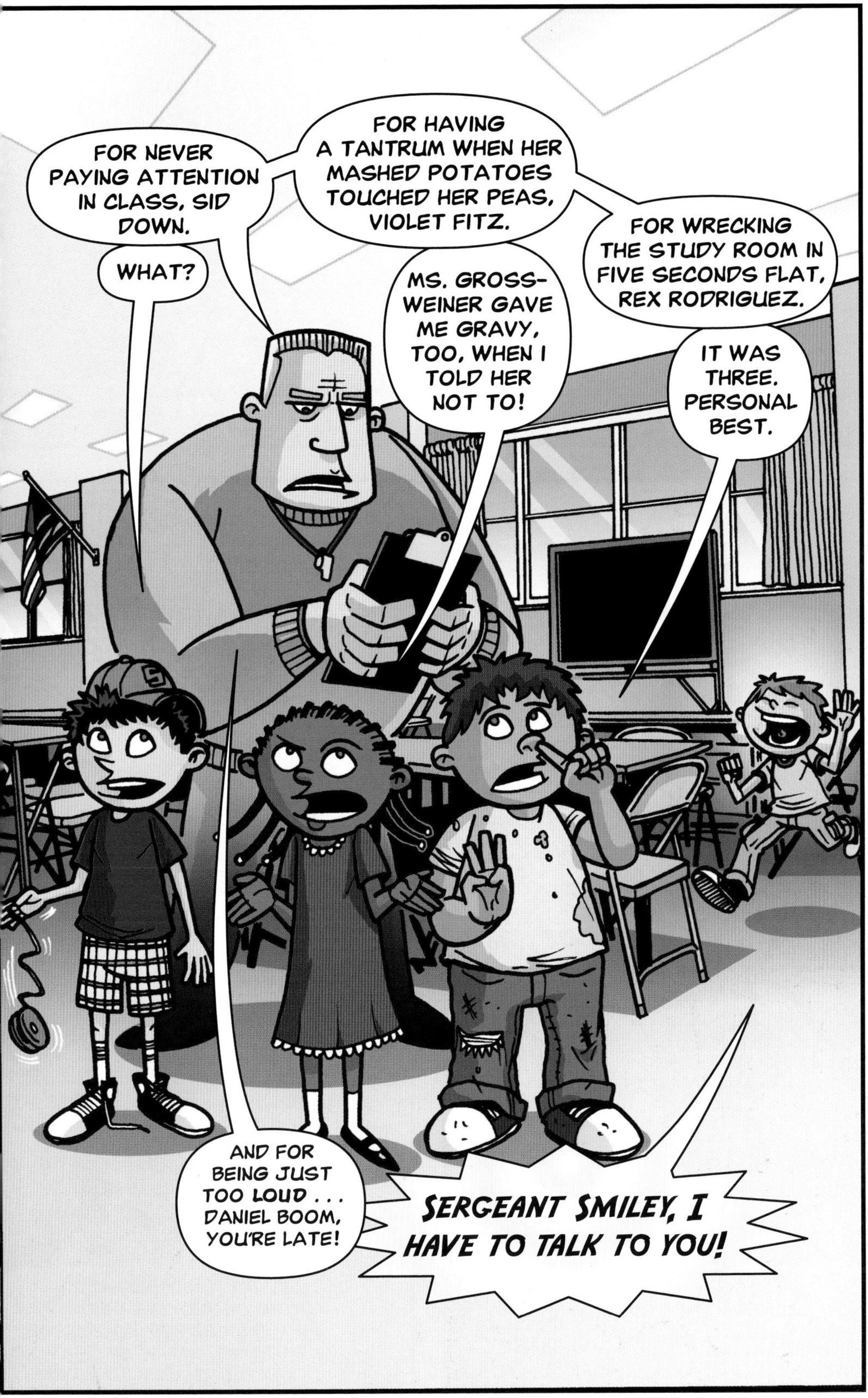
FOR NEVER PAYING ATTENTION IN CLASS, SID DOWN.
WHAT?
FOR HAVING A TANTRUM WHEN HER MASHED POTATOES TOUCHED HER PEAS, VIOLET FITZ.
MS. GROSS-WEINER GAVE ME GRAVY, TOO, WHEN I TOLD HER NOT TO!
FOR WRECKING THE STUDY ROOM IN FIVE SECONDS FLAT, REX RODRIGUEZ.
IT WAS THREE. PERSONAL BEST.
AND FOR BEING JUST TOO LOUD . . . DANIEL BOOM, YOU'RE LATE!
SERGEANT SMILEY, I HAVE TO TALK TO YOU!

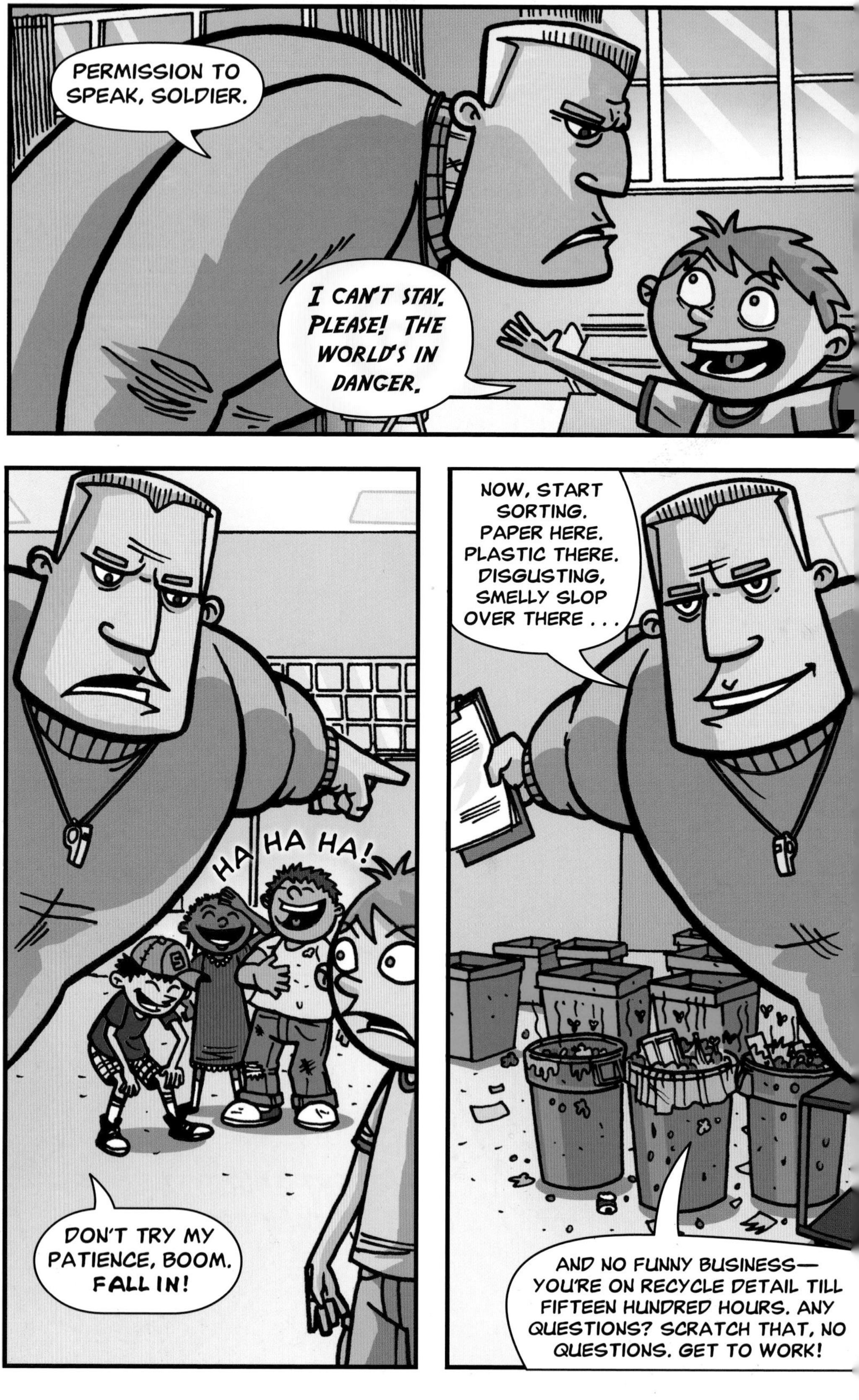
PERMISSION TO SPEAK, SOLDIER.
I CAN'T STAY. PLEASE! THE WORLD'S IN DANGER.
HA HA HA!
DON'T TRY MY PATIENCE, BOOM. FALL IN!
NOW, START SORTING. PAPER HERE. PLASTIC THERE. DISGUSTING, SMELLY SLOP OVER THERE . . .
AND NO FUNNY BUSINESS— YOU'RE ON RECYCLE DETAIL TILL FIFTEEN HUNDRED HOURS. ANY QUESTIONS? SCRATCH THAT, NO QUESTIONS. GET TO WORK!

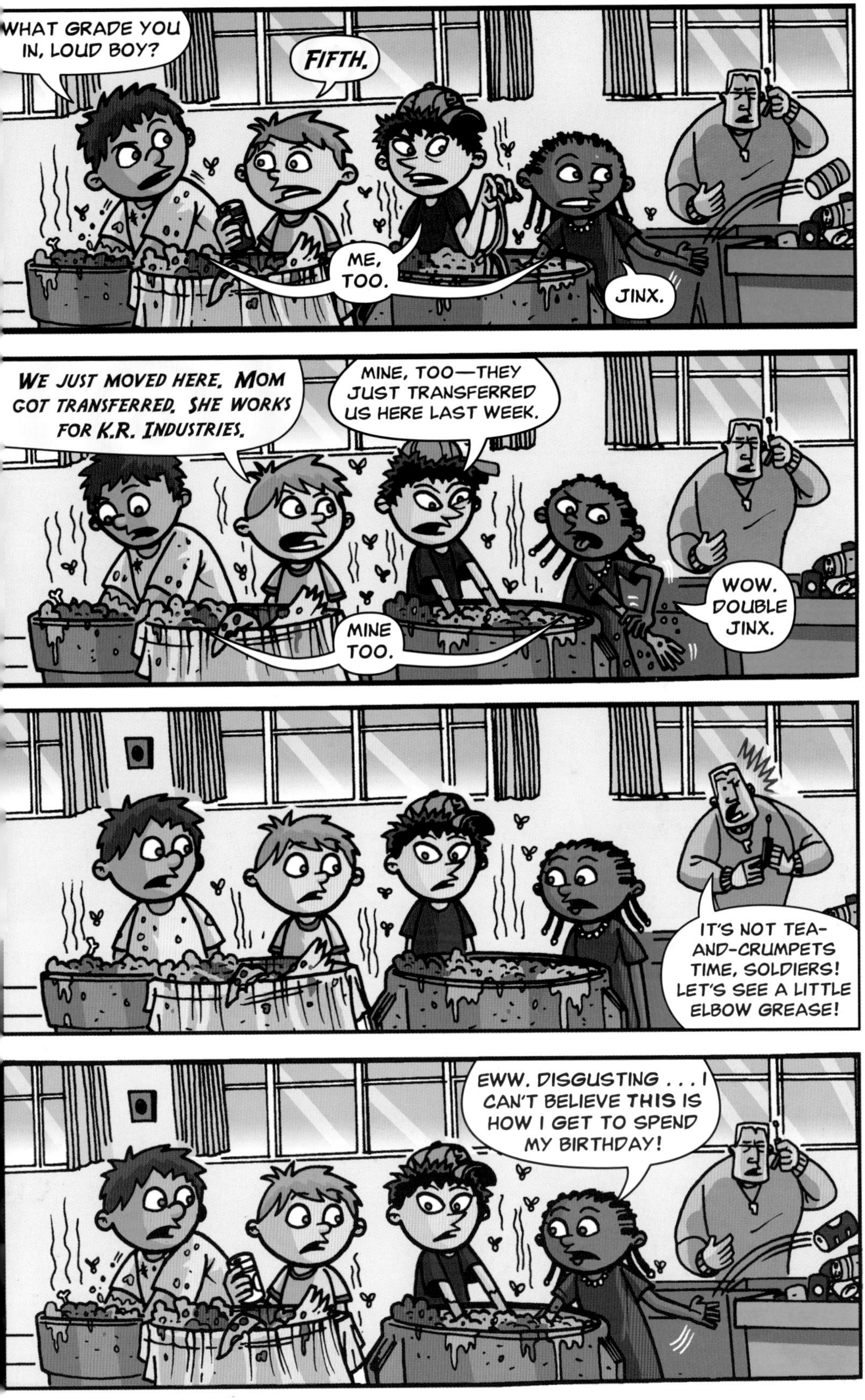
WHAT GRADE YOU IN, LOUD BOY?
FIFTH.
ME, TOO.
JINX.
WE JUST MOVED HERE. MOM GOT TRANSFERRED. SHE WORKS FOR K.R. INDUSTRIES.
MINE, TOO—THEY JUST TRANSFERRED US HERE LAST WEEK.
MINE TOO.
WOW. DOUBLE JINX.
IT'S NOT TEA-AND-CRUMPETS TIME, SOLDIERS! LET'S SEE A LITTLE ELBOW GREASE!
EWW. DISGUSTING . . . I CAN'T BELIEVE THIS IS HOW I GET TO SPEND MY BIRTHDAY!

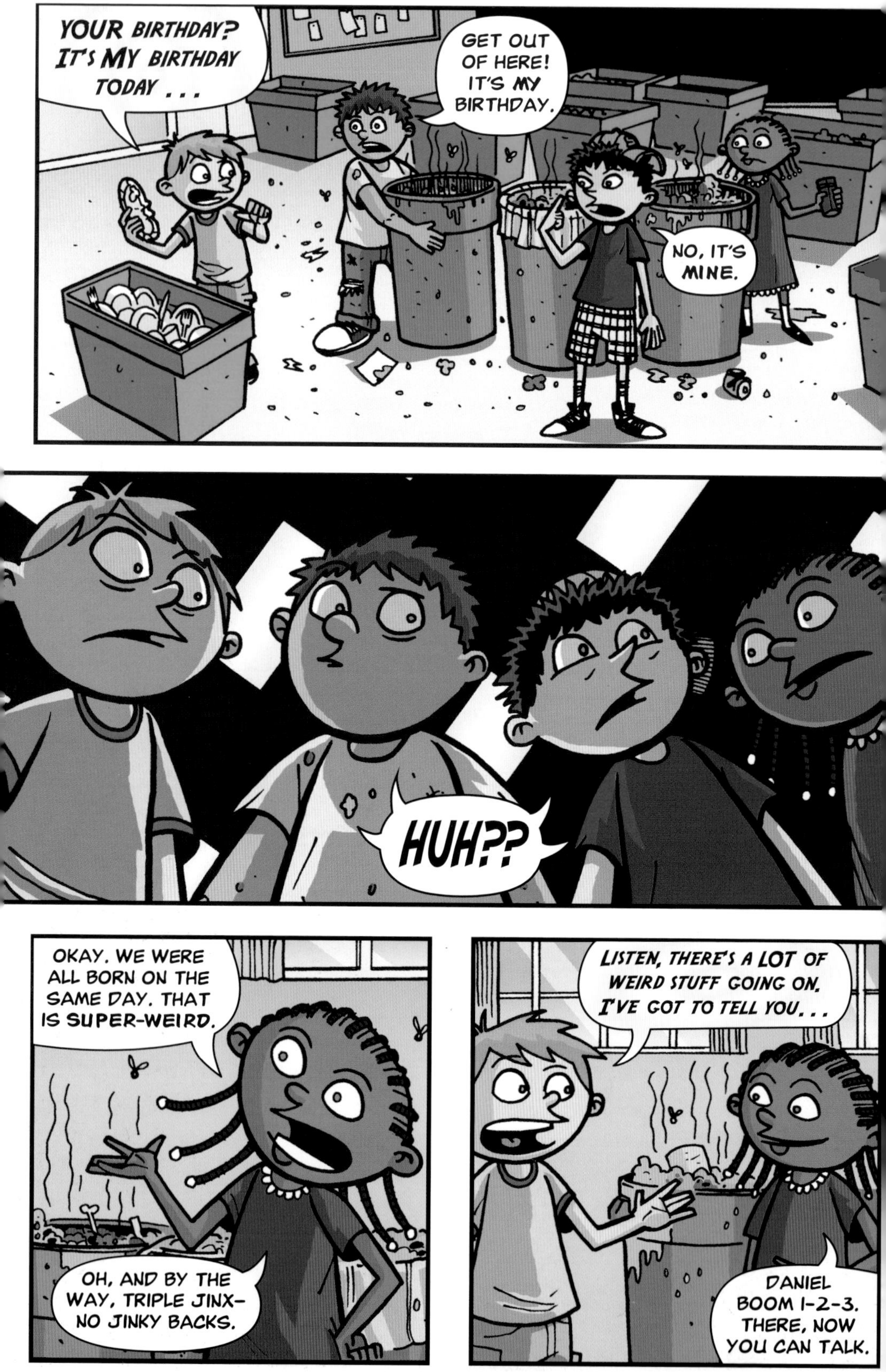
YOUR BIRTHDAY? IT'S MY BIRTHDAY TODAY . . .
GET OUT OF HERE! IT'S MY BIRTHDAY.
NO, IT'S MINE.
HUH??
OKAY. WE WERE ALL BORN ON THE SAME DAY. THAT IS SUPER-WEIRD.
OH, AND BY THE WAY, TRIPLE JINX-NO JINKY BACKS.
LISTEN, THERE'S A LOT OF WEIRD STUFF GOING ON. I'VE GOT TO TELL YOU . . .
DANIEL BOOM 1-2-3. THERE, NOW YOU CAN TALK.

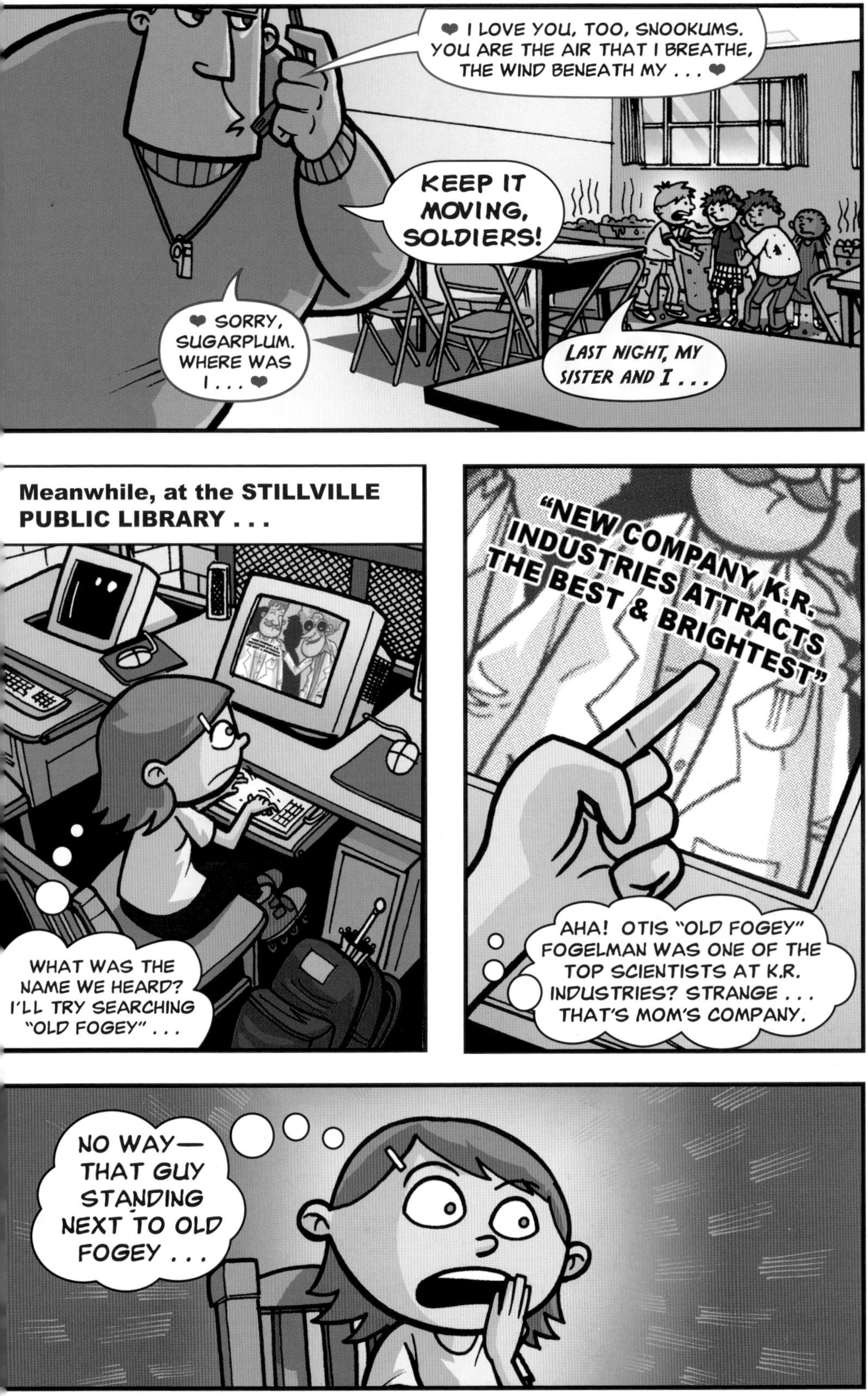
❤ I LOVE YOU, TOO, SNOOKUMS. YOU ARE THE AIR THAT I BREATHE, THE WIND BENEATH MY . . . ❤
KEEP IT MOVING, SOLDIERS!
❤ SORRY, SUGARPLUM. WHERE WAS I . . . ❤
LAST NIGHT, MY SISTER AND I . . .
Meanwhile, at the STILLVILLE PUBLIC LIBRARY . . .
WHAT WAS THE NAME WE HEARD? I'LL TRY SEARCHING "OLD FOGEY" . . .
"NEW COMPANY K.R. INDUSTRIES ATTRACTS THE BEST & BRIGHTEST"
AHA! OTIS "OLD FOGEY" FOGELMAN WAS ONE OF THE TOP SCIENTISTS AT K.R. INDUSTRIES? STRANGE . . . THAT'S MOM'S COMPANY.
NO WAY— THAT GUY STANDING NEXT TO OLD FOGEY . . .

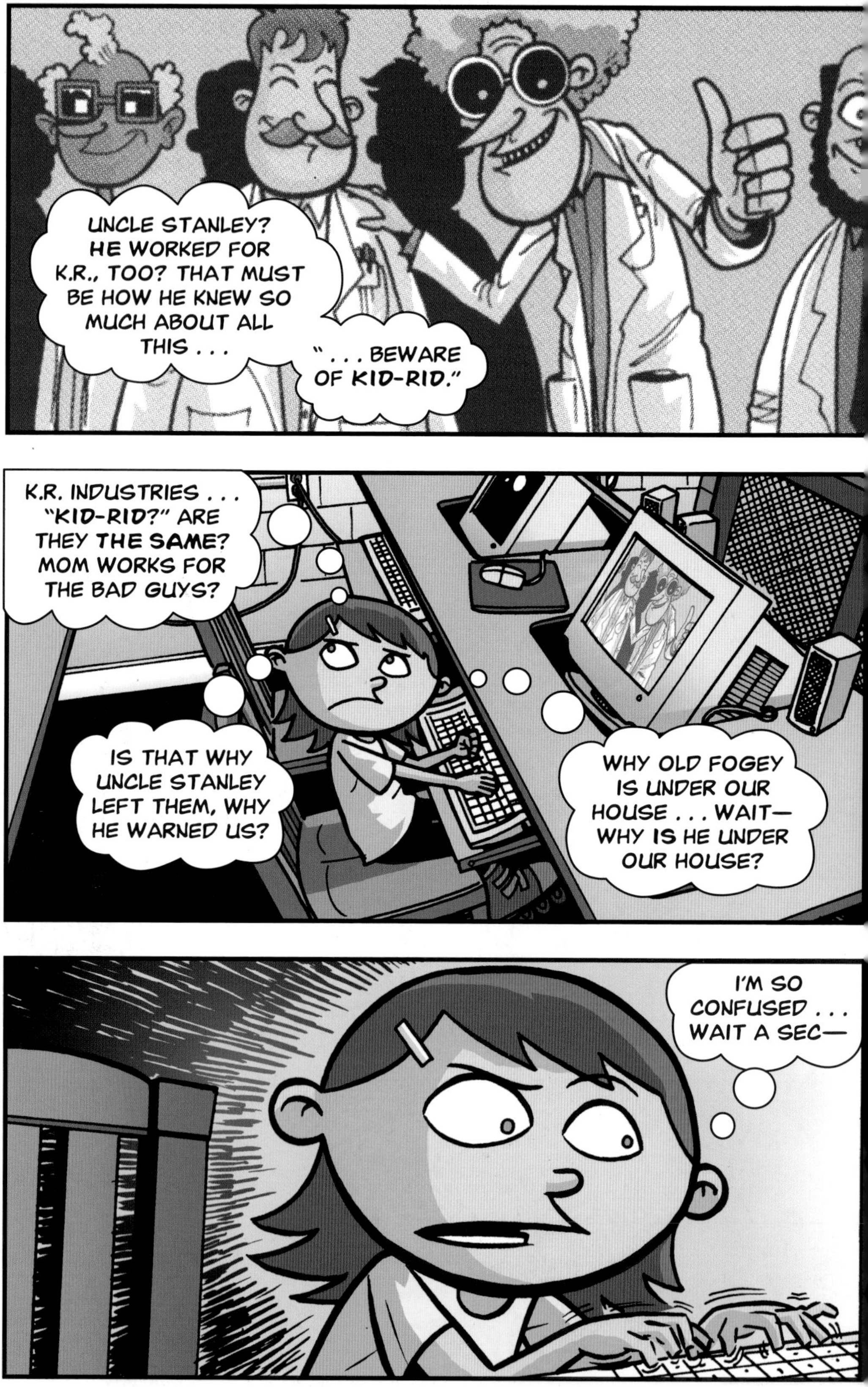
UNCLE STANLEY? HE WORKED FOR K.R., TOO? THAT MUST BE HOW HE KNEW SO MUCH ABOUT ALL THIS . . .
" . . . BEWARE OF KID-RID."
K.R. INDUSTRIES . . . "KID-RID?" ARE THEY THE SAME? MOM WORKS FOR THE BAD GUYS?
IS THAT WHY UNCLE STANLEY LEFT THEM, WHY HE WARNED US?
WHY OLD FOGEY IS UNDER OUR HOUSE . . . WAIT— WHY IS HE UNDER OUR HOUSE?
I'M SO CONFUSED . . . WAIT A SEC—

SCIENTIFIC TIMES, October 17, 1996.

FOGEY CHARGED WITH GRAND THEFT ESCAPES CUSTODY, POLICE BAFFLED

Respected scientist Otis Fogelman, known widely in the scientific community by the nickname "Old Fogey," escaped police custody Tuesday after charges were filed against the K.R. Industries veteran for the alleged heist of thousands of satellite dishes from Dishco's national warehouse. "We are as baffled by the theft as we are by Fogelman's perfect disappearing act," said Stillville Police Chief Rocky Rhodes in a statement later that day. "He has vanished literally without a trace."

Technology giant K.R. Industries disavowed any knowledge of Fogelman's criminal activity and promised to "help police in any and every way possible," according to a press statement released

(continued p. 25)

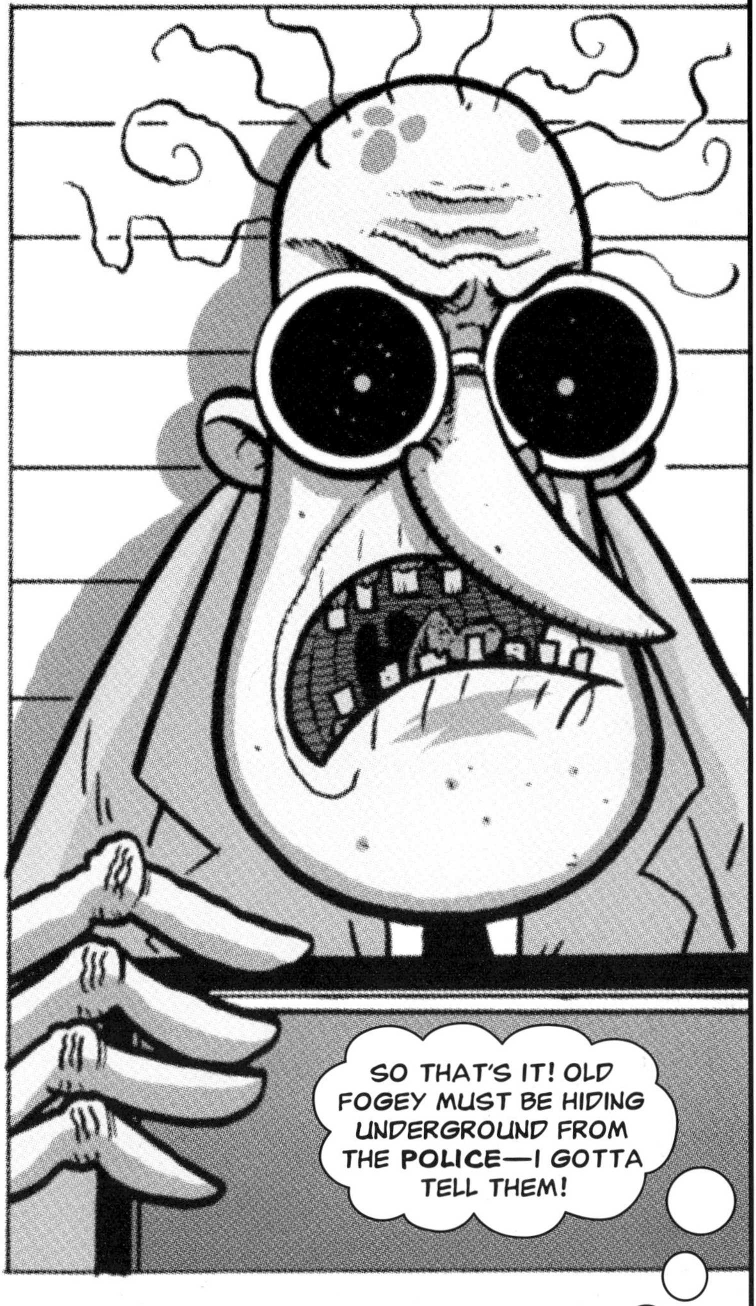
SO THAT'S IT! OLD FOGEY MUST BE HIDING UNDERGROUND FROM THE POLICE—I GOTTA TELL THEM!

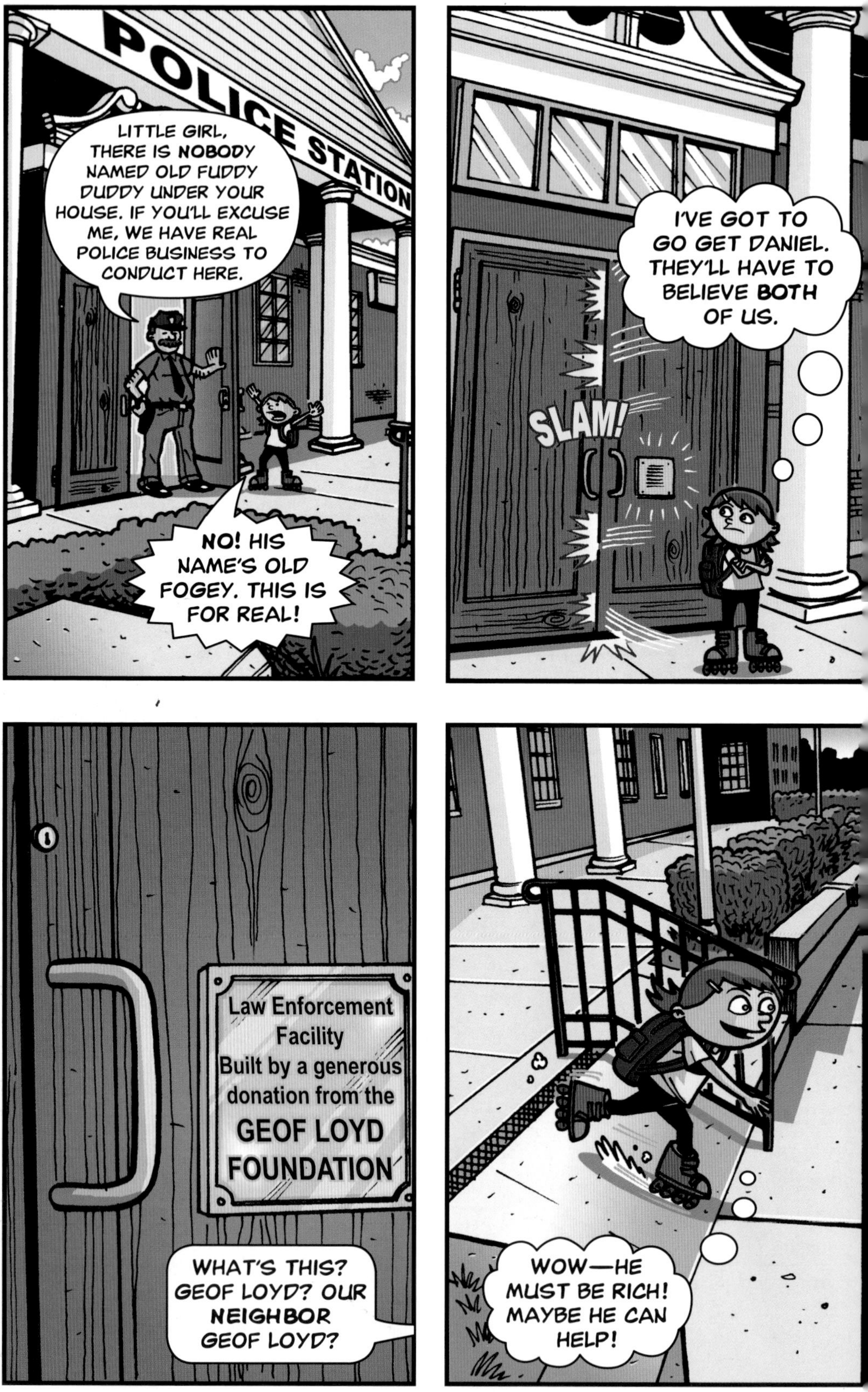
POLICE STATION
LITTLE GIRL, THERE IS NOBODY NAMED OLD FUDDY DUDDY UNDER YOUR HOUSE. IF YOU'LL EXCUSE ME, WE HAVE REAL POLICE BUSINESS TO CONDUCT HERE.
NO! HIS NAME'S OLD FOGEY. THIS IS FOR REAL!
I'VE GOT TO GO GET DANIEL. THEY'LL HAVE TO BELIEVE BOTH OF US.
SLAM!
Law Enforcement Facility Built by a generous donation from the GEOF LOYD FOUNDATION
WHAT'S THIS? GEOF LOYD? OUR NEIGHBOR GEOF LOYD?
WOW—HE MUST BE RICH! MAYBE HE CAN HELP!

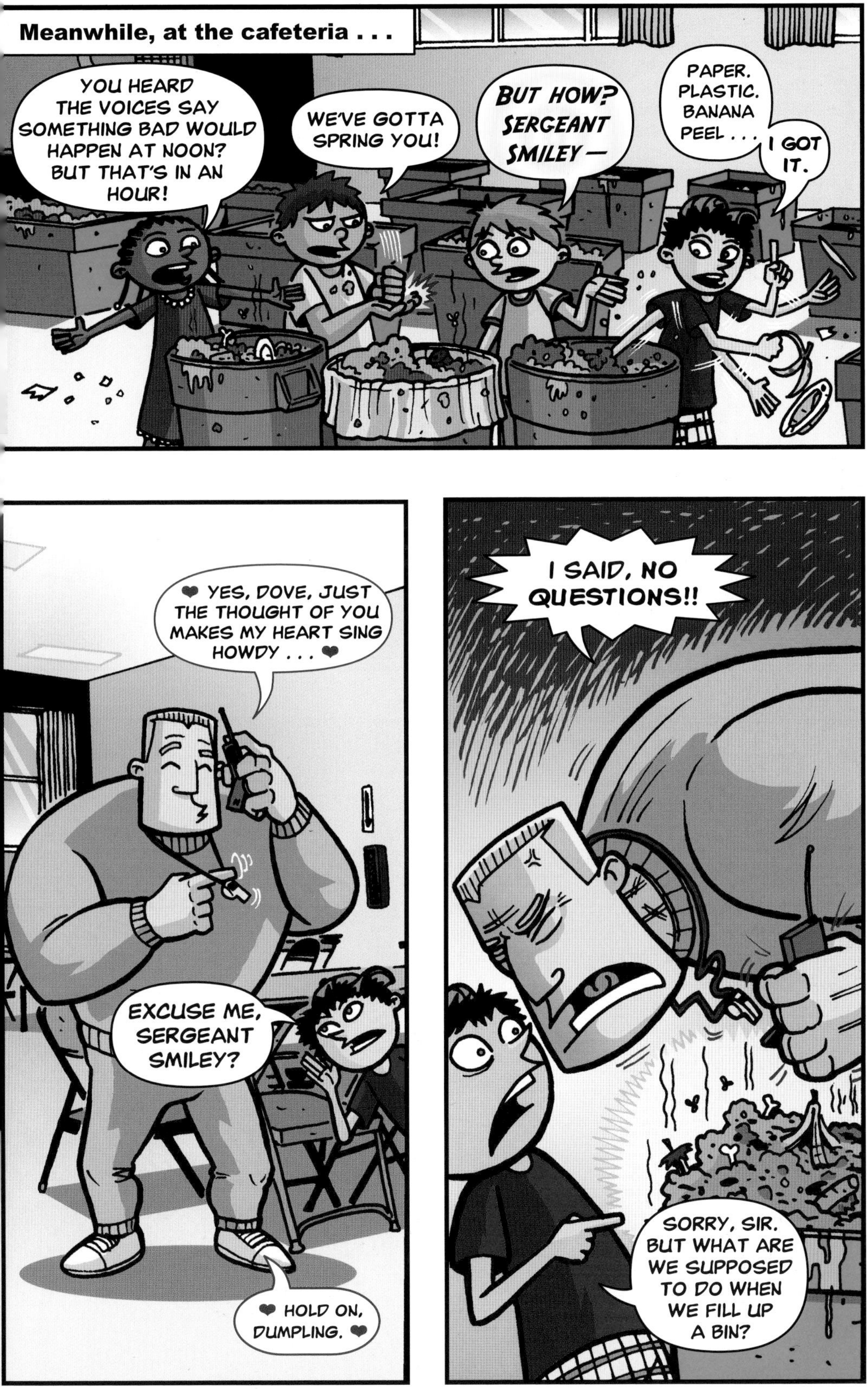
Meanwhile, at the cafeteria . . .
YOU HEARD THE VOICES SAY SOMETHING BAD WOULD HAPPEN AT NOON? BUT THAT'S IN AN HOUR!
WE'VE GOTTA SPRING YOU!
BUT HOW? SERGEANT SMILEY—
PAPER. PLASTIC. BANANA PEEL . . .
I GOT IT.
YES, DOVE, JUST THE THOUGHT OF YOU MAKES MY HEART SING HOWDY . . .
EXCUSE ME, SERGEANT SMILEY?
HOLD ON, DUMPLING.
I SAID, NO QUESTIONS!!
SORRY, SIR. BUT WHAT ARE WE SUPPOSED TO DO WHEN WE FILL UP A BIN?

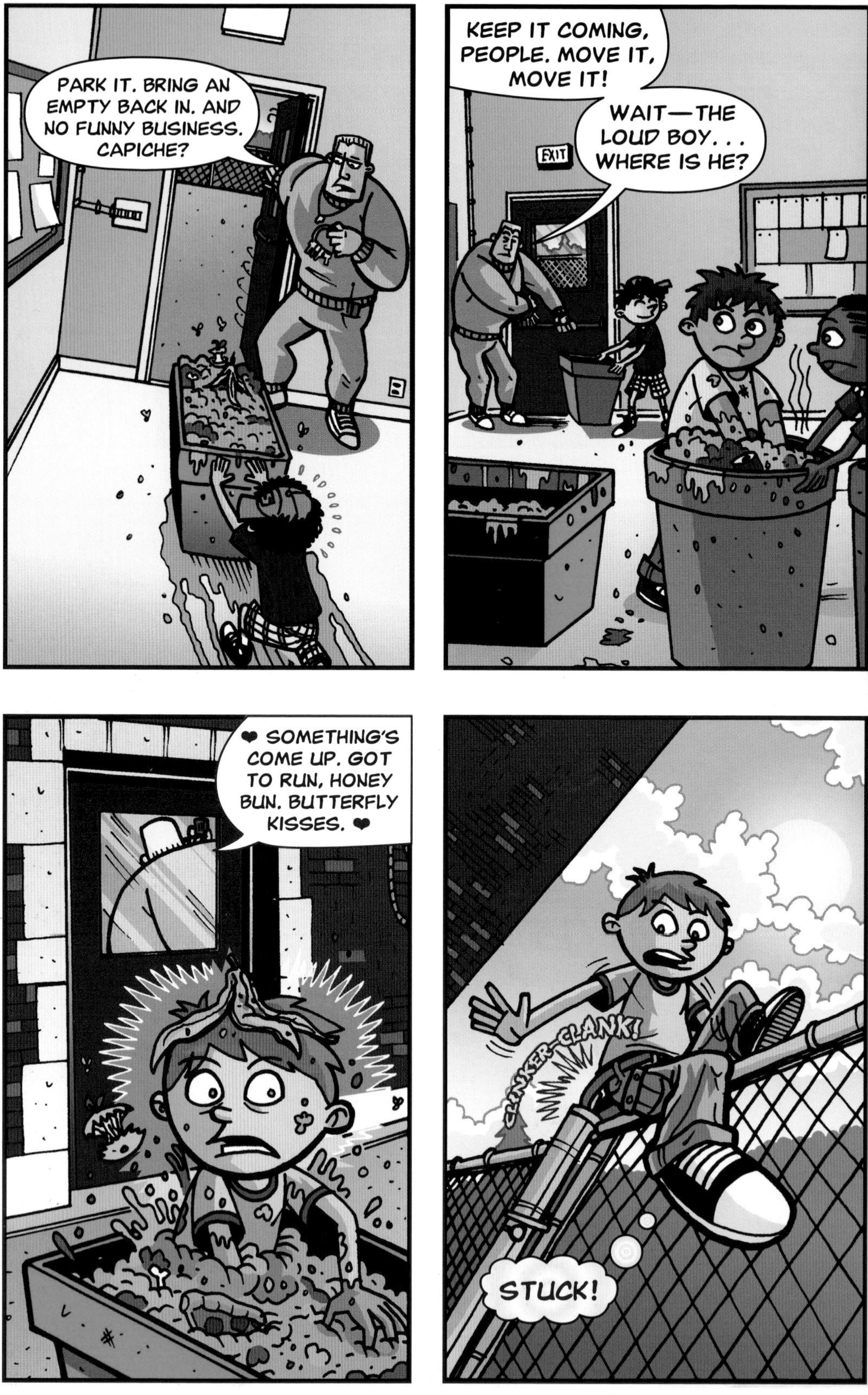
PARK IT. BRING AN EMPTY BACK IN. AND NO FUNNY BUSINESS. CAPICHE?
KEEP IT COMING, PEOPLE. MOVE IT, MOVE IT!
EXIT
WAIT—THE LOUD BOY . . . WHERE IS HE?
❤ SOMETHING'S COME UP. GOT TO RUN, HONEY BUN. BUTTERFLY KISSES. ❤
CLINKER-CLANK!
STUCK!

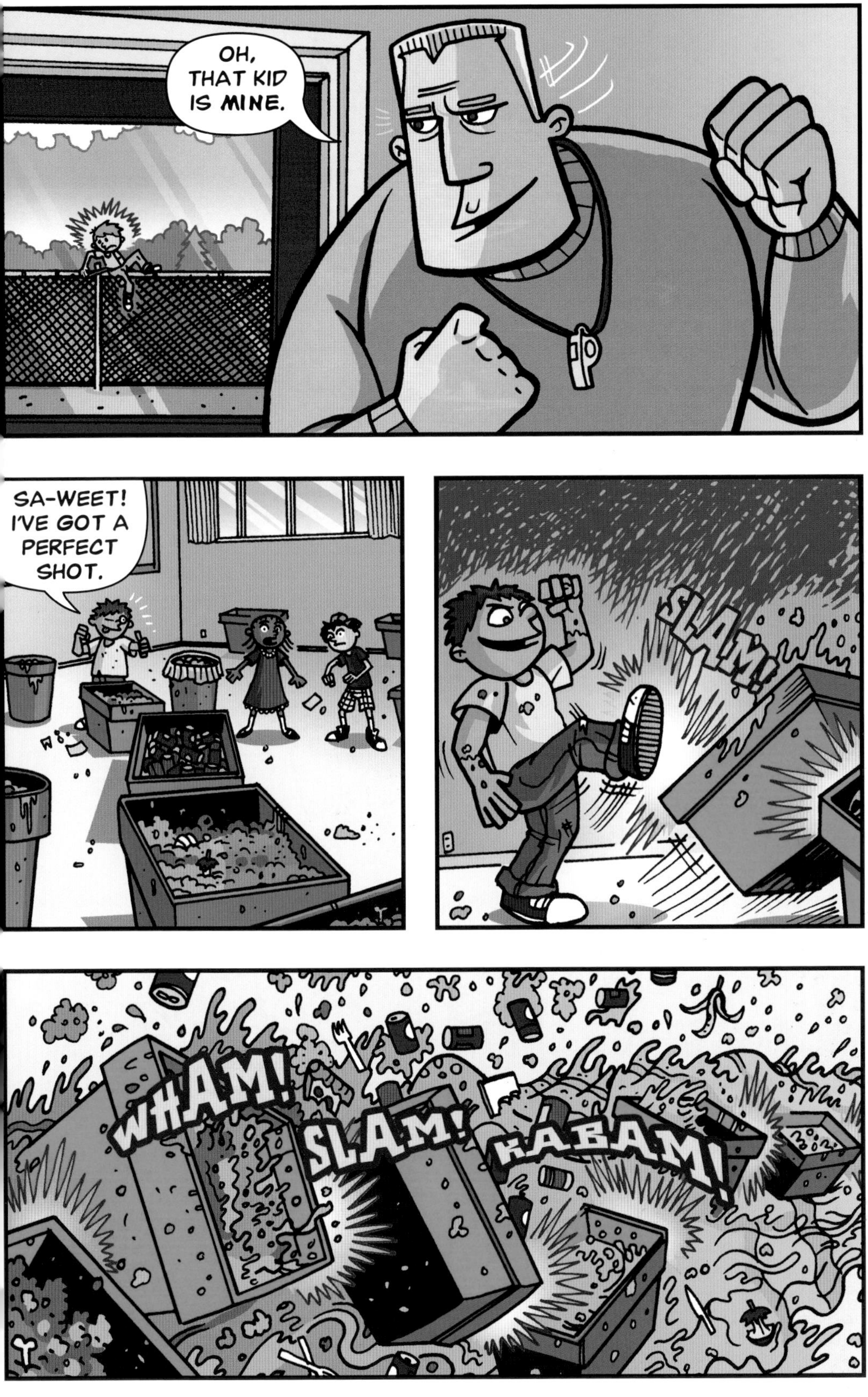
OH, THAT KID IS MINE.
SA-WEET! I'VE GOT A PERFECT SHOT.
SLAM!
WHAM!
SLAM!
KABAM!

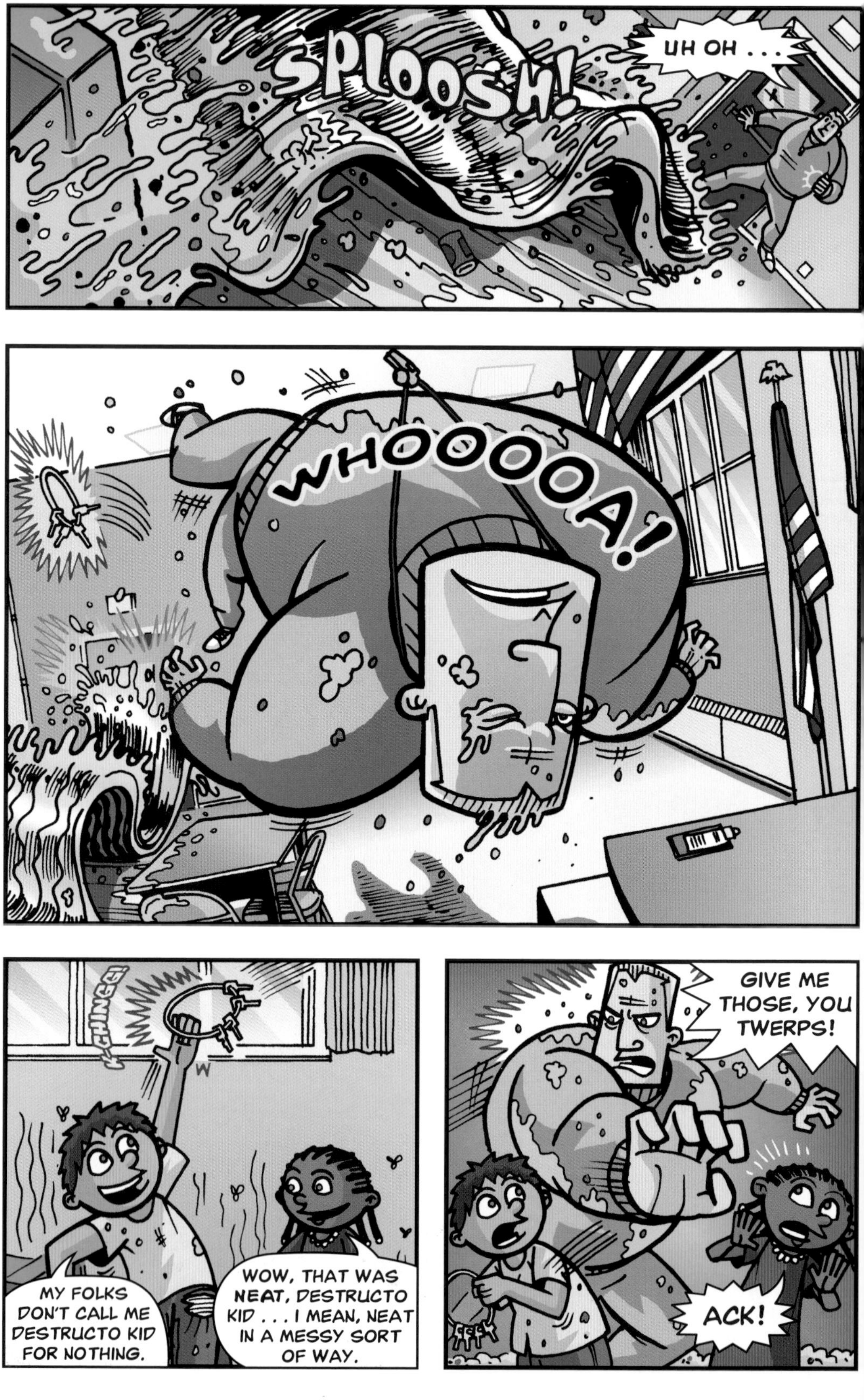
SPLOOSH!
UH OH . . .
WHOOOOA!
K-CHING!
MY FOLKS DON'T CALL ME DESTRUCTO KID FOR NOTHING.
WOW, THAT WAS NEAT, DESTRUCTO KID . . . I MEAN, NEAT IN A MESSY SORT OF WAY.
GIVE ME THOSE, YOU TWERPS!
ACK!

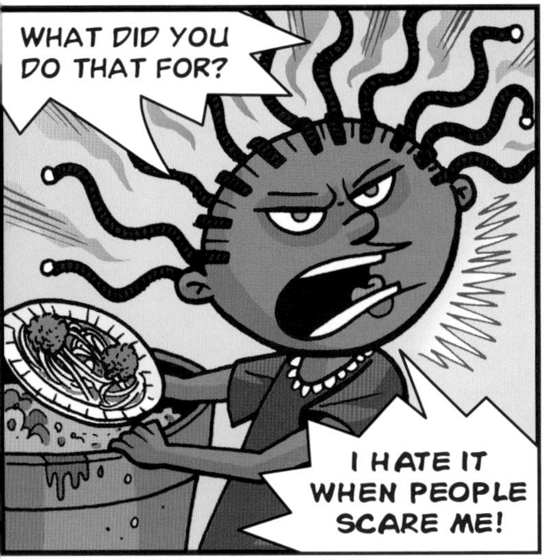
WHAT DID YOU DO THAT FOR?
I HATE IT WHEN PEOPLE SCARE ME!

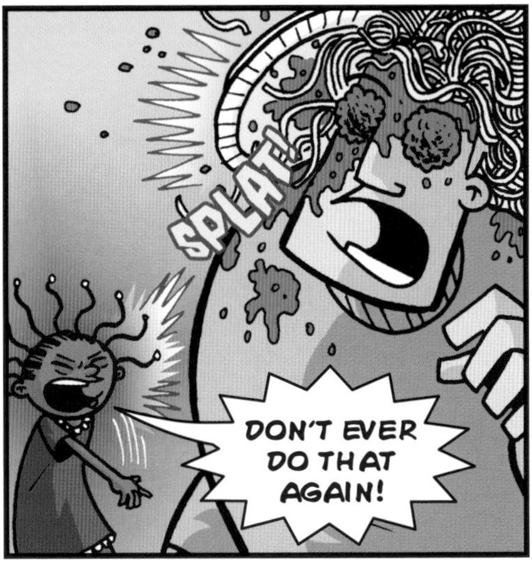
SPLAT!
DON'T EVER DO THAT AGAIN!

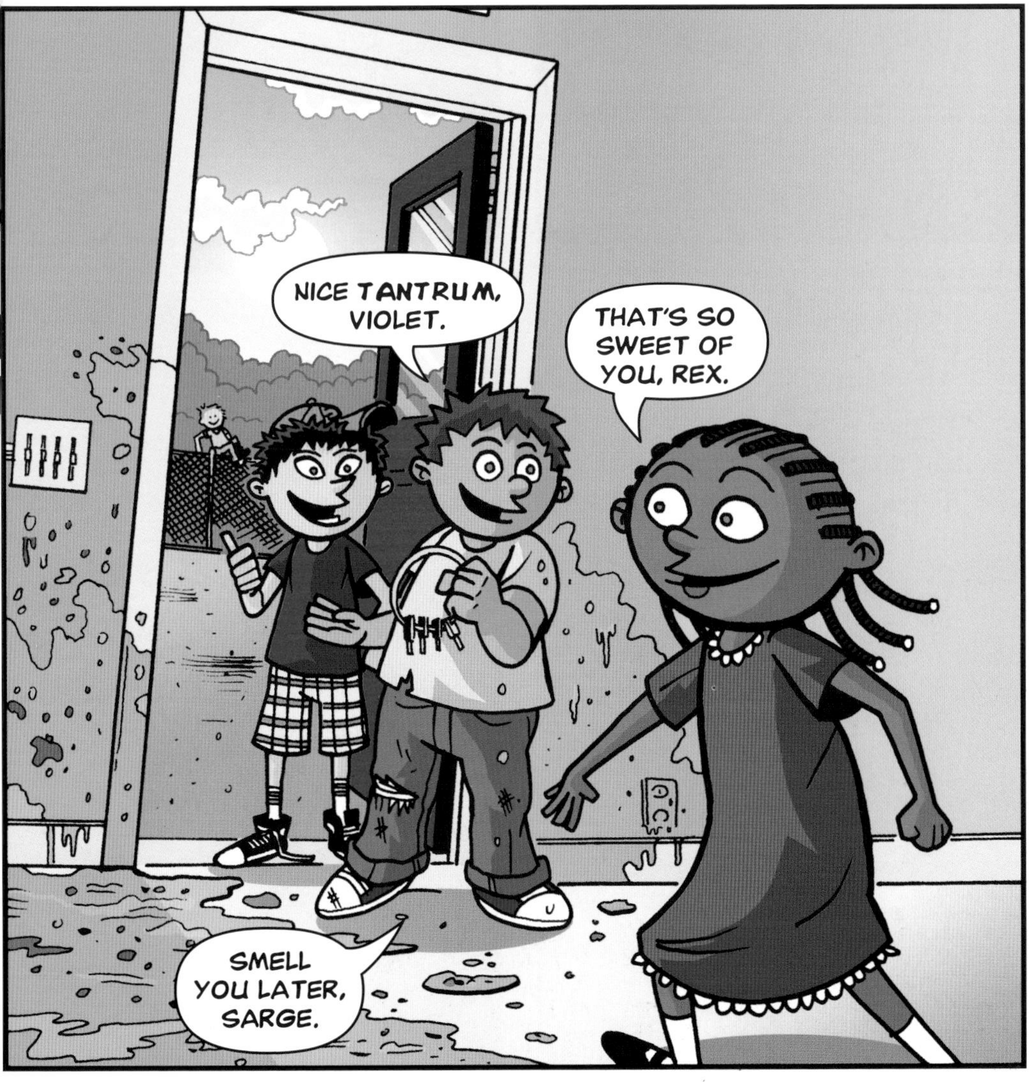
NICE TANTRUM, VIOLET.
THAT'S SO SWEET OF YOU, REX.
SMELL YOU LATER, SARGE.

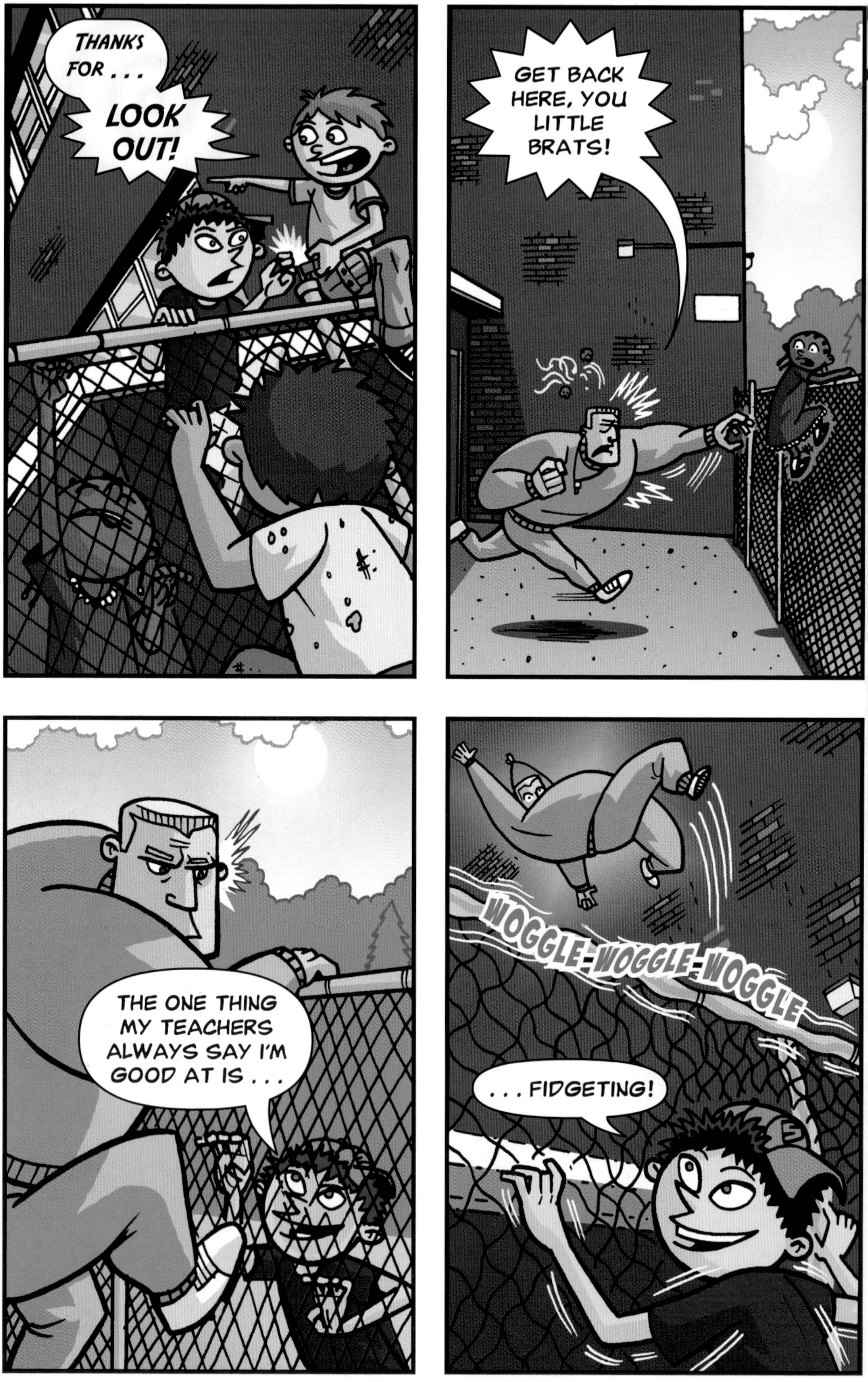
THANKS FOR . . .
LOOK OUT!
GET BACK HERE, YOU LITTLE BRATS!
THE ONE THING MY TEACHERS ALWAYS SAY I'M GOOD AT IS . . .
WOGGLE-WOGGLE-WOGGLE
. . . FIDGETING!

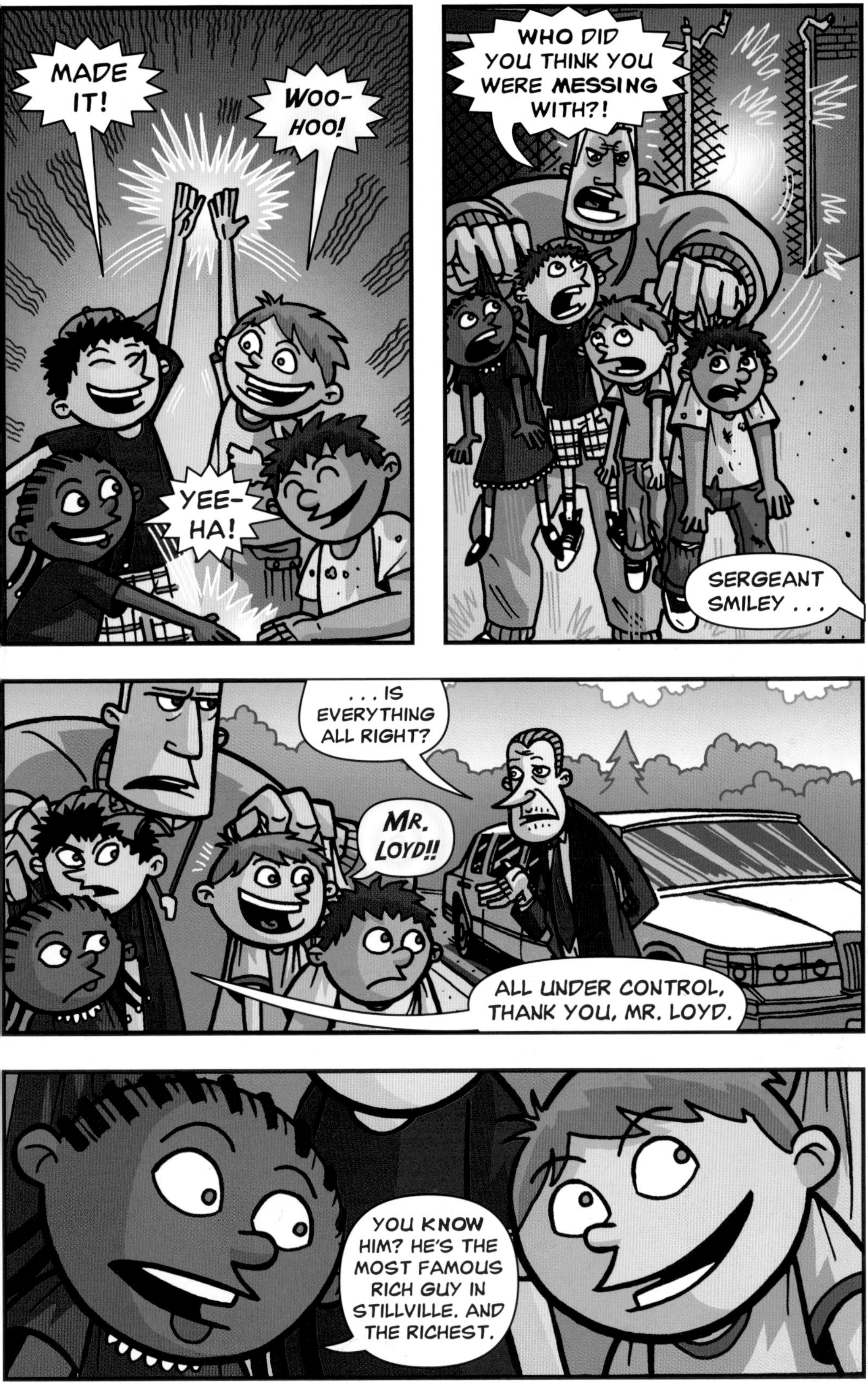
MADE IT!
WOO-HOO!
YEE-HA!
WHO DID YOU THINK YOU WERE MESSING WITH?!
SERGEANT SMILEY . . .
. . . IS EVERYTHING ALL RIGHT?
MR. LOYD!!
ALL UNDER CONTROL, THANK YOU, MR. LOYD.
YOU KNOW HIM? HE'S THE MOST FAMOUS RICH GUY IN STILLVILLE. AND THE RICHEST.

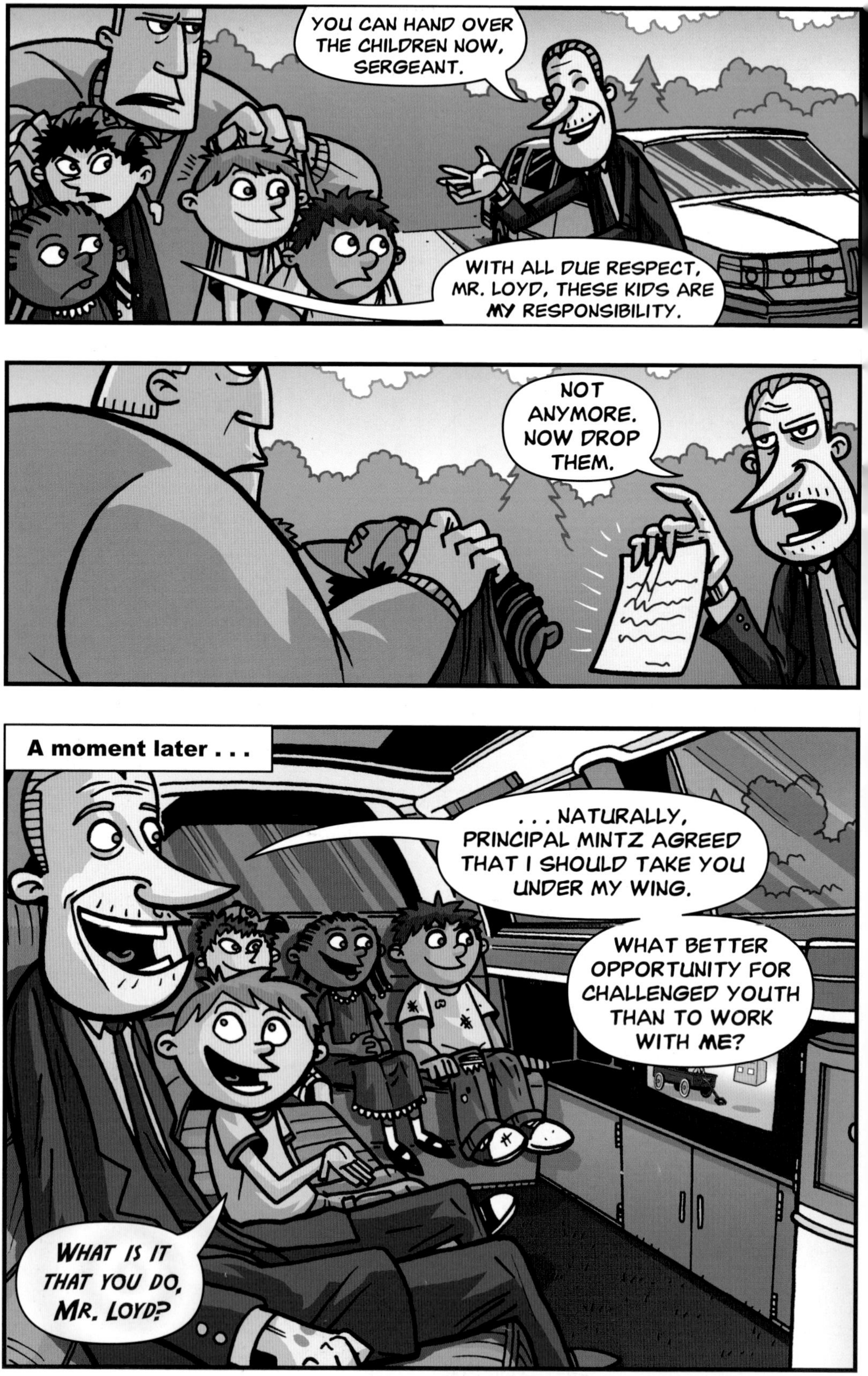
YOU CAN HAND OVER THE CHILDREN NOW, SERGEANT.
WITH ALL DUE RESPECT, MR. LOYD, THESE KIDS ARE MY RESPONSIBILITY.
NOT ANYMORE. NOW DROP THEM.
A moment later . . .
. . . NATURALLY, PRINCIPAL MINTZ AGREED THAT I SHOULD TAKE YOU UNDER MY WING.
WHAT BETTER OPPORTUNITY FOR CHALLENGED YOUTH THAN TO WORK WITH ME?
WHAT IS IT THAT YOU DO, MR. LOYD?

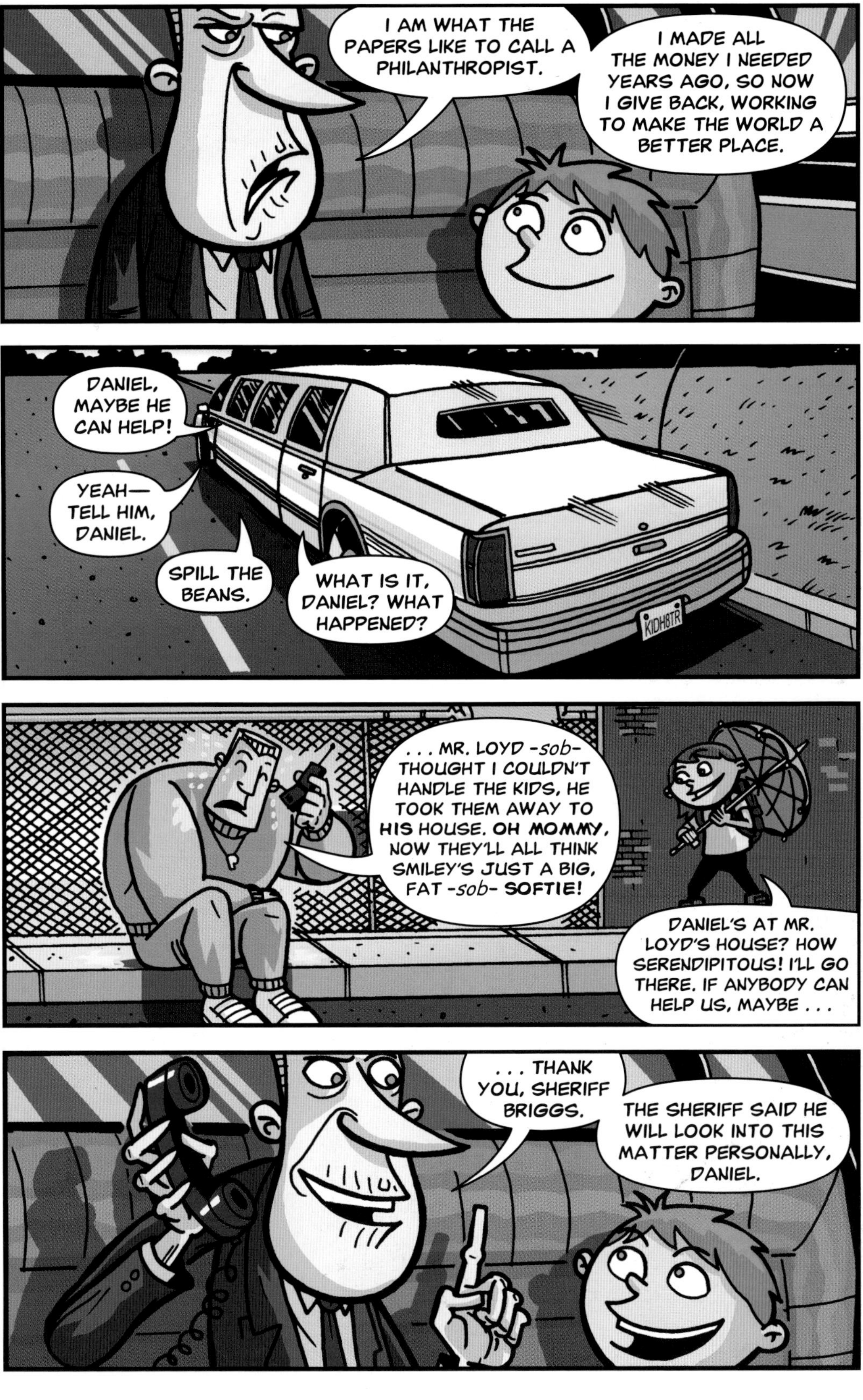
I AM WHAT THE PAPERS LIKE TO CALL A PHILANTHROPIST.
I MADE ALL THE MONEY I NEEDED YEARS AGO, SO NOW I GIVE BACK, WORKING TO MAKE THE WORLD A BETTER PLACE.
DANIEL, MAYBE HE CAN HELP!
YEAH— TELL HIM, DANIEL.
SPILL THE BEANS.
WHAT IS IT, DANIEL? WHAT HAPPENED?
KIDH8TR
. . . MR. LOYD *-sob-* THOUGHT I COULDN'T HANDLE THE KIDS, HE TOOK THEM AWAY TO **HIS** HOUSE. **OH MOMMY**, NOW THEY'LL ALL THINK SMILEY'S JUST A BIG, FAT *-sob-* **SOFTIE**!
DANIEL'S AT MR. LOYD'S HOUSE? HOW SERENDIPITOUS! I'LL GO THERE. IF ANYBODY CAN HELP US, MAYBE . . .
. . . THANK YOU, SHERIFF BRIGGS.
THE SHERIFF SAID HE WILL LOOK INTO THIS MATTER PERSONALLY, DANIEL.

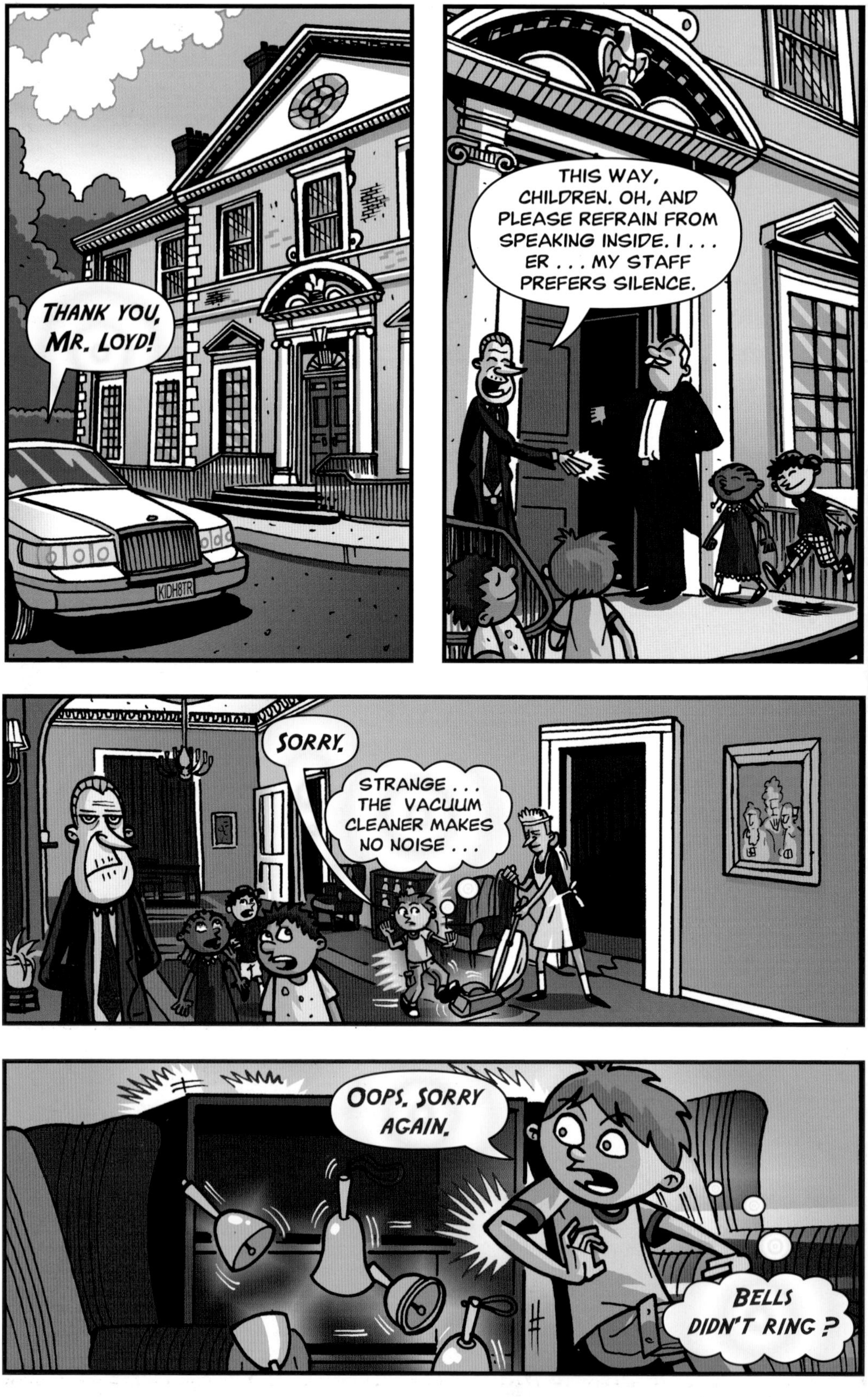

THANK YOU, MR. LOYD!
KIDH8TR
THIS WAY, CHILDREN. OH, AND PLEASE REFRAIN FROM SPEAKING INSIDE. I . . . ER . . . MY STAFF PREFERS SILENCE.
SORRY.
STRANGE . . . THE VACUUM CLEANER MAKES NO NOISE . . .
OOPS. SORRY AGAIN.
BELLS DIDN'T RING?

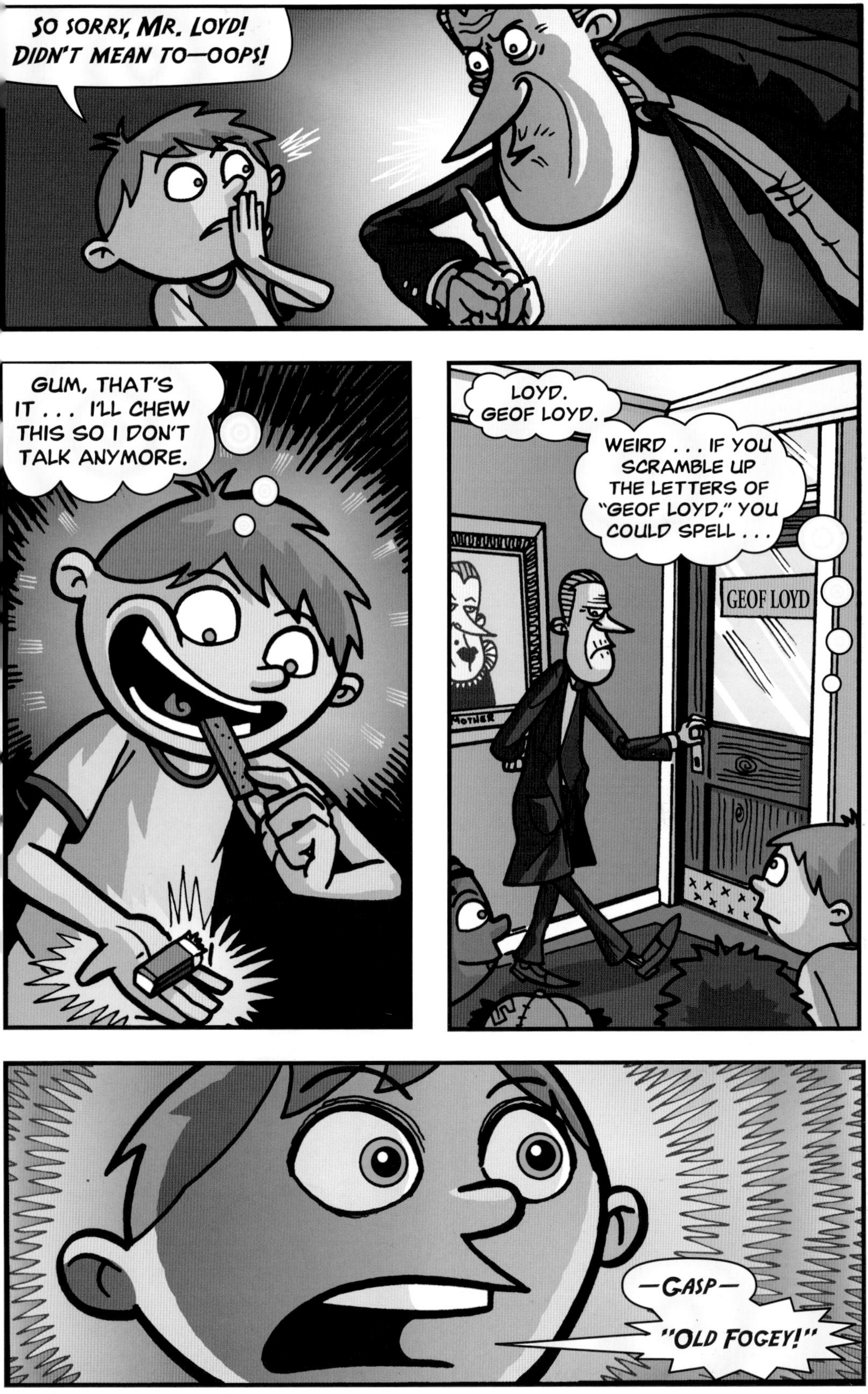
SO SORRY, MR. LOYD! DIDN'T MEAN TO—OOPS!
GUM, THAT'S IT . . . I'LL CHEW THIS SO I DON'T TALK ANYMORE.
LOYD. GEOF LOYD.
WEIRD . . . IF YOU SCRAMBLE UP THE LETTERS OF "GEOF LOYD," YOU COULD SPELL . . .
GEOF LOYD
MOTHER
—GASP—
"OLD FOGEY!"

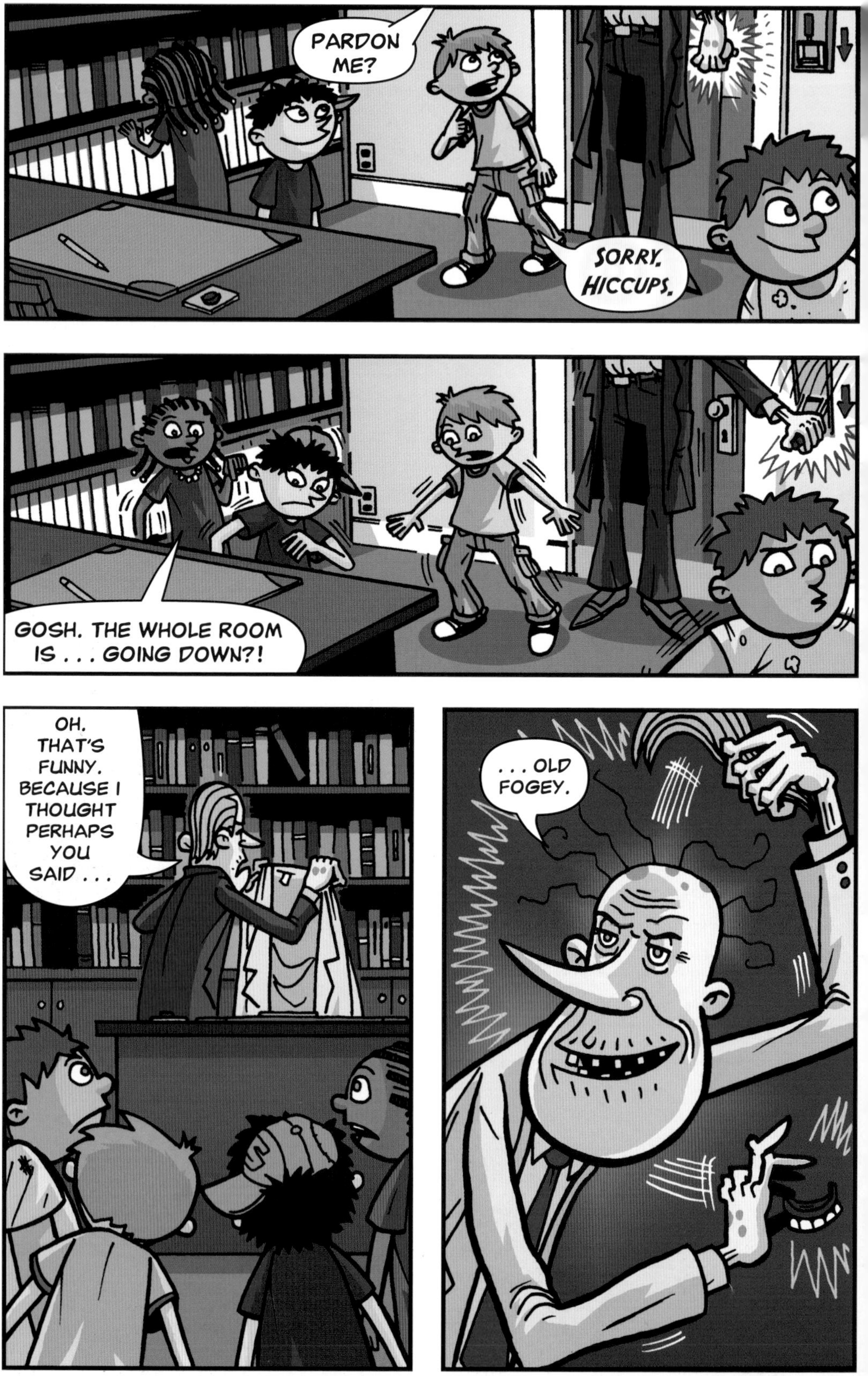

PARDON ME?
SORRY. HICCUPS.
GOSH. THE WHOLE ROOM IS . . . GOING DOWN?!
OH. THAT'S FUNNY. BECAUSE I THOUGHT PERHAPS YOU SAID . . .
. . . OLD FOGEY.

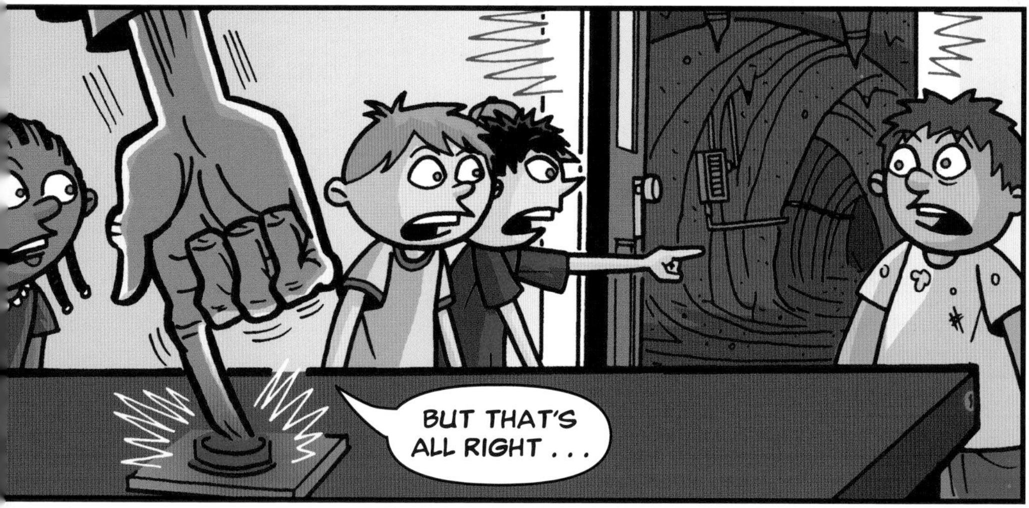
BUT THAT'S ALL RIGHT . . .

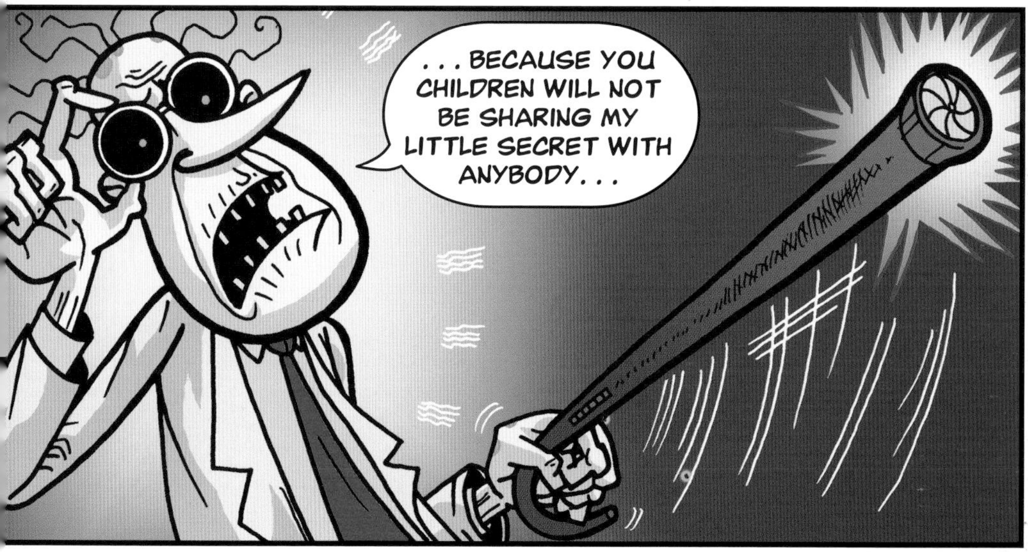
. . . BECAUSE YOU CHILDREN WILL NOT BE SHARING MY LITTLE SECRET WITH ANYBODY. . .

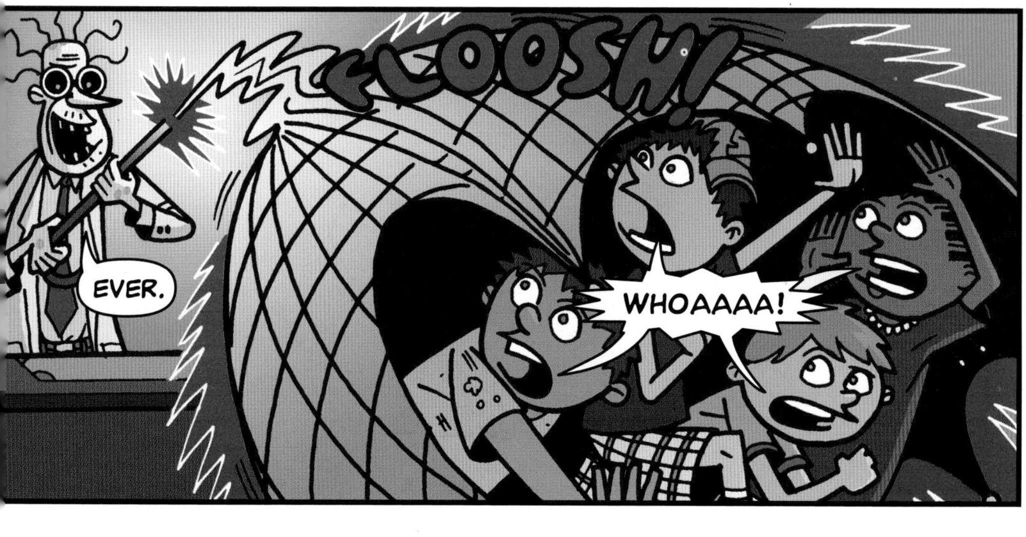
FLOOSH!
EVER.
WHOAAAA!

NO TIME TO STOP HOME . . . GOTTA GET TO MR. LOYD'S. BUT—

HUH?

CHARLIE??

HIS COLLAR . . .

CHARLIE— WHERE ARE YOU? CHARLIE?

Back in Old Fogey's underground lair . . .

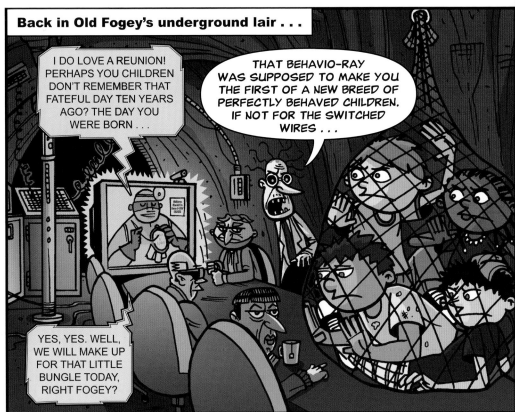

I DO LOVE A REUNION! PERHAPS YOU CHILDREN DON'T REMEMBER THAT FATEFUL DAY TEN YEARS AGO? THE DAY YOU WERE BORN . . .

THAT BEHAVIO-RAY WAS SUPPOSED TO MAKE YOU THE FIRST OF A NEW BREED OF PERFECTLY BEHAVED CHILDREN. IF NOT FOR THE SWITCHED WIRES . . .

YES, YES. WELL, WE WILL MAKE UP FOR THAT LITTLE BUNGLE TODAY, RIGHT FOGEY?

TECHNOLOGY HAS COME A **LONG** WAY IN TEN YEARS. BEHOLD . . .

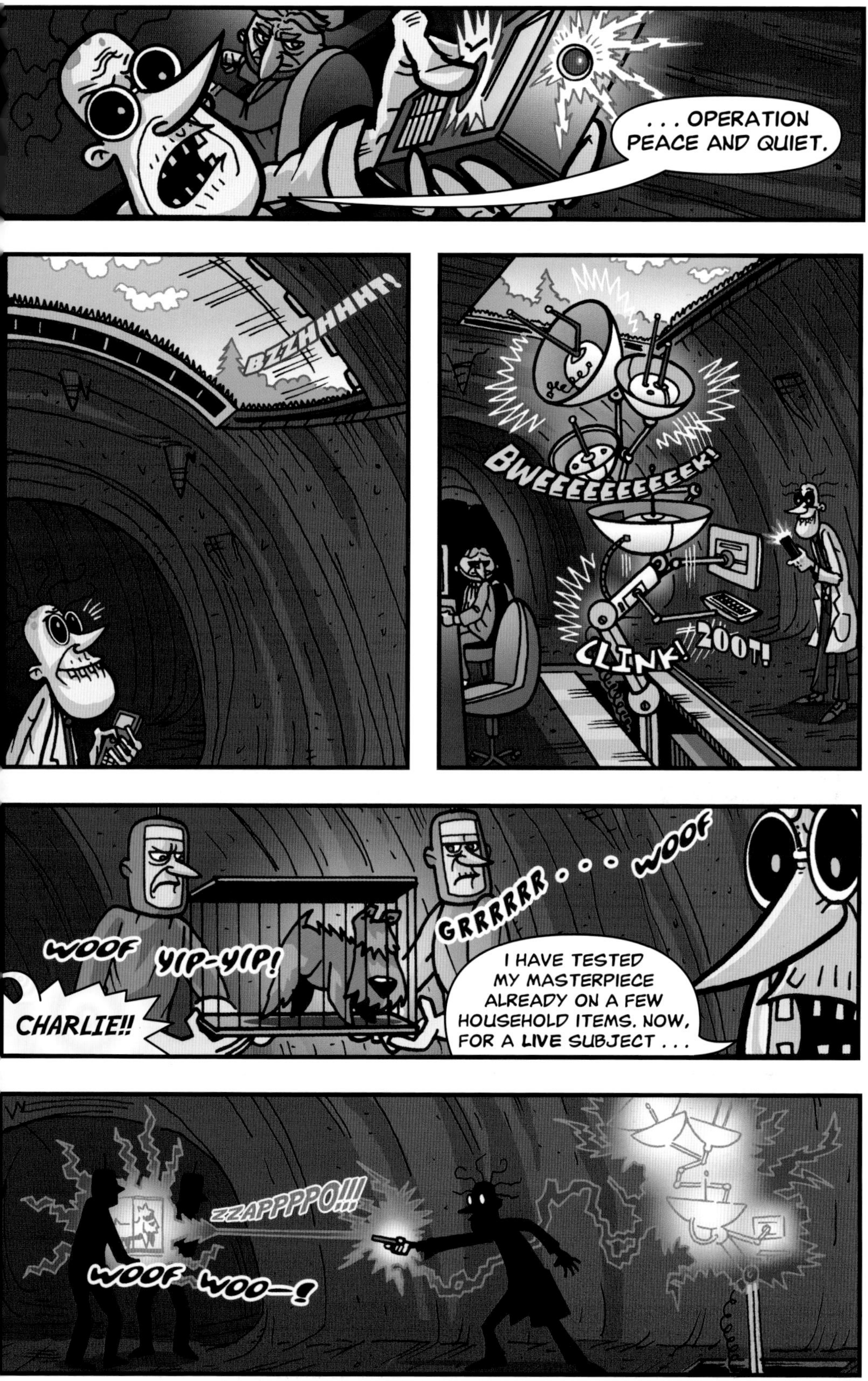
. . . OPERATION PEACE AND QUIET.
BZZHHHHT!
BWEEEEEEEEEEK!
CLINK!
ZOOT!
GRRRRRR . . . WOOF
WOOF
YIP-YIP!
CHARLIE!!
I HAVE TESTED MY MASTERPIECE ALREADY ON A FEW HOUSEHOLD ITEMS. NOW, FOR A LIVE SUBJECT . . .
ZZAPPPPO!!!
WOOF WOO—!

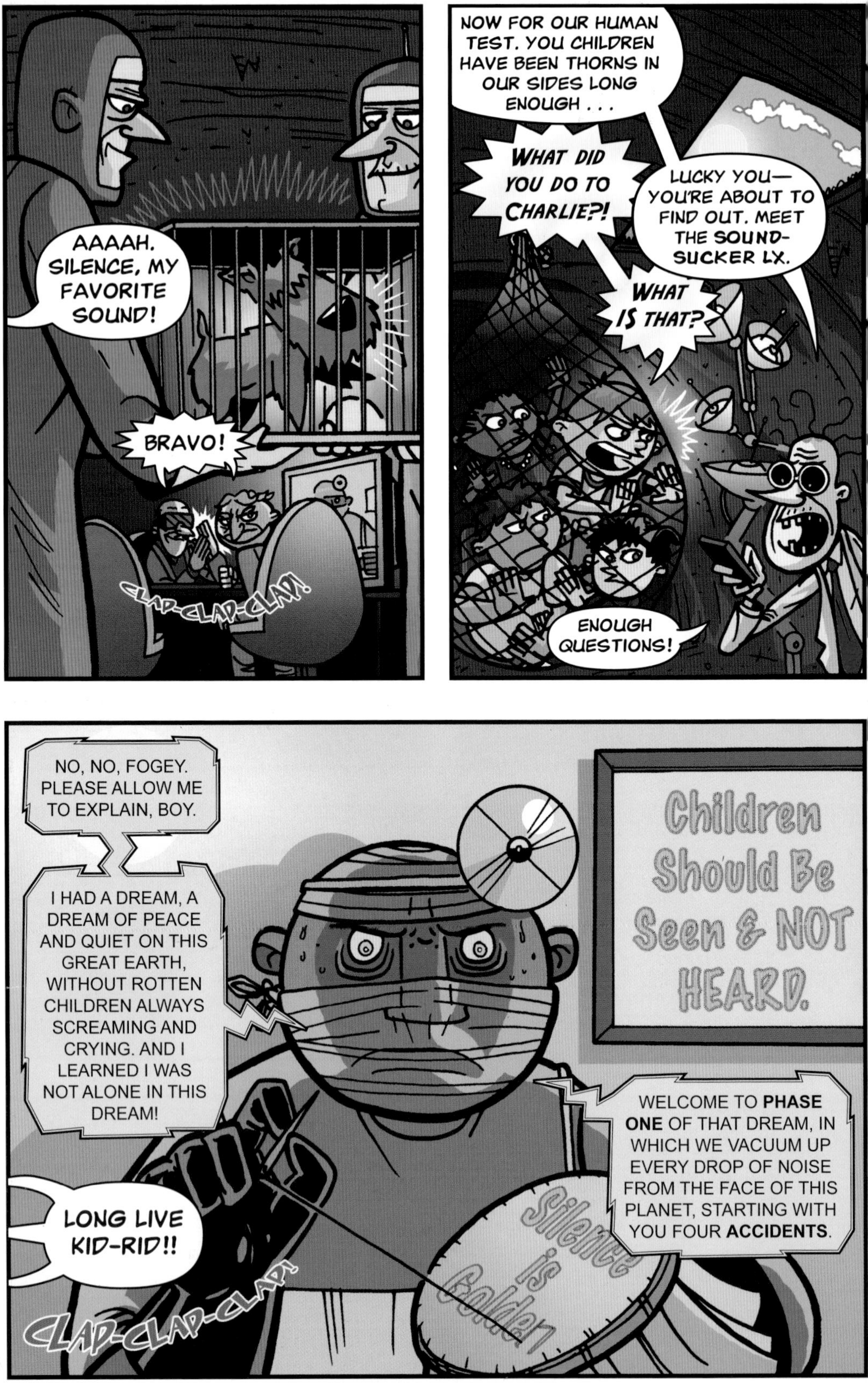
AAAAH. SILENCE, MY FAVORITE SOUND!
BRAVO!
CLAP-CLAP-CLAP!
NOW FOR OUR HUMAN TEST. YOU CHILDREN HAVE BEEN THORNS IN OUR SIDES LONG ENOUGH . . .
WHAT DID YOU DO TO CHARLIE?!
LUCKY YOU— YOU'RE ABOUT TO FIND OUT. MEET THE SOUND-SUCKER LX.
WHAT IS THAT?
ENOUGH QUESTIONS!
NO, NO, FOGEY. PLEASE ALLOW ME TO EXPLAIN, BOY.
I HAD A DREAM, A DREAM OF PEACE AND QUIET ON THIS GREAT EARTH, WITHOUT ROTTEN CHILDREN ALWAYS SCREAMING AND CRYING. AND I LEARNED I WAS NOT ALONE IN THIS DREAM!
Children Should Be Seen & NOT HEARD.
WELCOME TO PHASE ONE OF THAT DREAM, IN WHICH WE VACUUM UP EVERY DROP OF NOISE FROM THE FACE OF THIS PLANET, STARTING WITH YOU FOUR ACCIDENTS.
LONG LIVE KID-RID!!
Silence is Golden
CLAP-CLAP-CLAP!

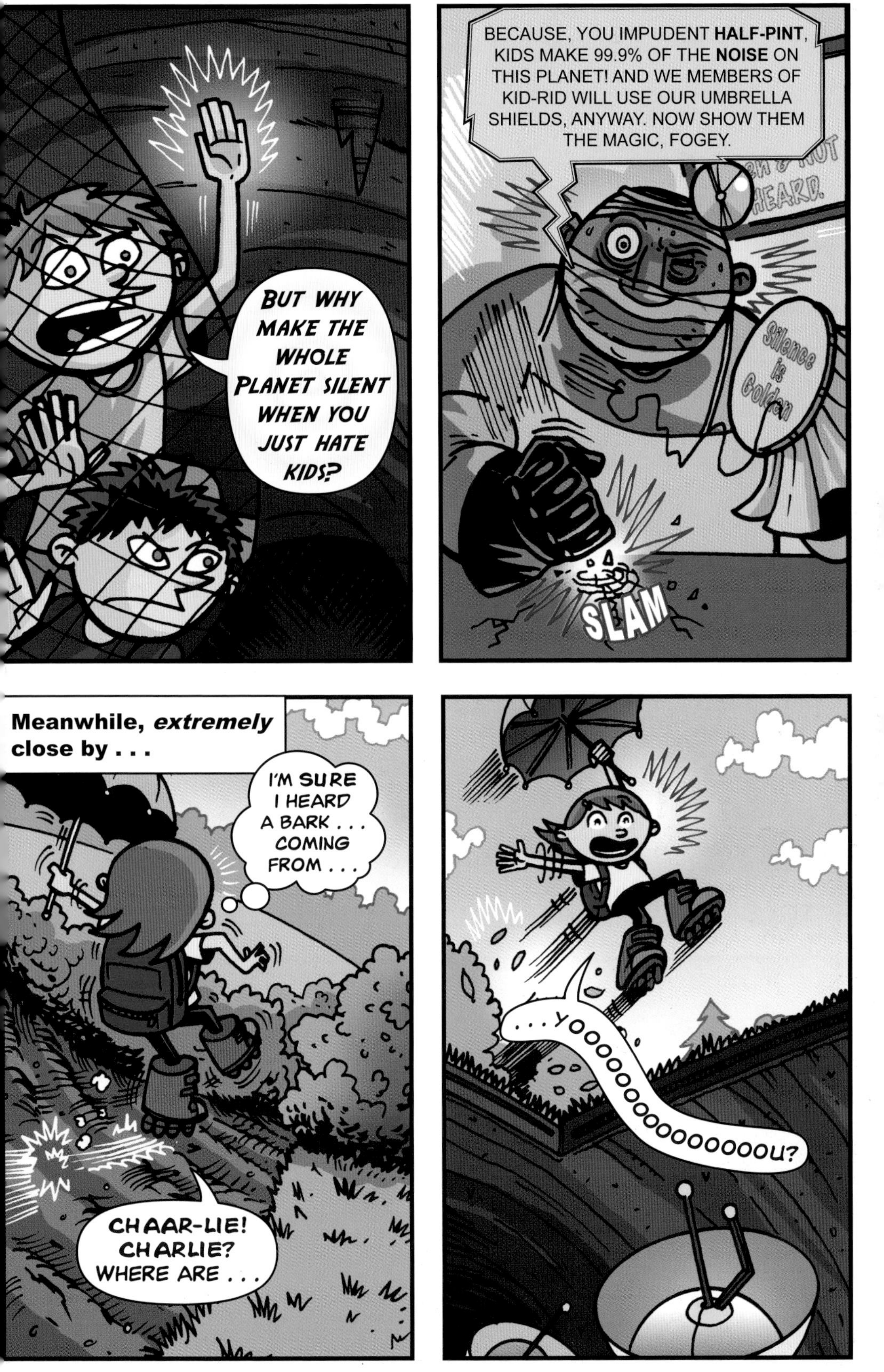
BUT WHY MAKE THE WHOLE PLANET SILENT WHEN YOU JUST HATE KIDS?
BECAUSE, YOU IMPUDENT HALF-PINT, KIDS MAKE 99.9% OF THE NOISE ON THIS PLANET! AND WE MEMBERS OF KID-RID WILL USE OUR UMBRELLA SHIELDS, ANYWAY. NOW SHOW THEM THE MAGIC, FOGEY.
Silence is Golden
SLAM
Meanwhile, extremely close by . . .
I'M SURE I HEARD A BARK . . . COMING FROM . . .
CHAAR-LIE! CHARLIE? WHERE ARE . . .
. . . YOOOOOOOOOOOOOOOOOOOU?

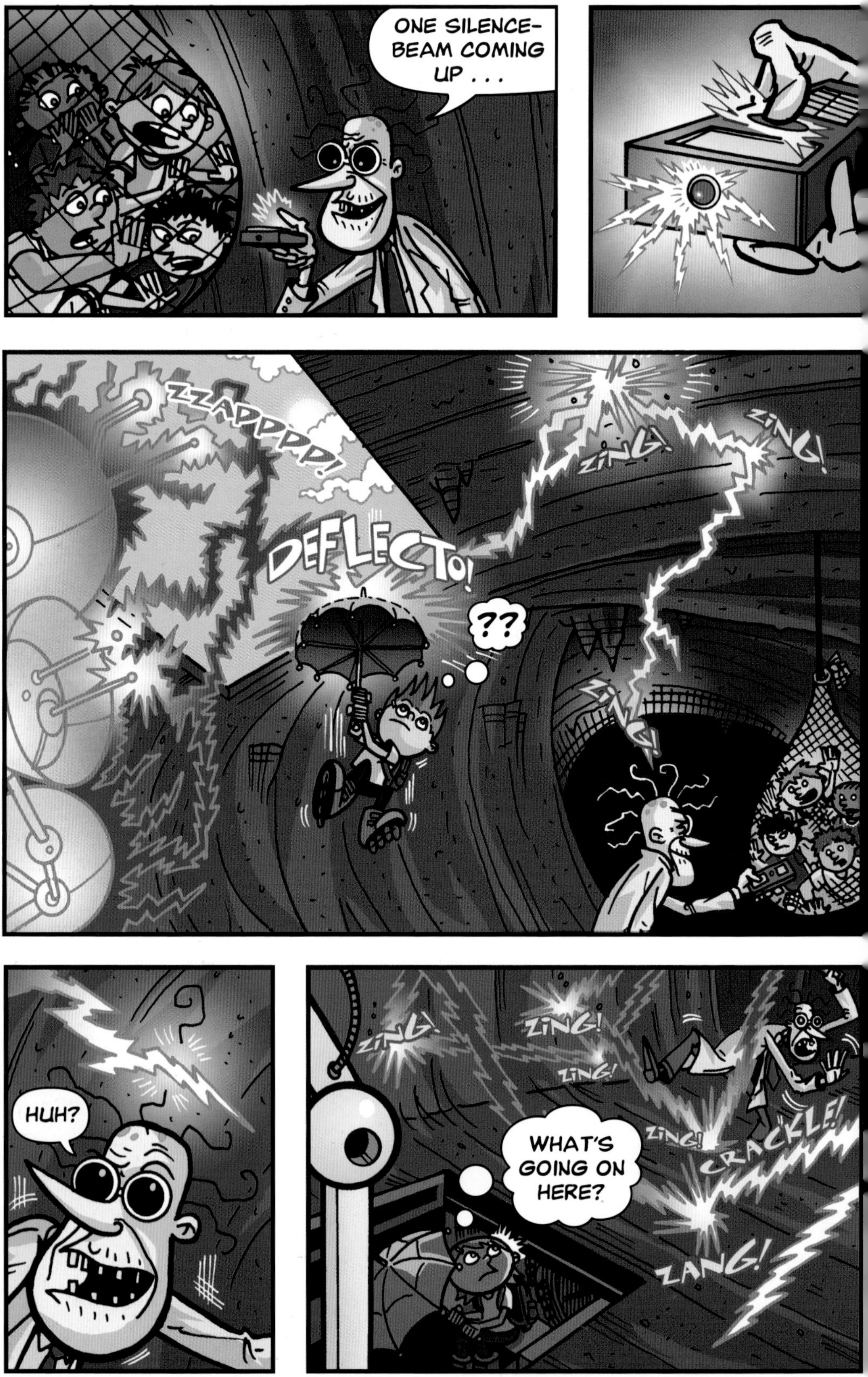
ONE SILENCE-BEAM COMING UP . . .
ZZAPPPPP!
DEFLECTO!
ZING!
ZING!
??
ZING!
HUH?
ZING!
ZING!
ZING!
WHAT'S GOING ON HERE?
ZING!
CRACKLE!
ZANG!

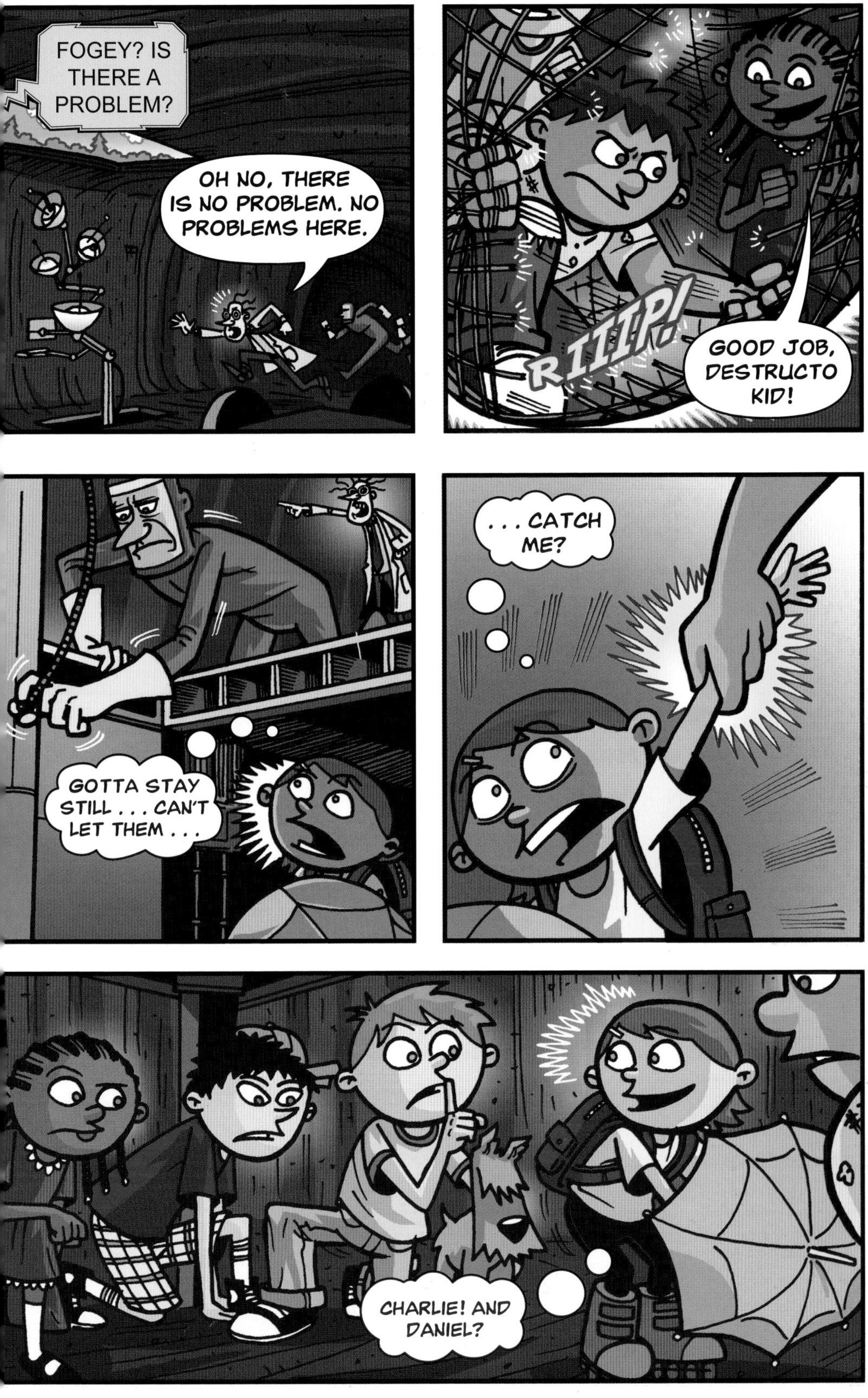
FOGEY? IS THERE A PROBLEM?
OH NO, THERE IS NO PROBLEM. NO PROBLEMS HERE.
RIIIP!
GOOD JOB, DESTRUCTO KID!
GOTTA STAY STILL . . . CAN'T LET THEM . . .
. . . CATCH ME?
CHARLIE! AND DANIEL?

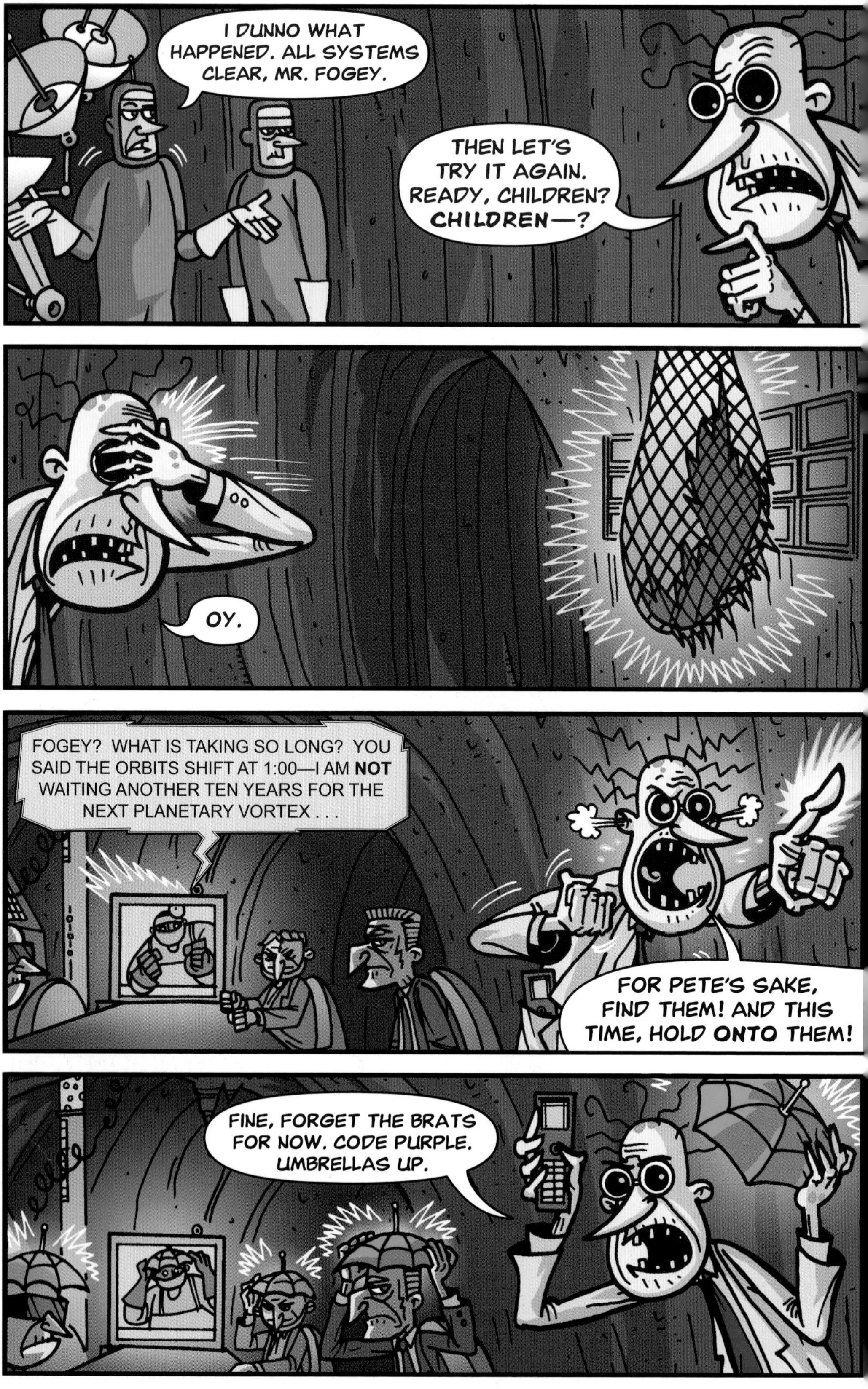
I DUNNO WHAT HAPPENED. ALL SYSTEMS CLEAR, MR. FOGEY.
THEN LET'S TRY IT AGAIN. READY, CHILDREN? CHILDREN—?
OY.
FOGEY? WHAT IS TAKING SO LONG? YOU SAID THE ORBITS SHIFT AT 1:00—I AM NOT WAITING ANOTHER TEN YEARS FOR THE NEXT PLANETARY VORTEX . . .
FOR PETE'S SAKE, FIND THEM! AND THIS TIME, HOLD ONTO THEM!
FINE, FORGET THE BRATS FOR NOW. CODE PURPLE. UMBRELLAS UP.

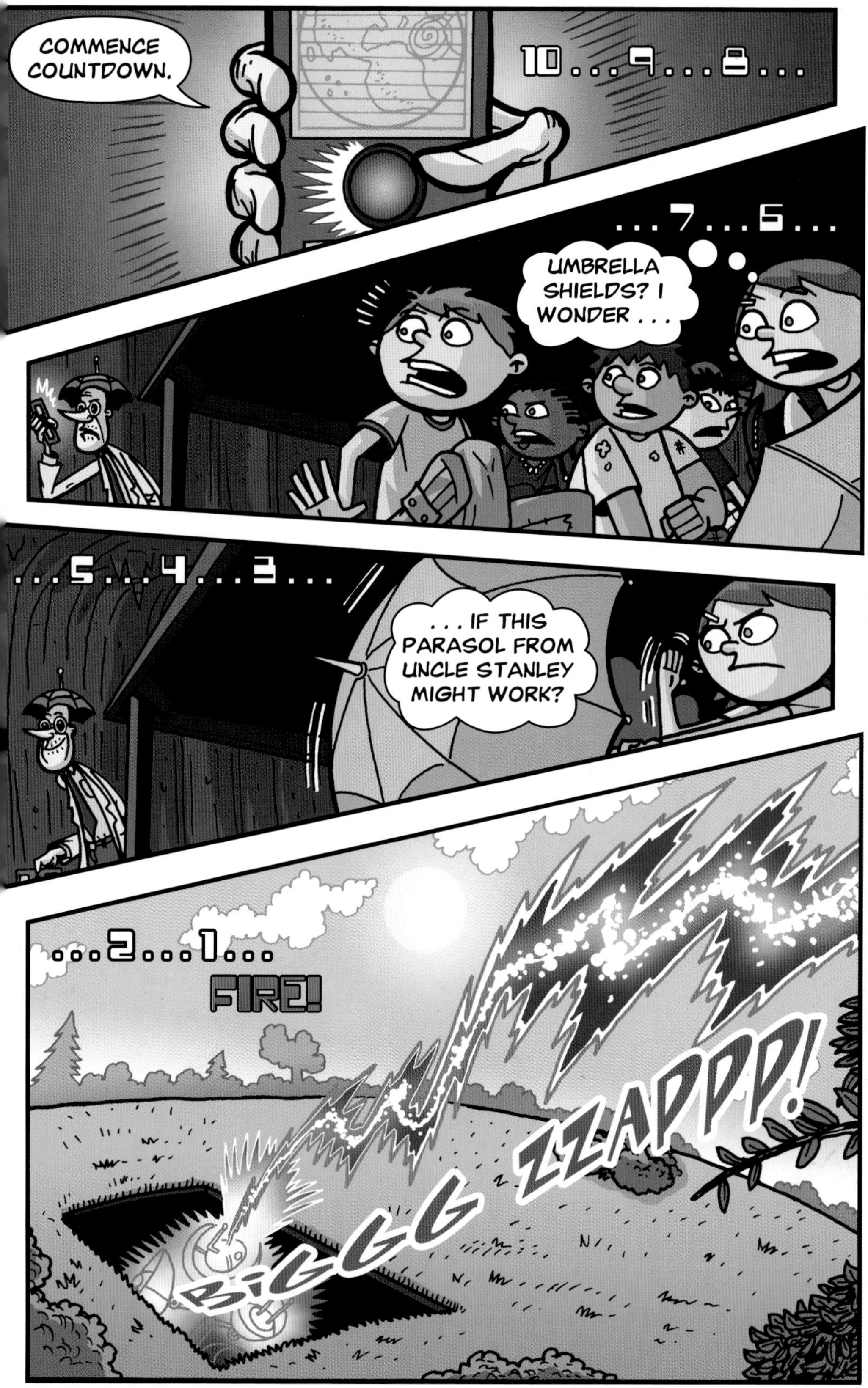
COMMENCE COUNTDOWN.
10 . . . 9 . . . 8 . . .
. . . 7 . . . 6 . . .
UMBRELLA SHIELDS? I WONDER . . .
. . . 5 . . . 4 . . . 3 . . .
. . . IF THIS PARASOL FROM UNCLE STANLEY MIGHT WORK?
. . . 2 . . . 1 . . .
FIRE!
BIGGG ZZAPPP!

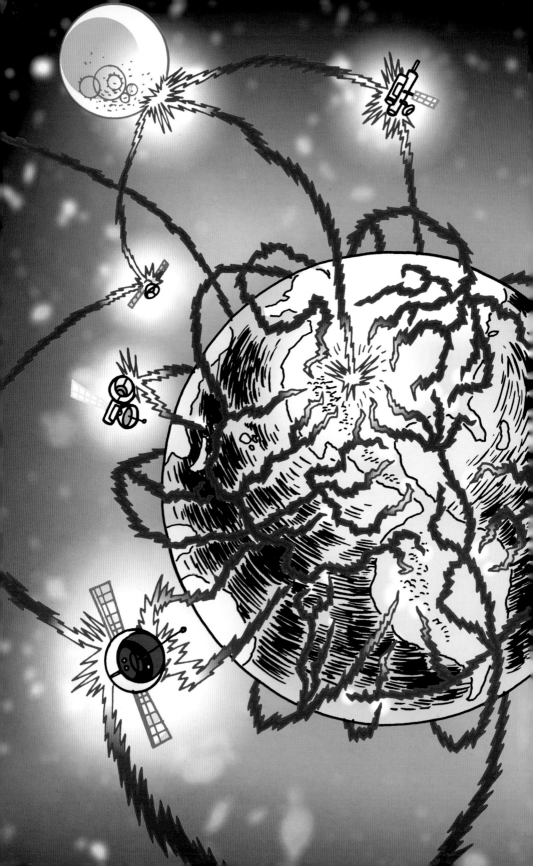

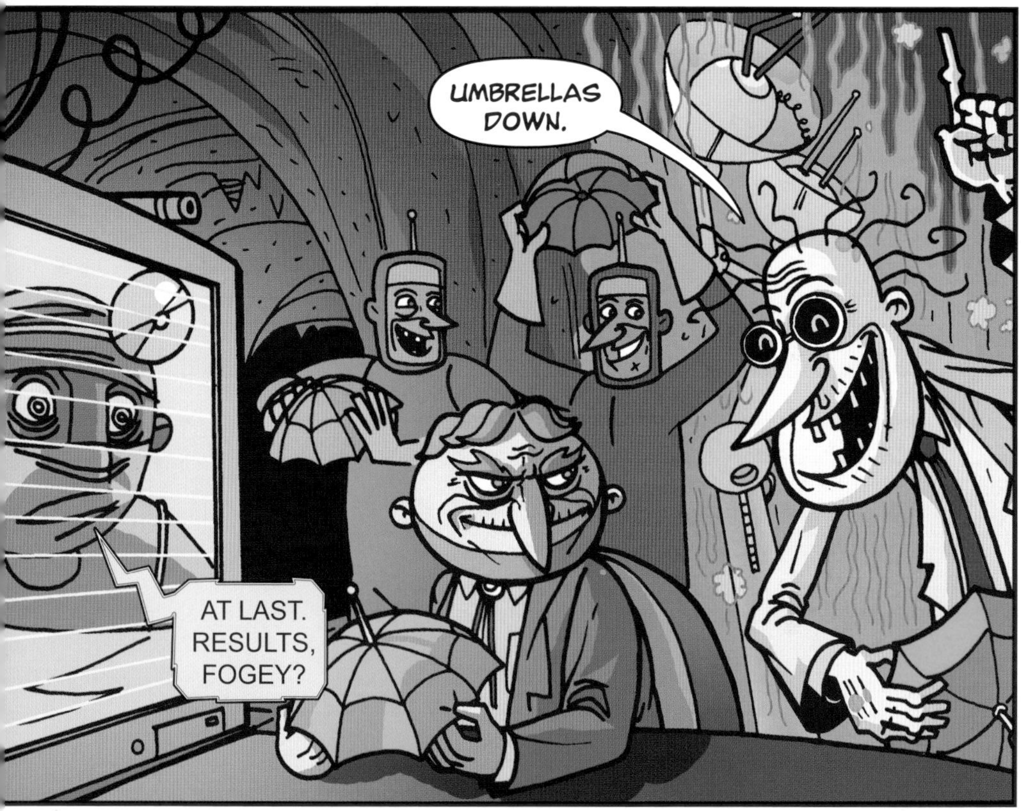
UMBRELLAS DOWN.
AT LAST. RESULTS, FOGEY?

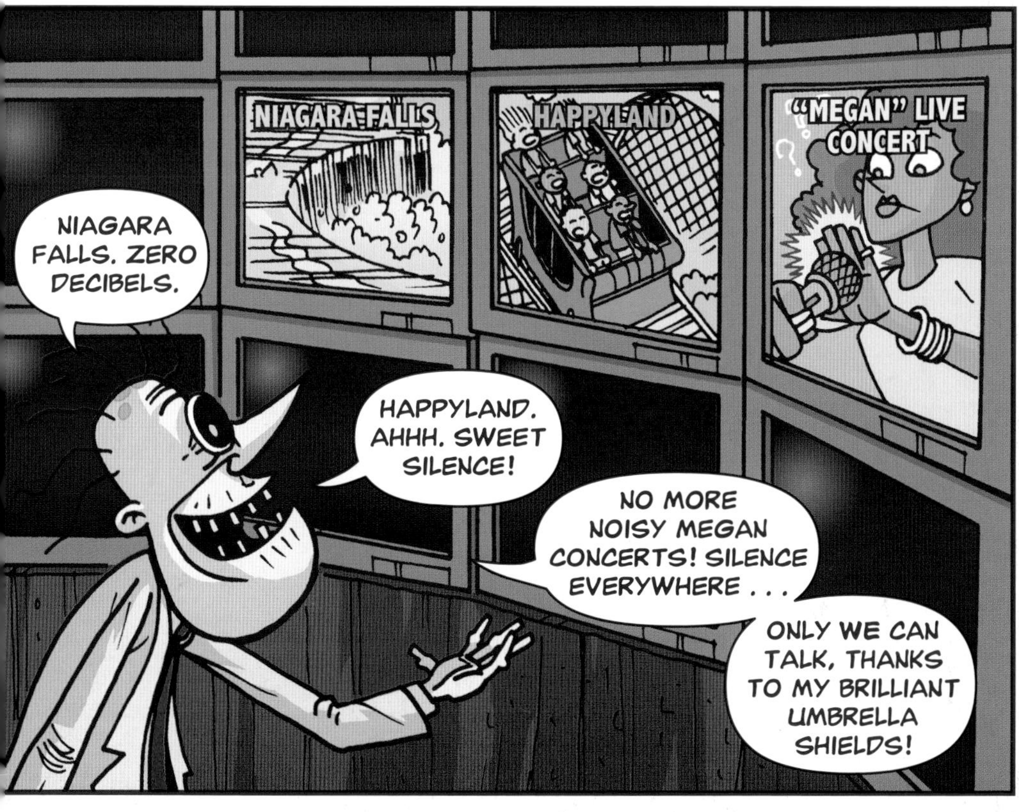
NIAGARA FALLS
HAPPYLAND
"MEGAN" LIVE CONCERT
NIAGARA FALLS. ZERO DECIBELS.
HAPPYLAND. AHHH. SWEET SILENCE!
NO MORE NOISY MEGAN CONCERTS! SILENCE EVERYWHERE . . .
ONLY WE CAN TALK, THANKS TO MY BRILLIANT UMBRELLA SHIELDS!

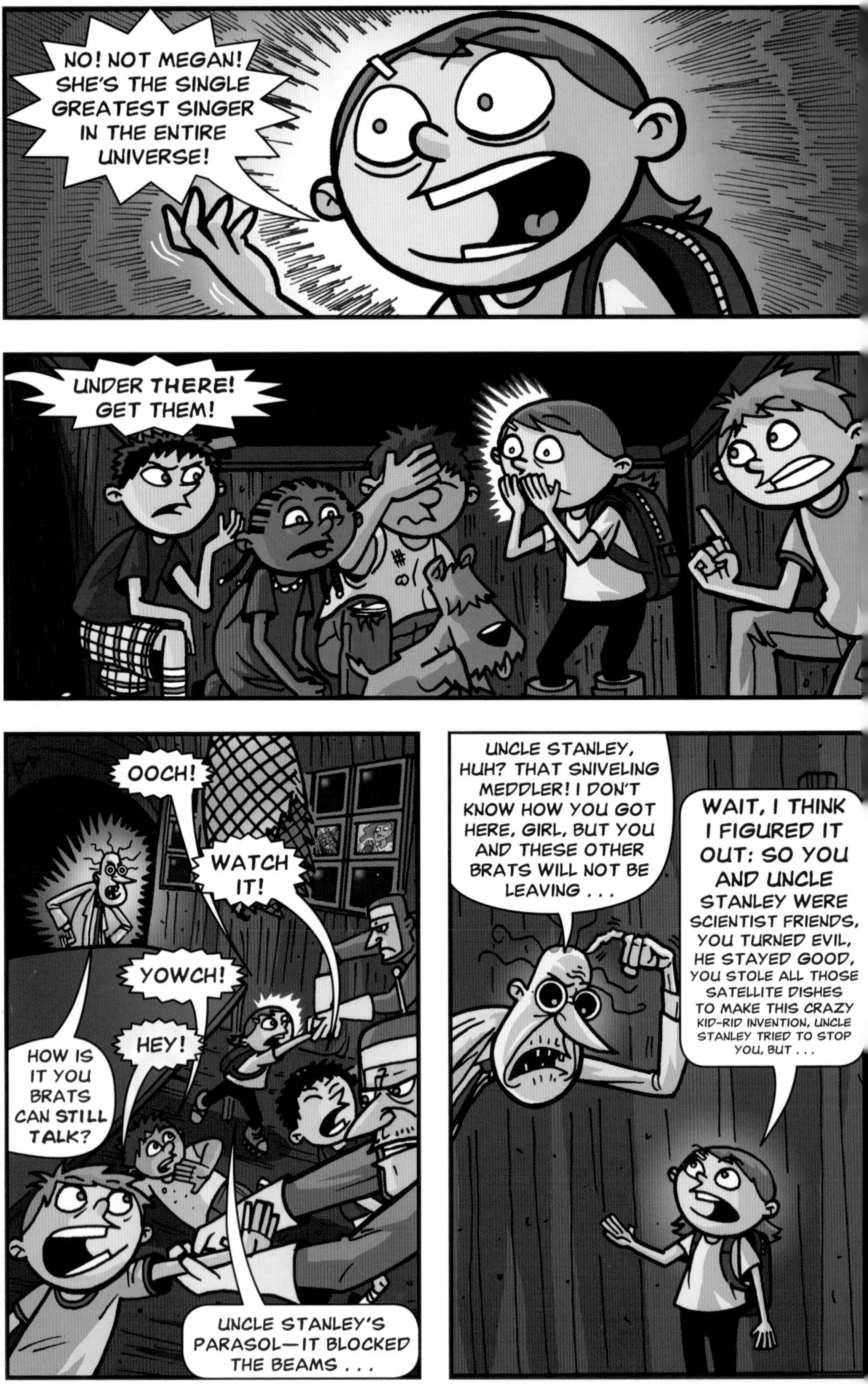
NO! NOT MEGAN! SHE'S THE SINGLE GREATEST SINGER IN THE ENTIRE UNIVERSE!
UNDER THERE! GET THEM!
OOCH!
WATCH IT!
YOWCH!
HEY!
HOW IS IT YOU BRATS CAN STILL TALK?
UNCLE STANLEY'S PARASOL—IT BLOCKED THE BEAMS . . .
UNCLE STANLEY, HUH? THAT SNIVELING MEDDLER! I DON'T KNOW HOW YOU GOT HERE, GIRL, BUT YOU AND THESE OTHER BRATS WILL NOT BE LEAVING . . .
WAIT, I THINK I FIGURED IT OUT: SO YOU AND UNCLE STANLEY WERE SCIENTIST FRIENDS, YOU TURNED EVIL, HE STAYED GOOD, YOU STOLE ALL THOSE SATELLITE DISHES TO MAKE THIS CRAZY KID-RID INVENTION, UNCLE STANLEY TRIED TO STOP YOU, BUT . . .

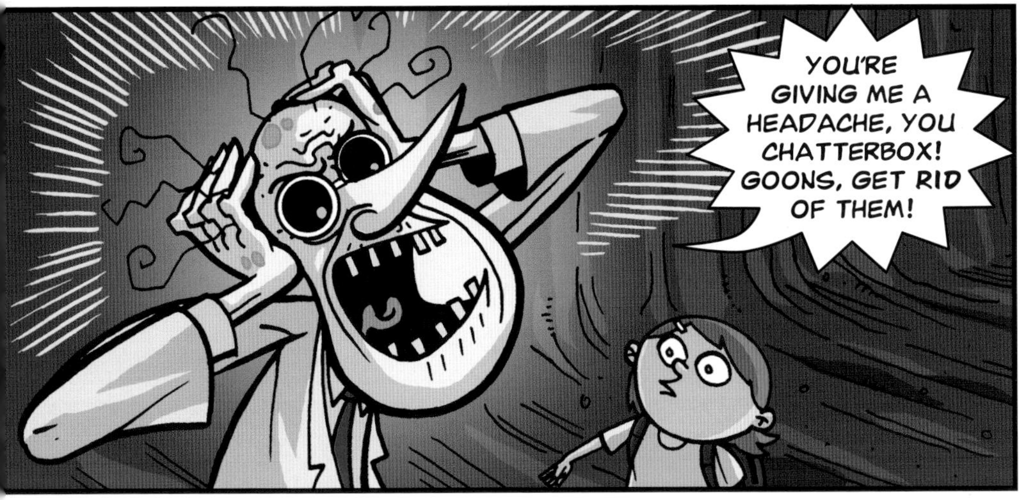
YOU'RE GIVING ME A HEADACHE, YOU CHATTERBOX! GOONS, GET RID OF THEM!

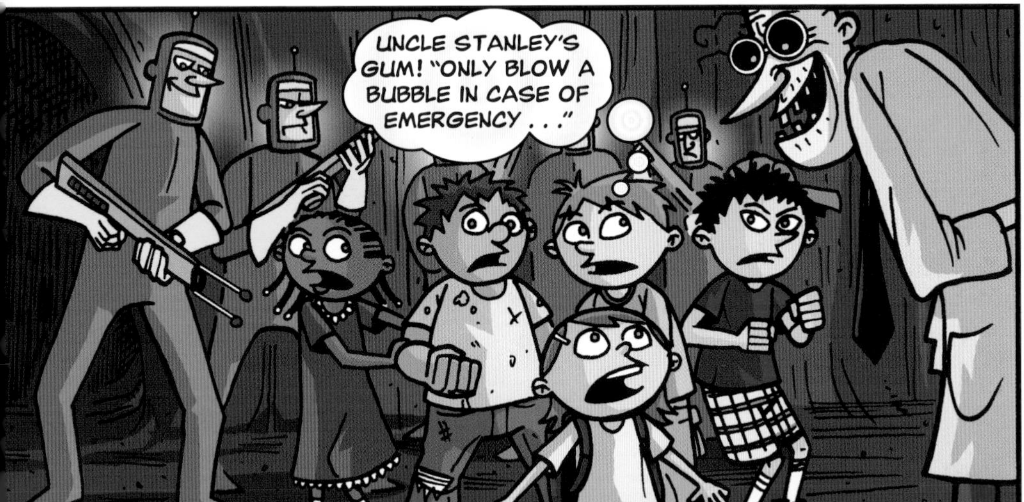
UNCLE STANLEY'S GUM! "ONLY BLOW A BUBBLE IN CASE OF EMERGENCY . . ."

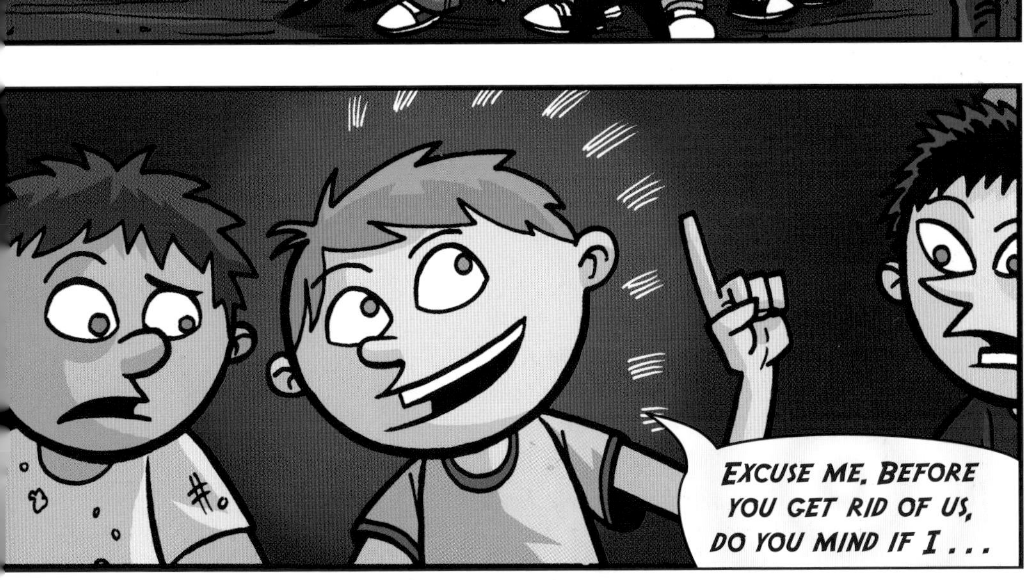
EXCUSE ME. BEFORE YOU GET RID OF US, DO YOU MIND IF I . . .

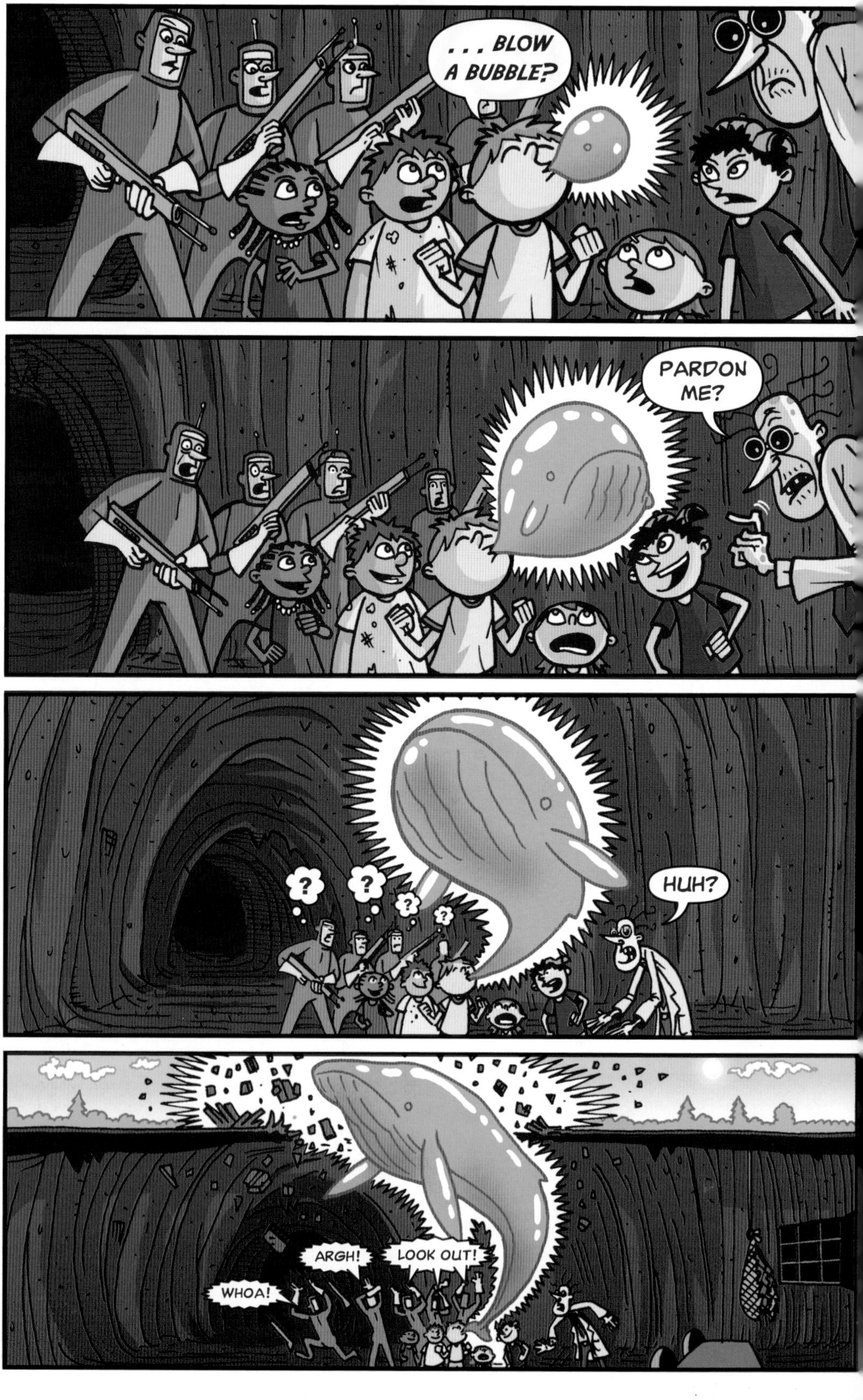
. . . BLOW A BUBBLE?
PARDON ME?
HUH?
ARGH!
LOOK OUT!
WHOA!

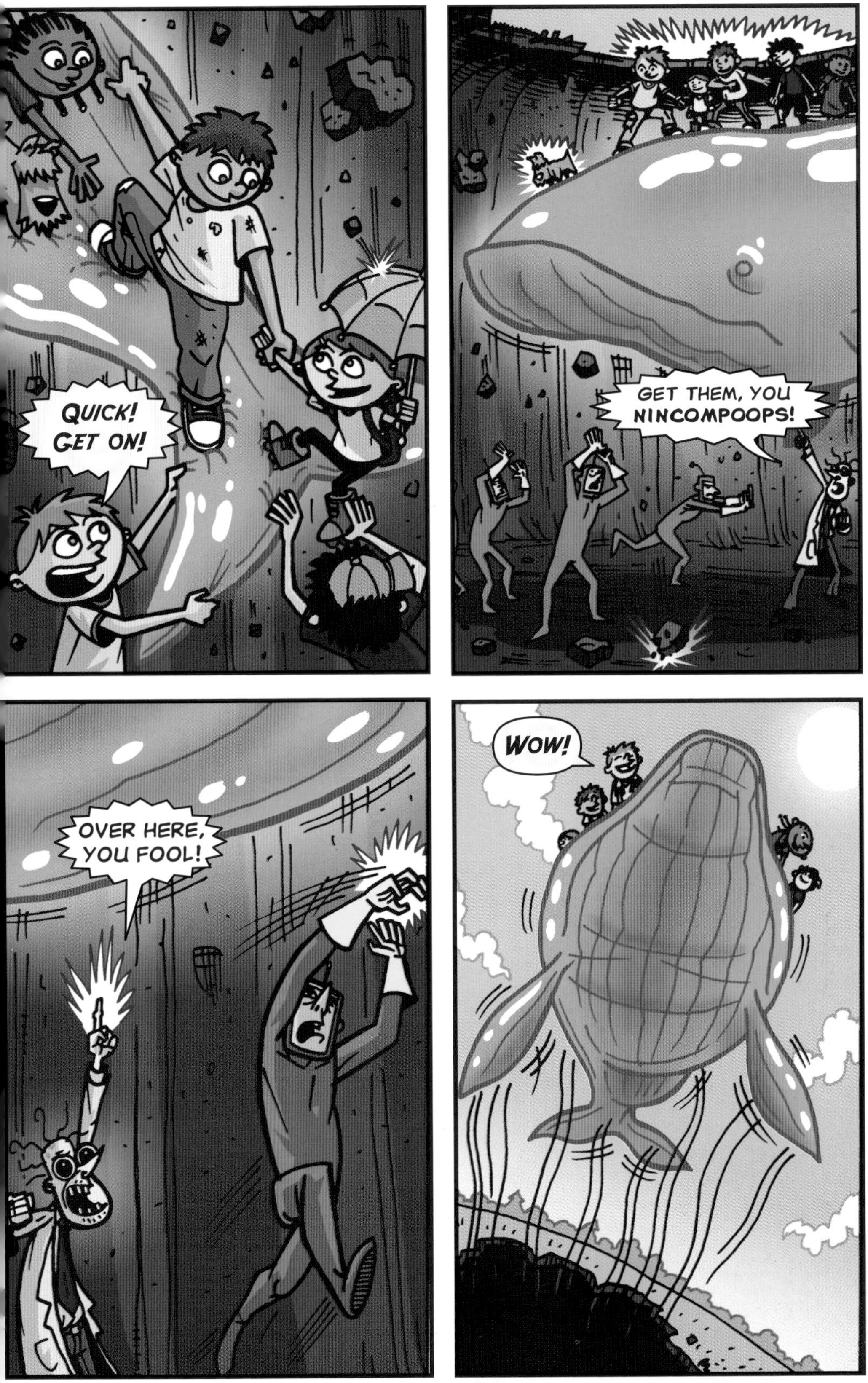
QUICK! GET ON!
GET THEM, YOU NINCOMPOOPS!
OVER HERE, YOU FOOL!
WOW!

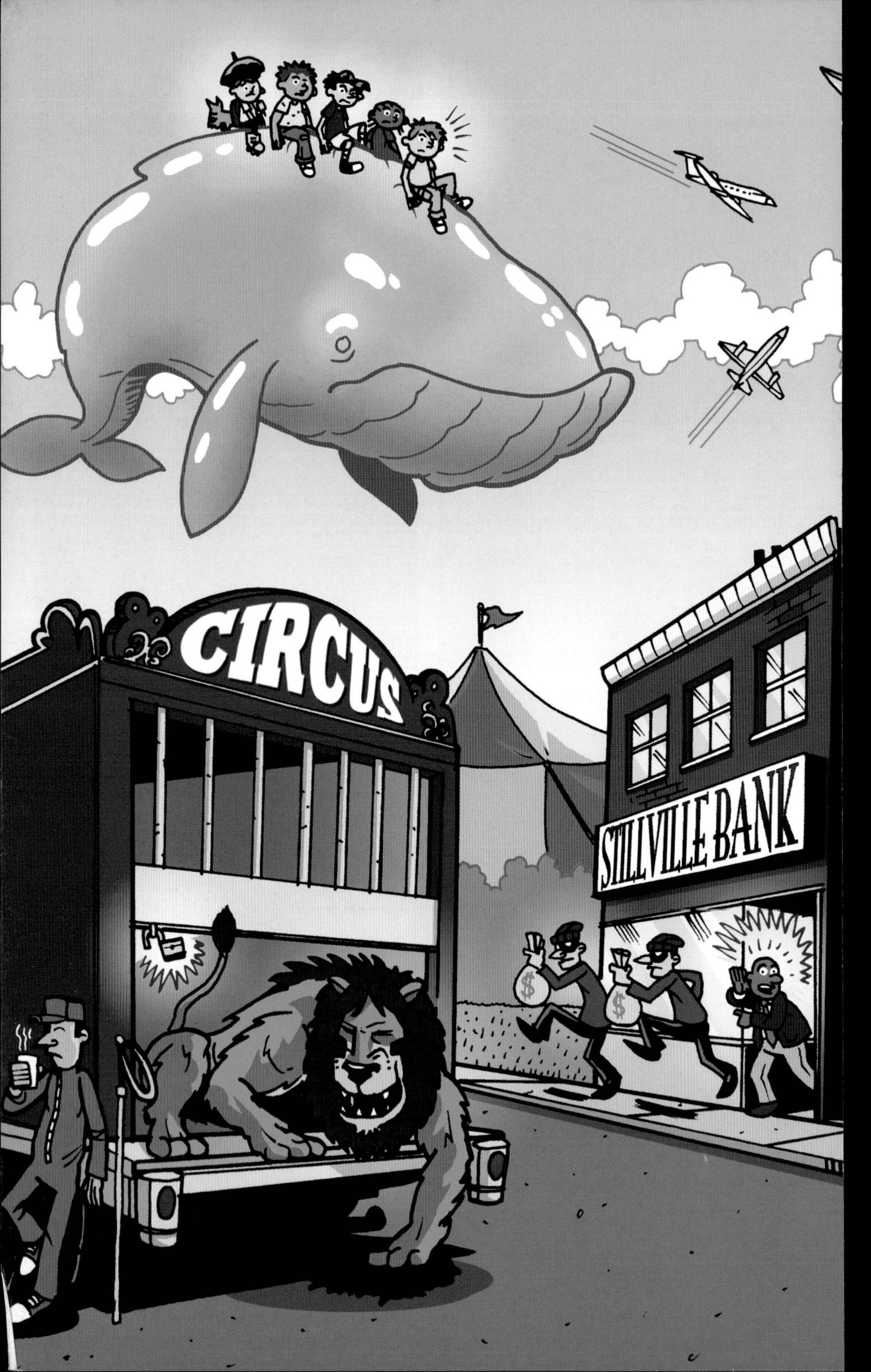
CIRCUS
STILLVILLE BANK

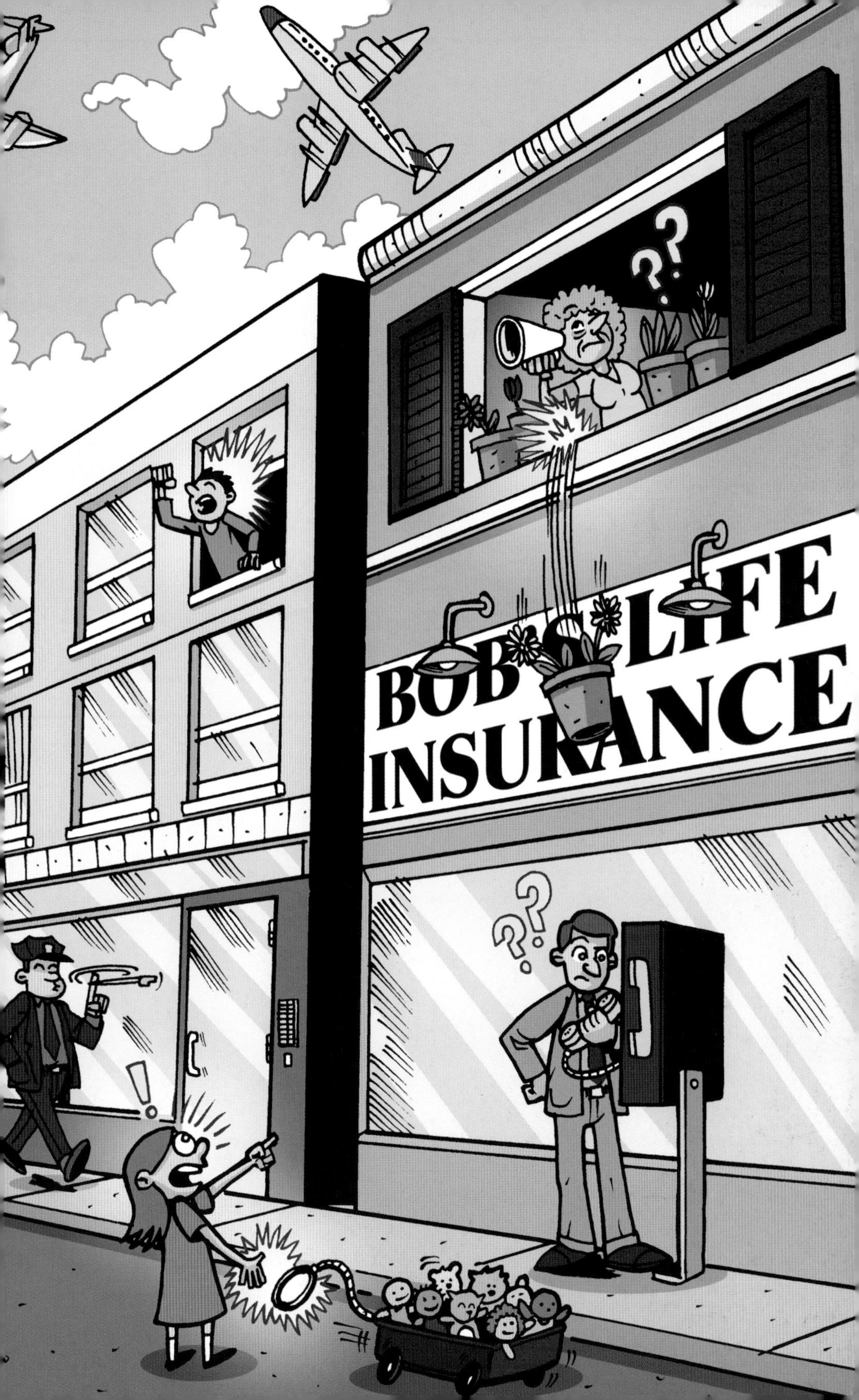
BOB
LIFE
INSURANCE

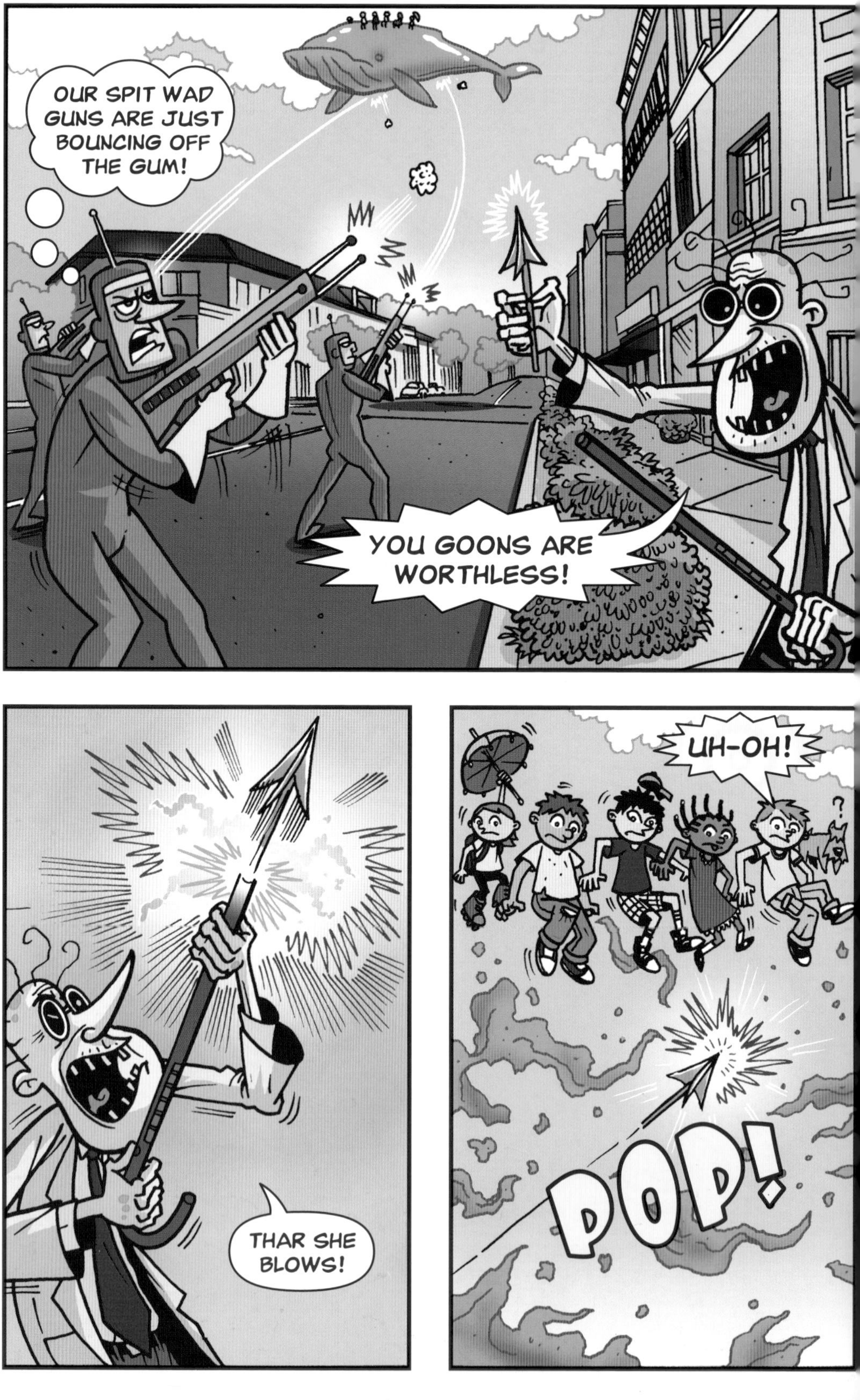
OUR SPIT WAD GUNS ARE JUST BOUNCING OFF THE GUM!
YOU GOONS ARE WORTHLESS!
THAR SHE BLOWS!
UH-OH!
POP!

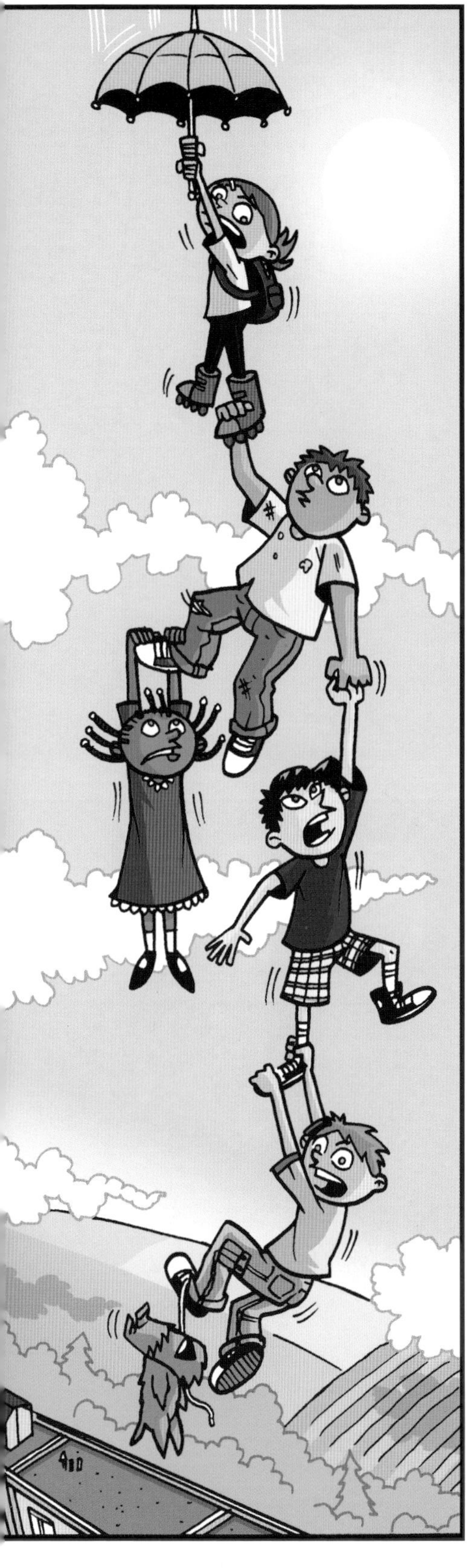

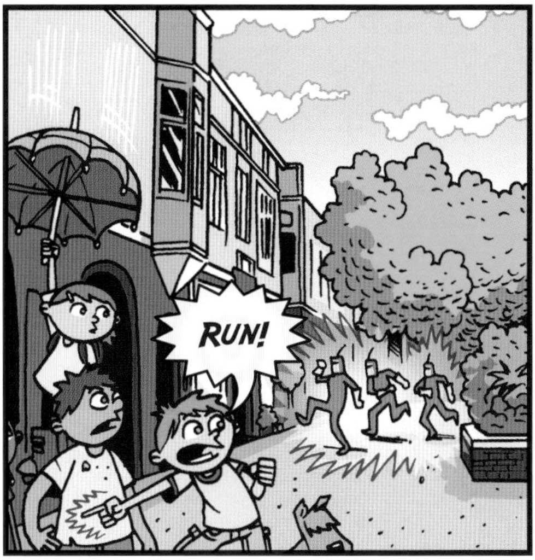
RUN!

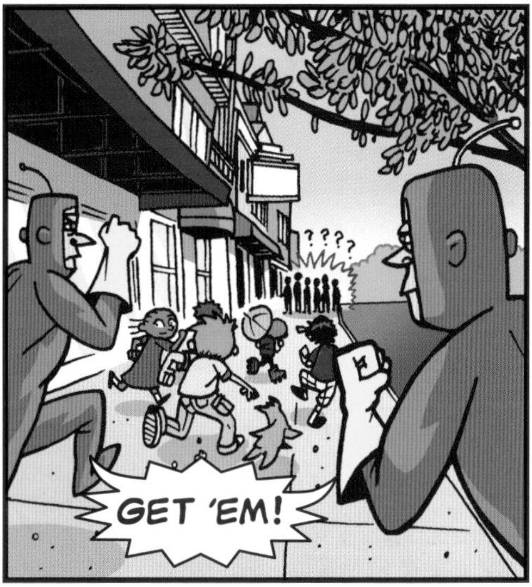
????
GET 'EM!

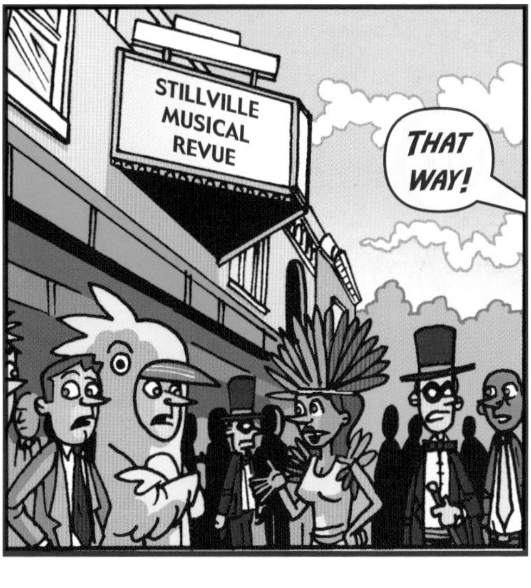
STILLVILLE
MUSICAL
REVUE
THAT WAY!

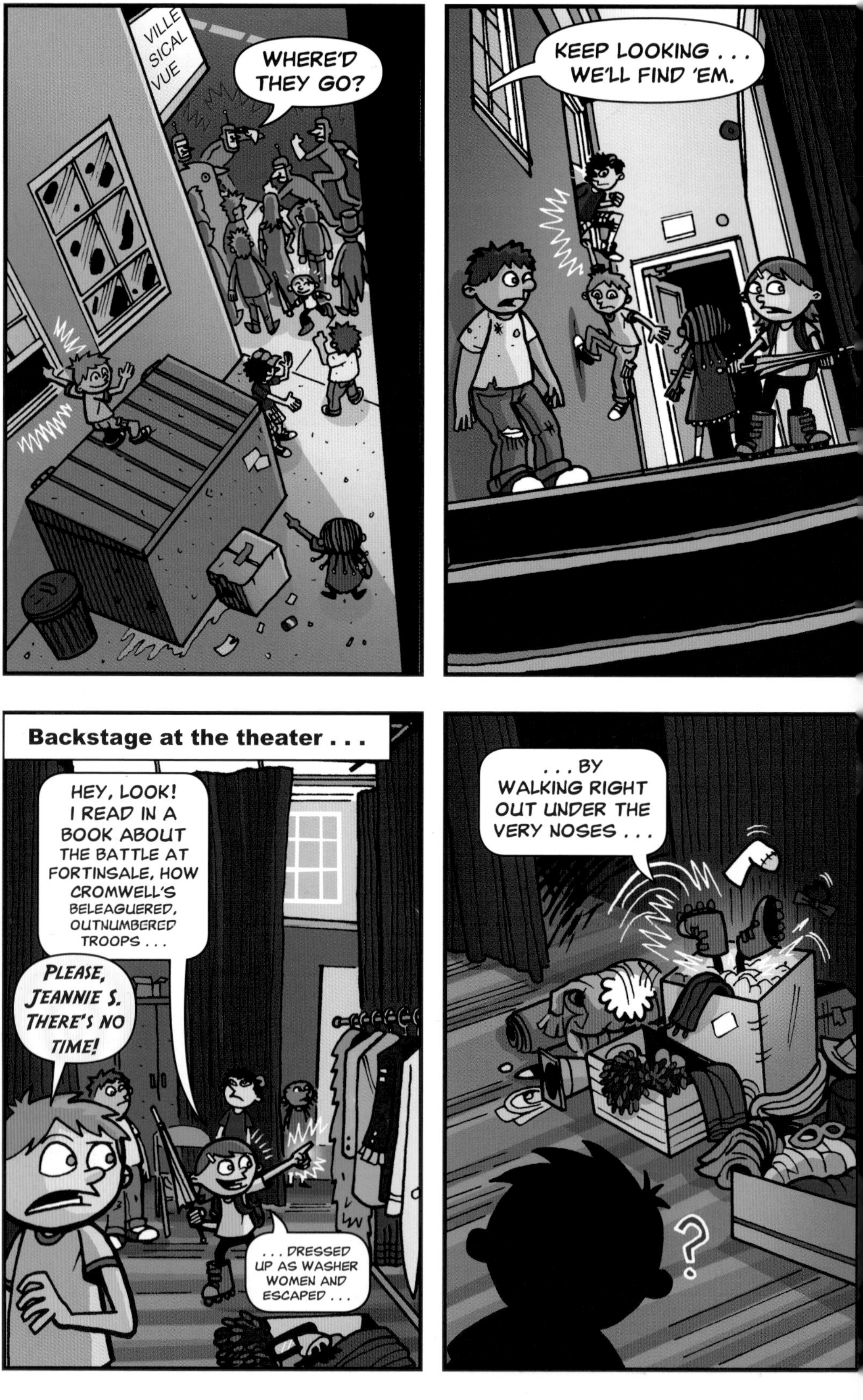
VILLE SICAL VUE
WHERE'D THEY GO?
KEEP LOOKING . . . WE'LL FIND 'EM.
Backstage at the theater . . .
HEY, LOOK! I READ IN A BOOK ABOUT THE BATTLE AT FORTINSALE, HOW CROMWELL'S BELEAGUERED, OUTNUMBERED TROOPS . . .
PLEASE, JEANNIE S. THERE'S NO TIME!
. . . DRESSED UP AS WASHER WOMEN AND ESCAPED . . .
. . . BY WALKING RIGHT OUT UNDER THE VERY NOSES . . .
?

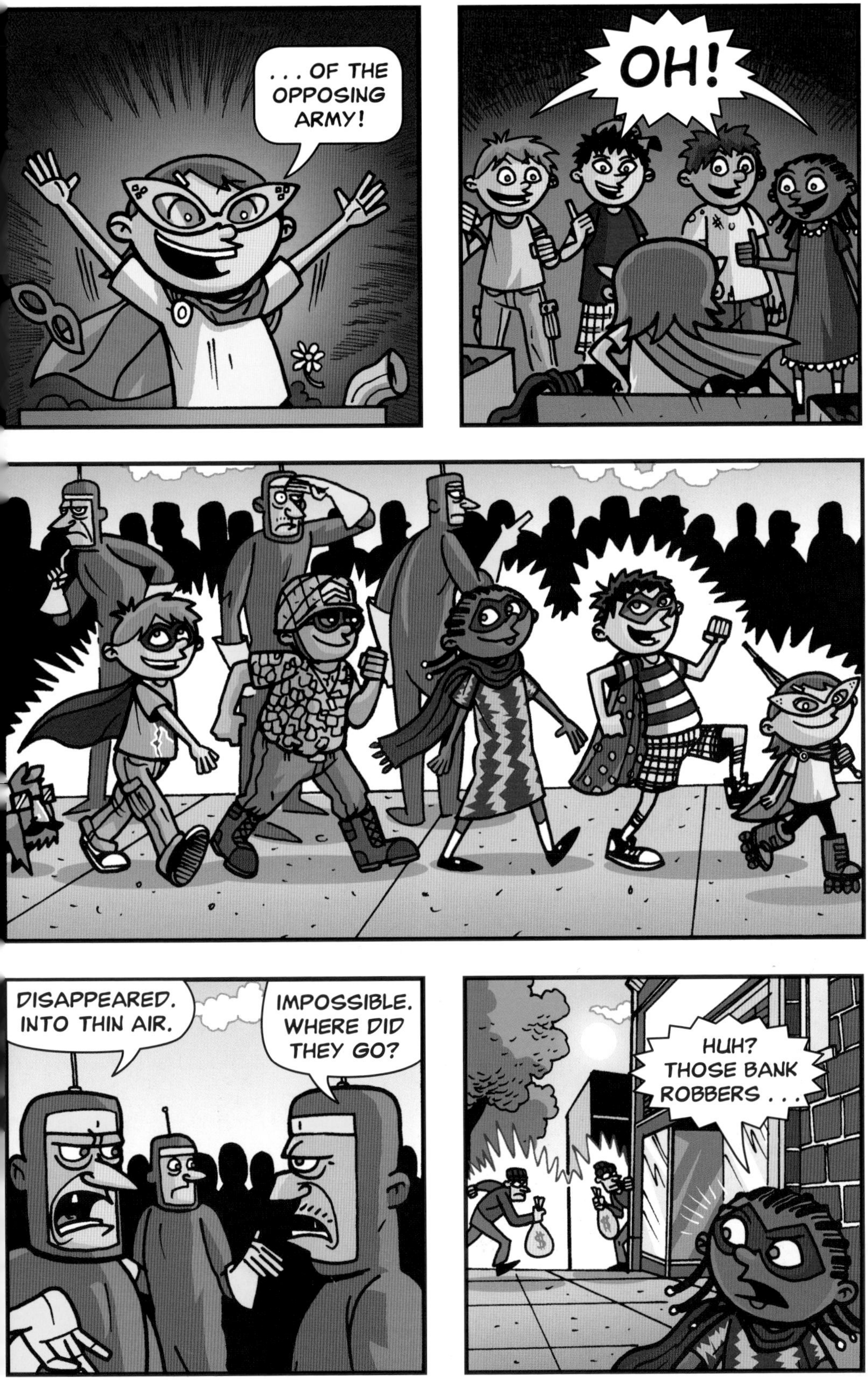
. . . OF THE OPPOSING ARMY!
OH!
DISAPPEARED. INTO THIN AIR.
IMPOSSIBLE. WHERE DID THEY GO?
HUH? THOSE BANK ROBBERS . . .

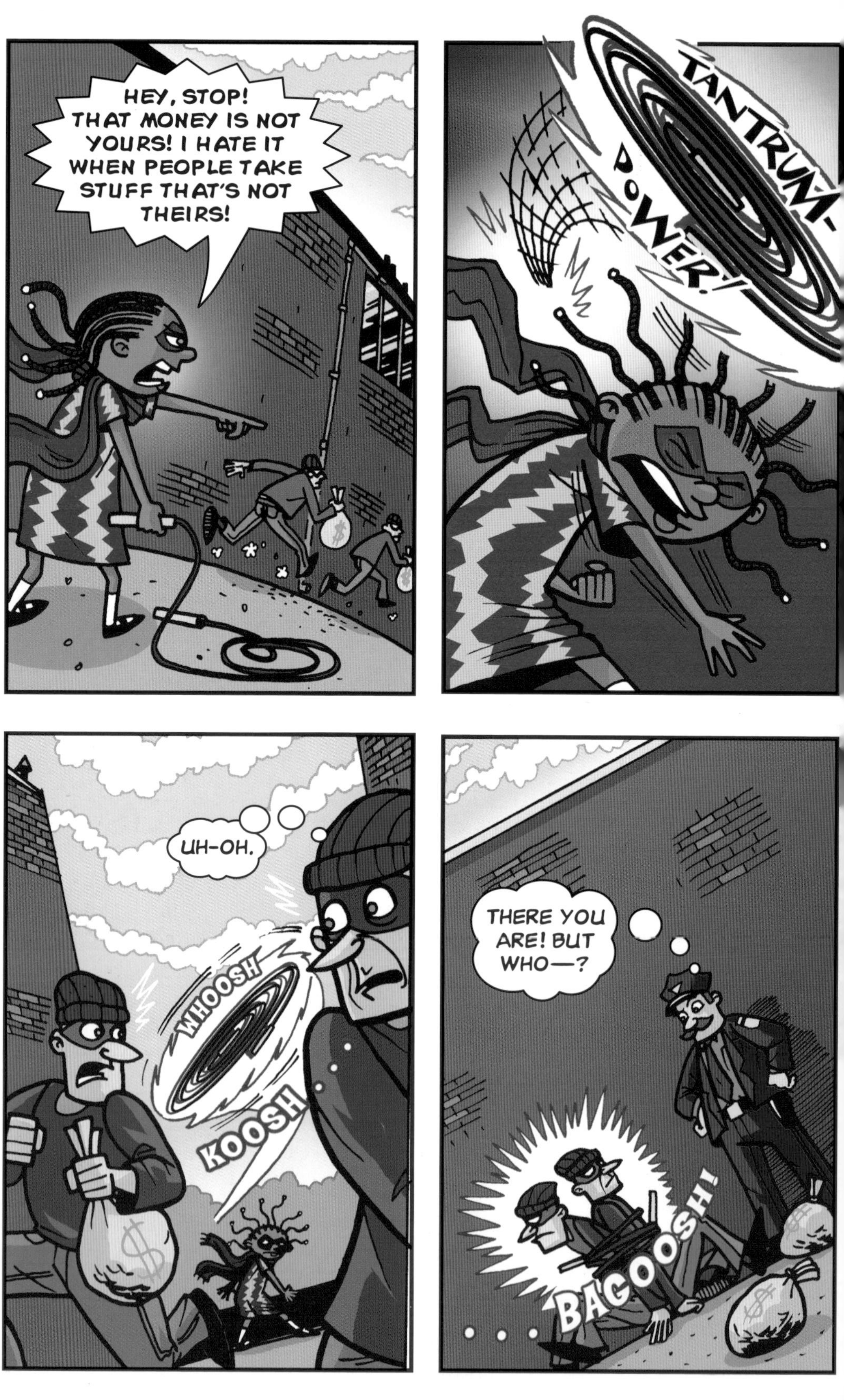
HEY, STOP! THAT MONEY IS NOT YOURS! I HATE IT WHEN PEOPLE TAKE STUFF THAT'S NOT THEIRS!
TANTRUM-POWER!
UH-OH.
WHOOSH
KOOSH
THERE YOU ARE! BUT WHO—?
BAGOOSH!

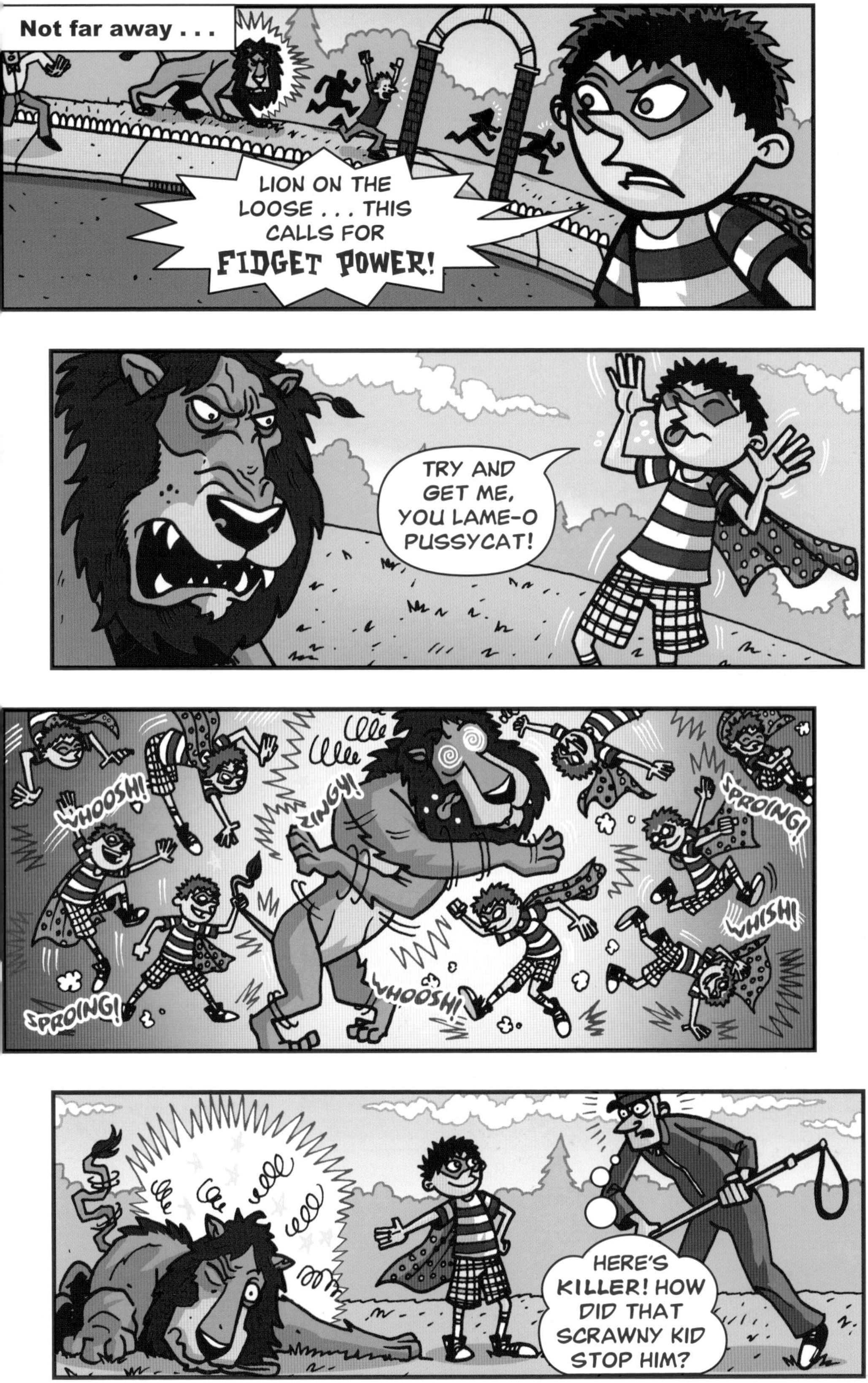
Not far away . . .
LION ON THE LOOSE . . . THIS CALLS FOR FIDGET POWER!
TRY AND GET ME, YOU LAME-O PUSSYCAT!
WHOOSH!
ZINGY!
SPROING!
WHISH!
SPROING!
WHOOSH!
HERE'S KILLER! HOW DID THAT SCRAWNY KID STOP HIM?

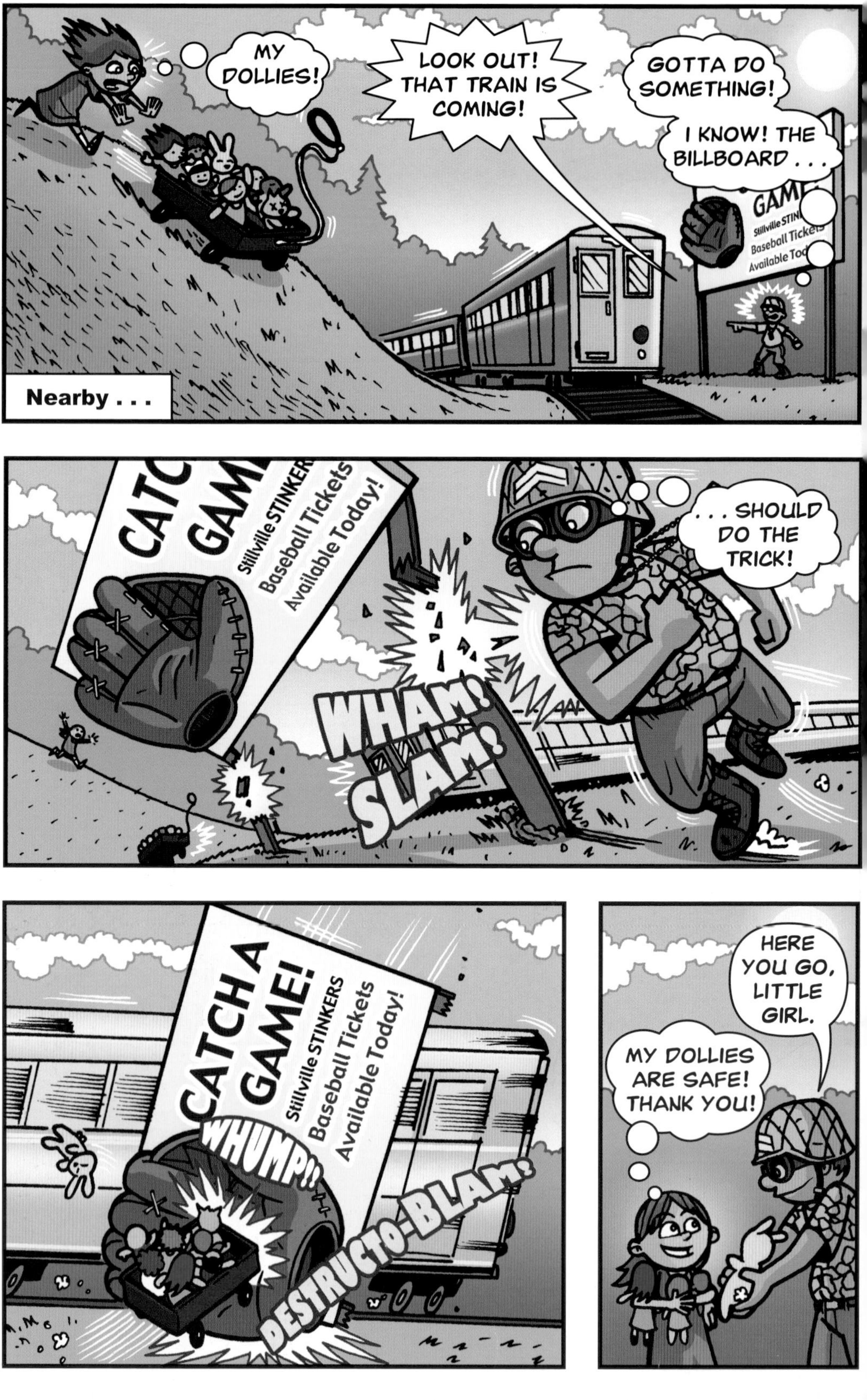
MY DOLLIES!
LOOK OUT! THAT TRAIN IS COMING!
GOTTA DO SOMETHING!
I KNOW! THE BILLBOARD . . .
Nearby . . .
. . . SHOULD DO THE TRICK!
CATCH A GAME! Stillville STINKERS Baseball Tickets Available Today!
WHAM!
SLAM!
WHUMP!!
DESTRUCTO-BLAM!
HERE YOU GO, LITTLE GIRL.
MY DOLLIES ARE SAFE! THANK YOU!

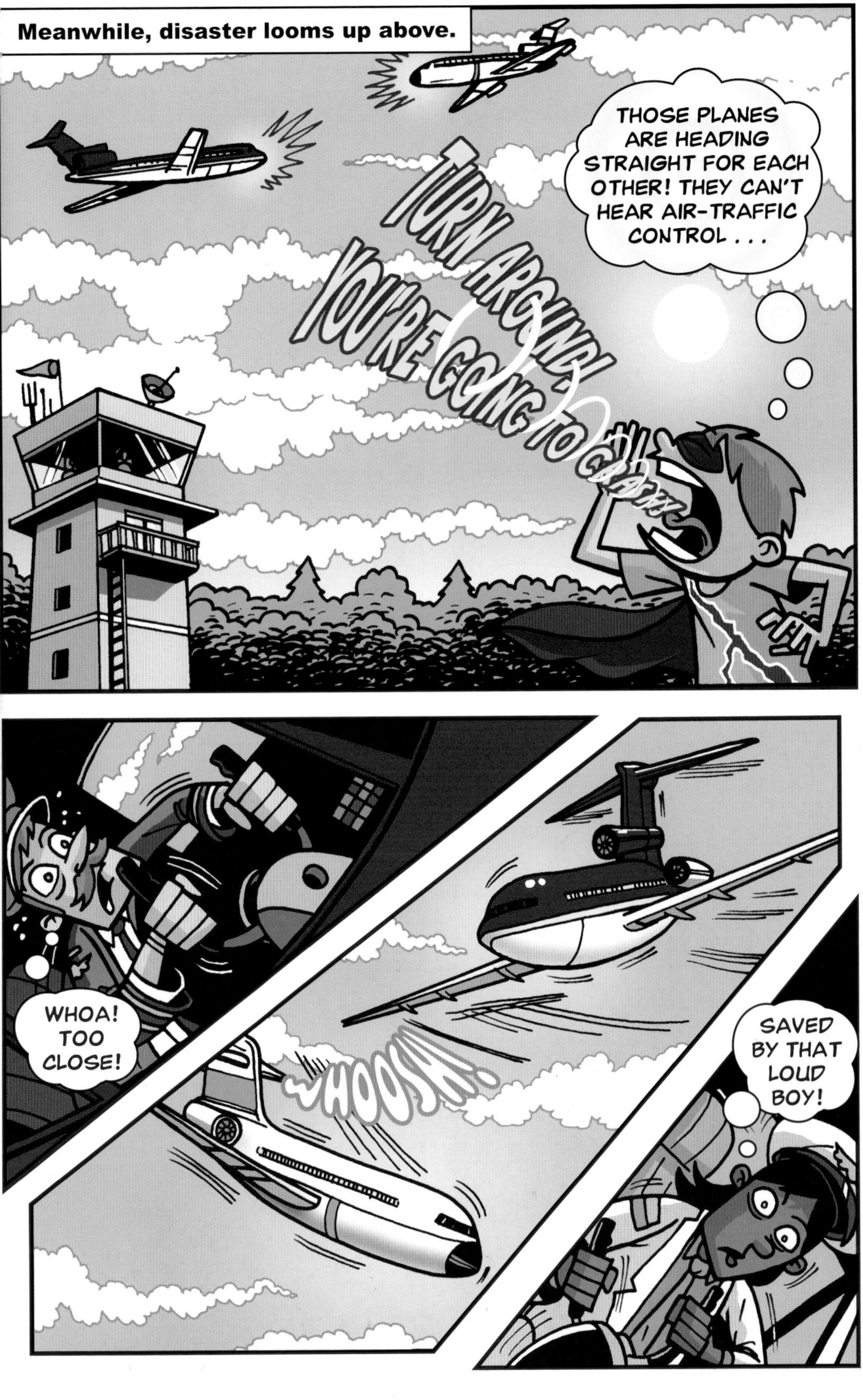
Meanwhile, disaster looms up above.
THOSE PLANES ARE HEADING STRAIGHT FOR EACH OTHER! THEY CAN'T HEAR AIR-TRAFFIC CONTROL . . .
TURN AROUND! YOU'RE GOING TO CRASH!!
WHOA! TOO CLOSE!
WHOOSH!
SAVED BY THAT LOUD BOY!

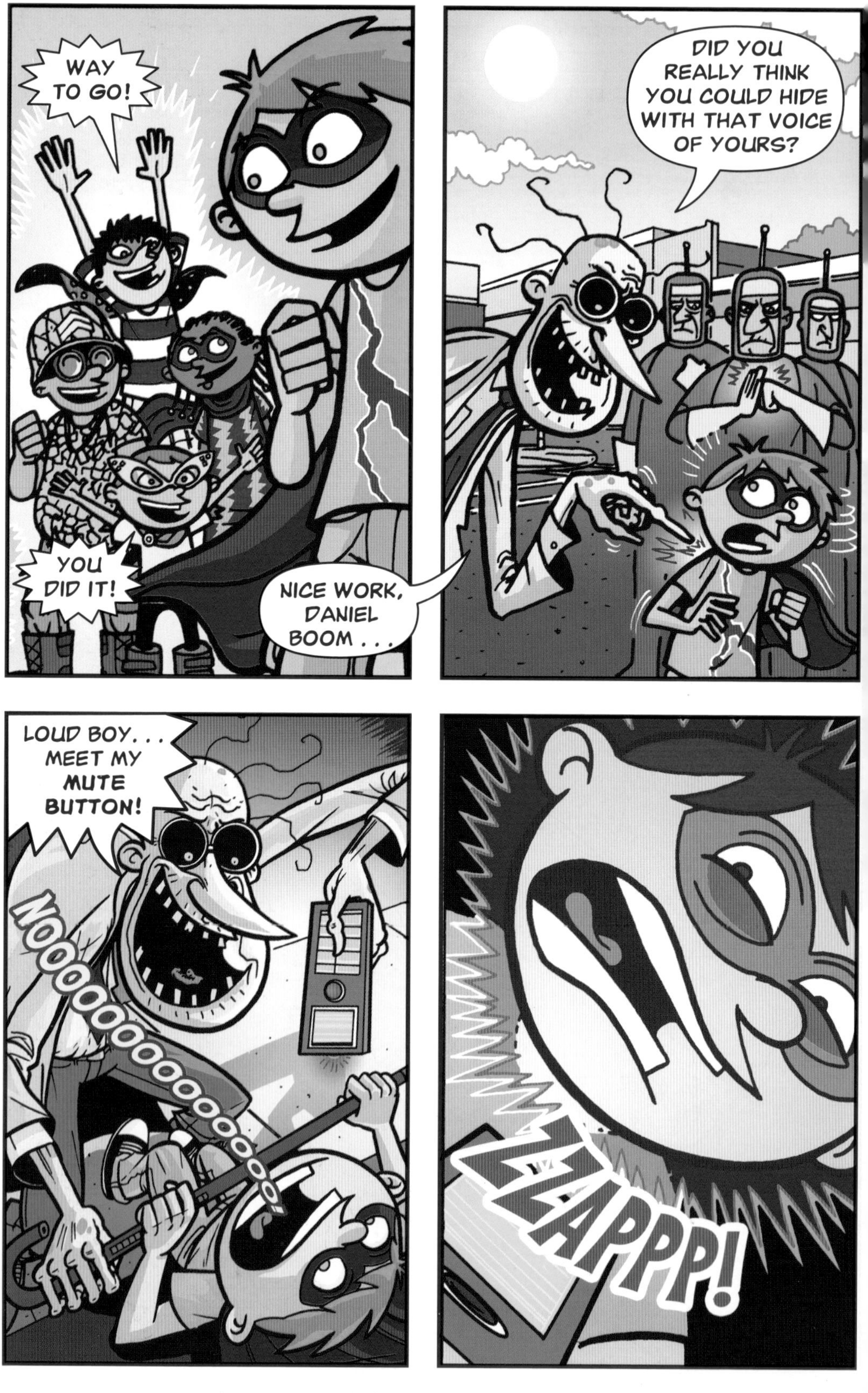
WAY TO GO!
YOU DID IT!
NICE WORK, DANIEL BOOM . . .
DID YOU REALLY THINK YOU COULD HIDE WITH THAT VOICE OF YOURS?
LOUD BOY. . . MEET MY MUTE BUTTON!
NOOOOOOOOOOOOOOOO!
ZZAPPP!

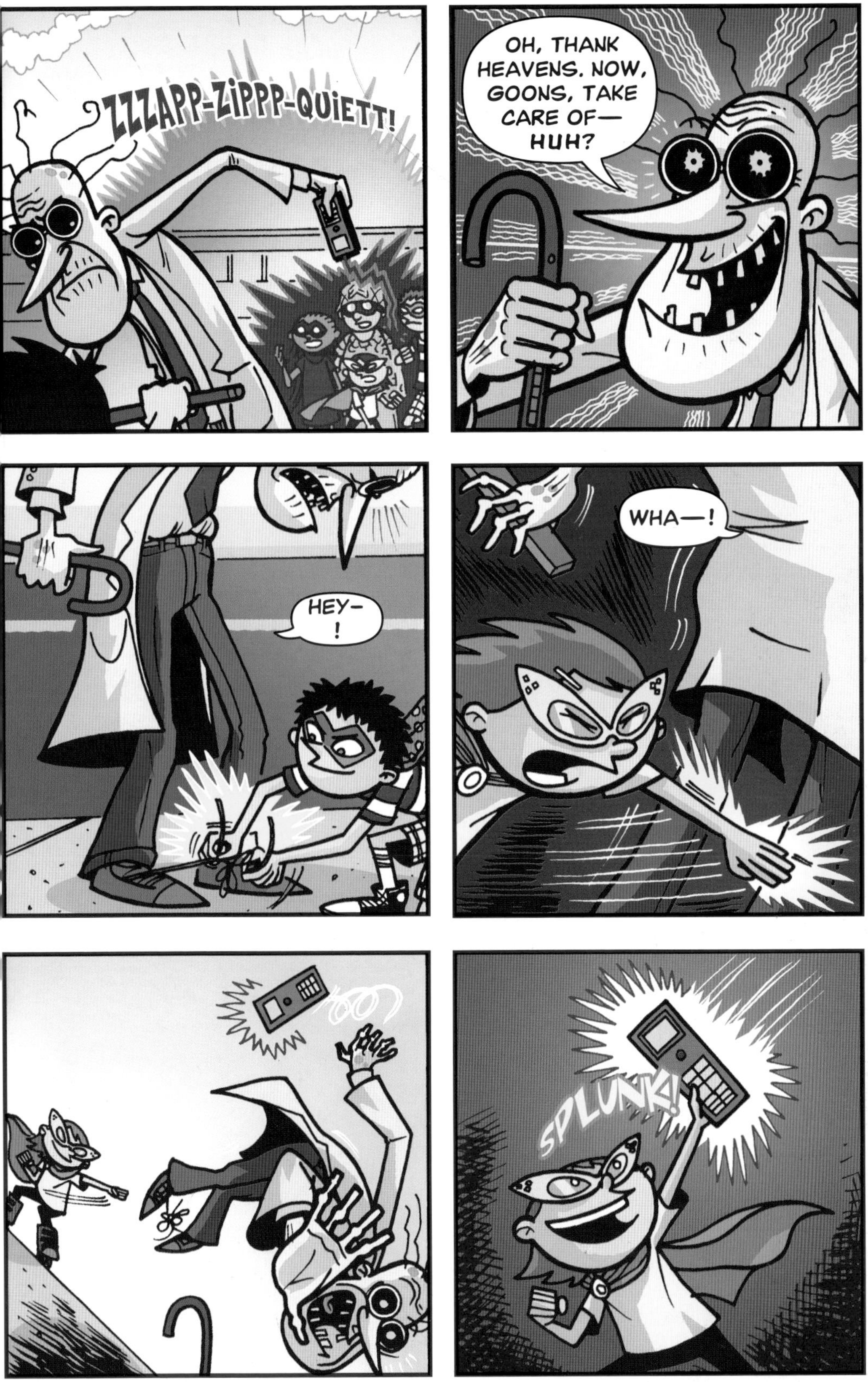
ZZZAPP-ZIPPP-QUIETT!
OH, THANK HEAVENS. NOW, GOONS, TAKE CARE OF— HUH?
HEY- !
WHA—!
SPLUNK!

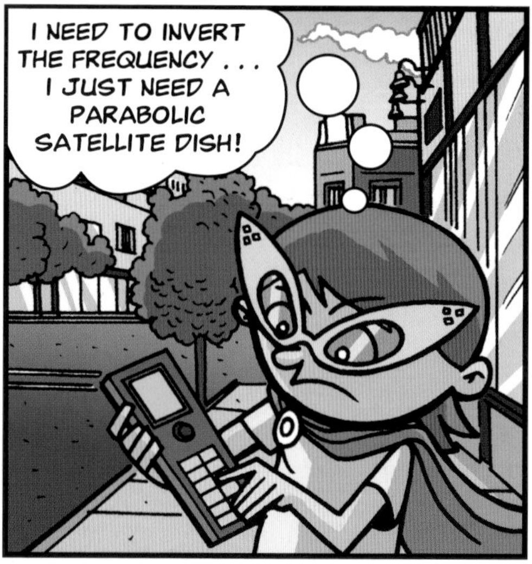
I NEED TO INVERT THE FREQUENCY . . . I JUST NEED A PARABOLIC SATELLITE DISH!

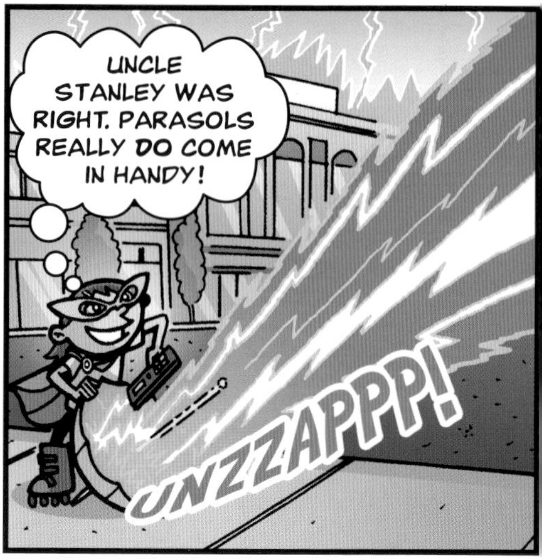
UNCLE STANLEY WAS RIGHT. PARASOLS REALLY DO COME IN HANDY!
UNZZAPPP!

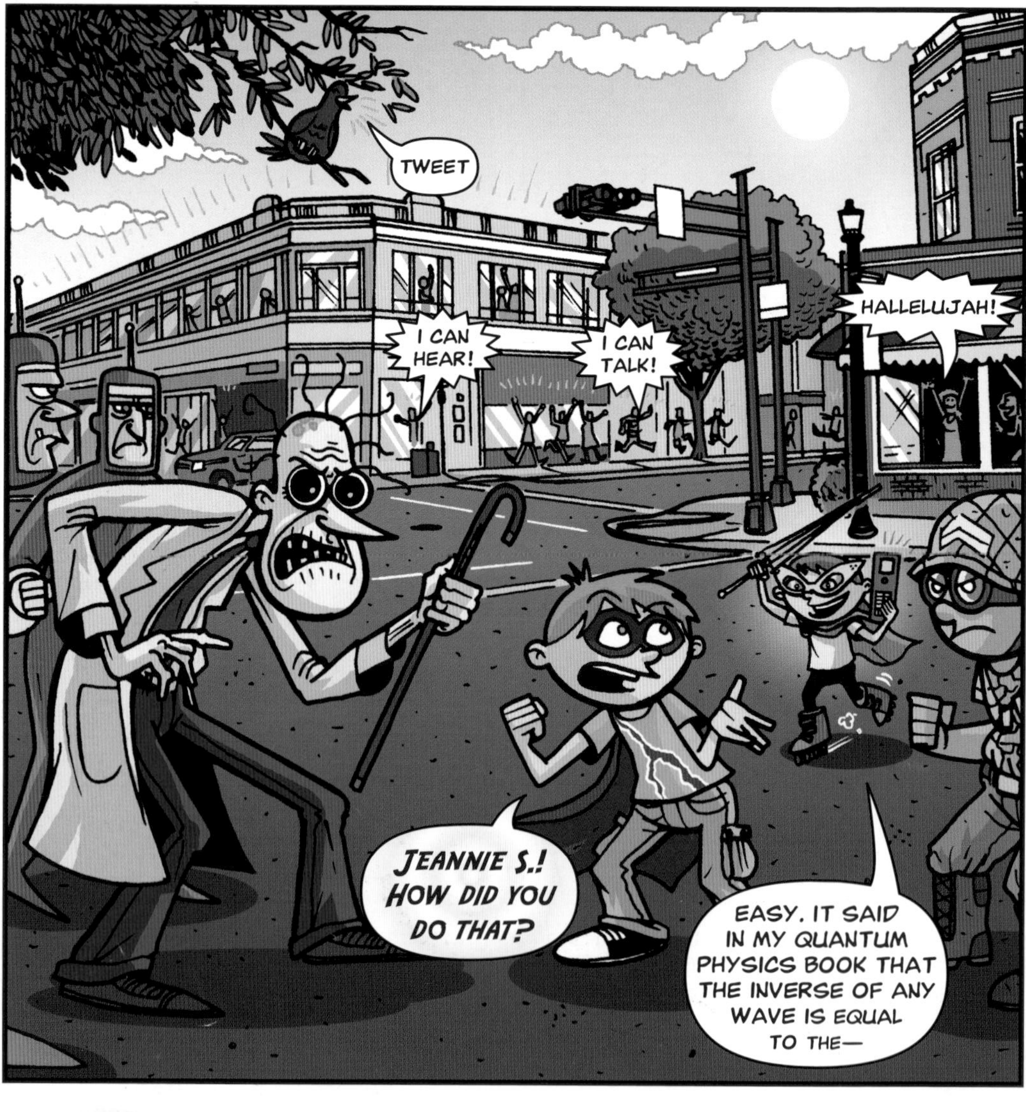
TWEET
I CAN HEAR!
I CAN TALK!
HALLELUJAH!
JEANNIE S.! HOW DID YOU DO THAT?
EASY. IT SAID IN MY QUANTUM PHYSICS BOOK THAT THE INVERSE OF ANY WAVE IS EQUAL TO THE—

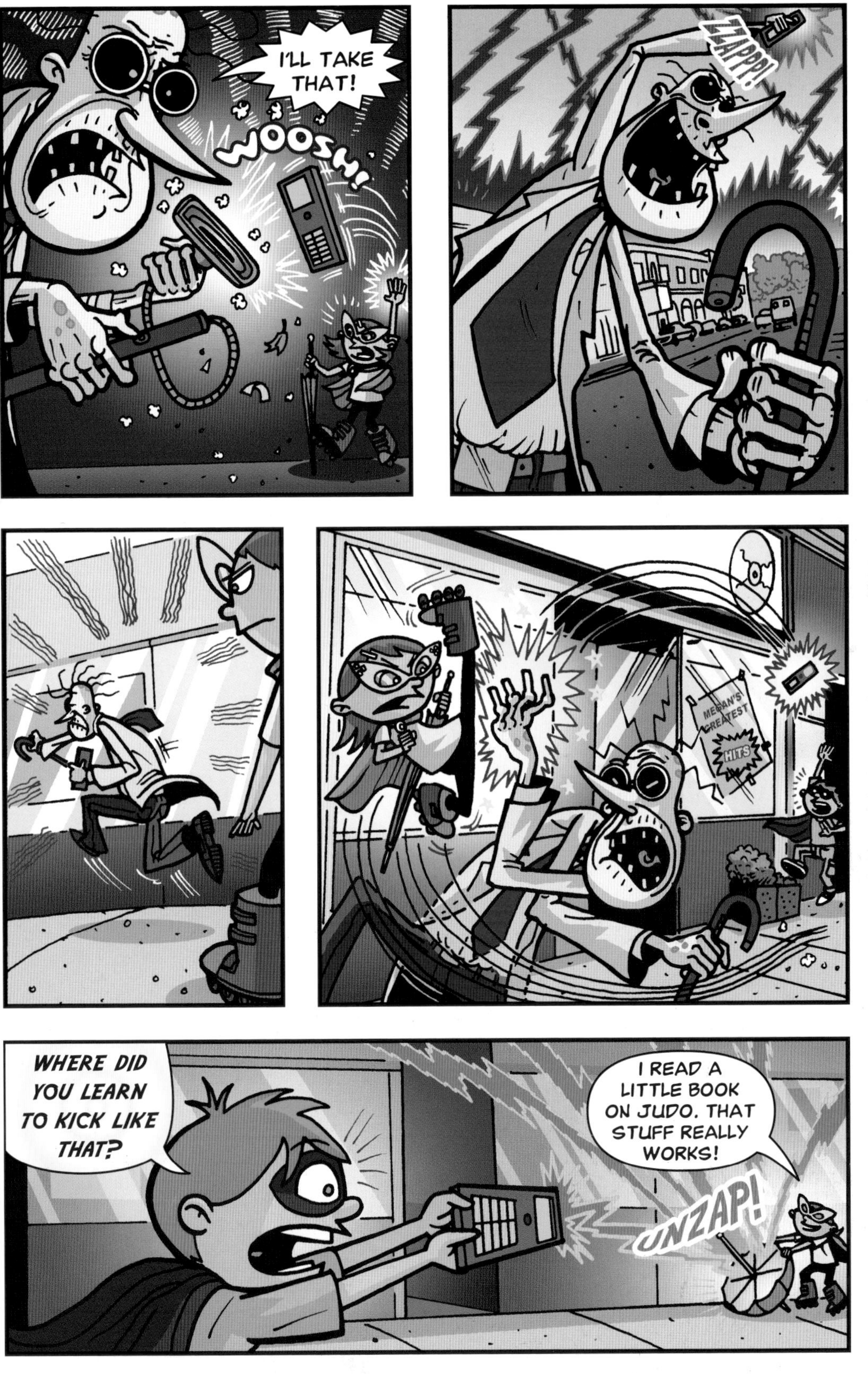
I'LL TAKE THAT!
WOOSH!
ZZAPPP!
MEGAN'S GREATEST HITS
WHERE DID YOU LEARN TO KICK LIKE THAT?
I READ A LITTLE BOOK ON JUDO. THAT STUFF REALLY WORKS!
UNZAP!

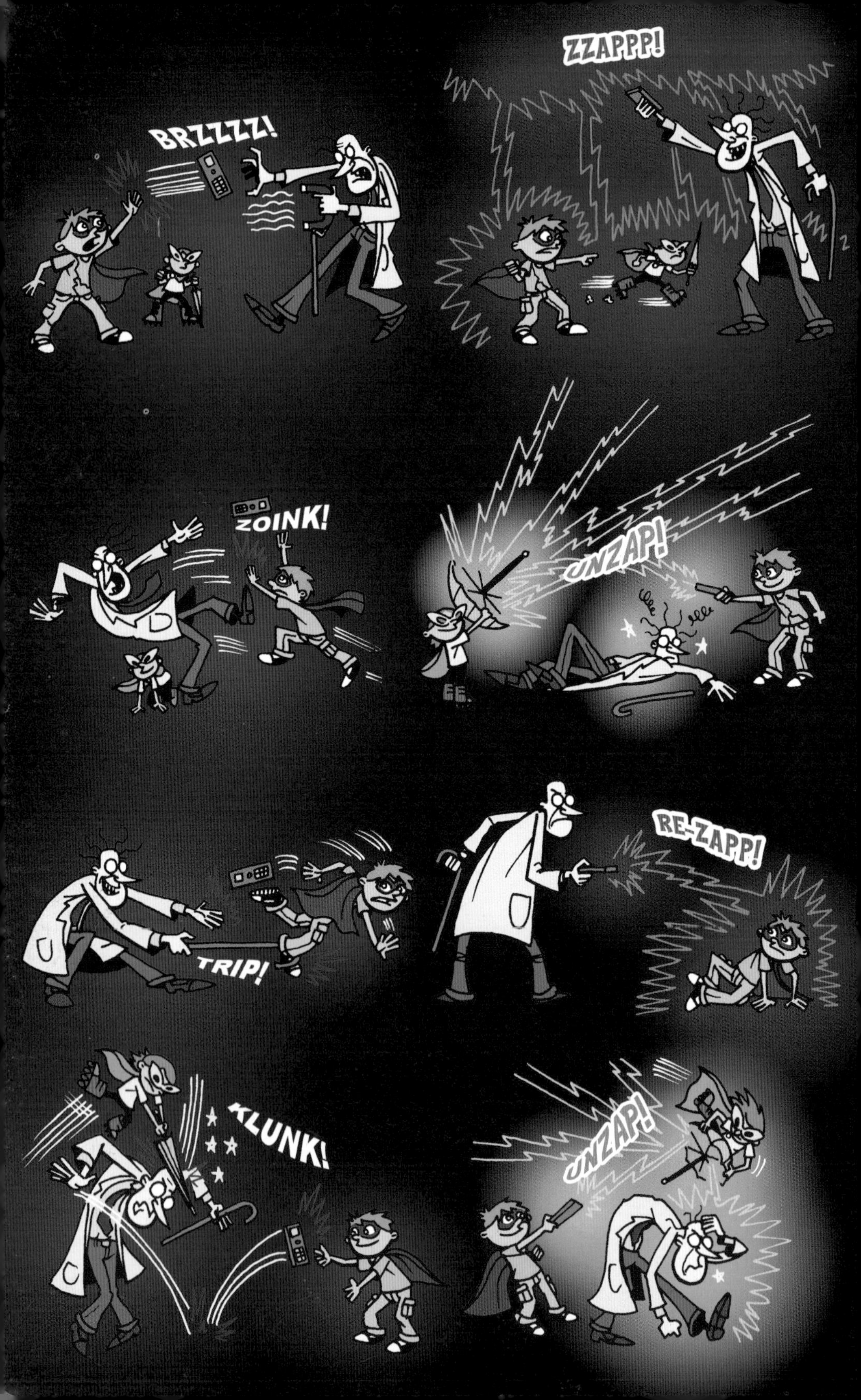
BRZZZZZ!
ZZAPPP!
ZOINK!
UNZAP!
TRIP!
RE-ZAPP!
KLUNK!
UNZAP!

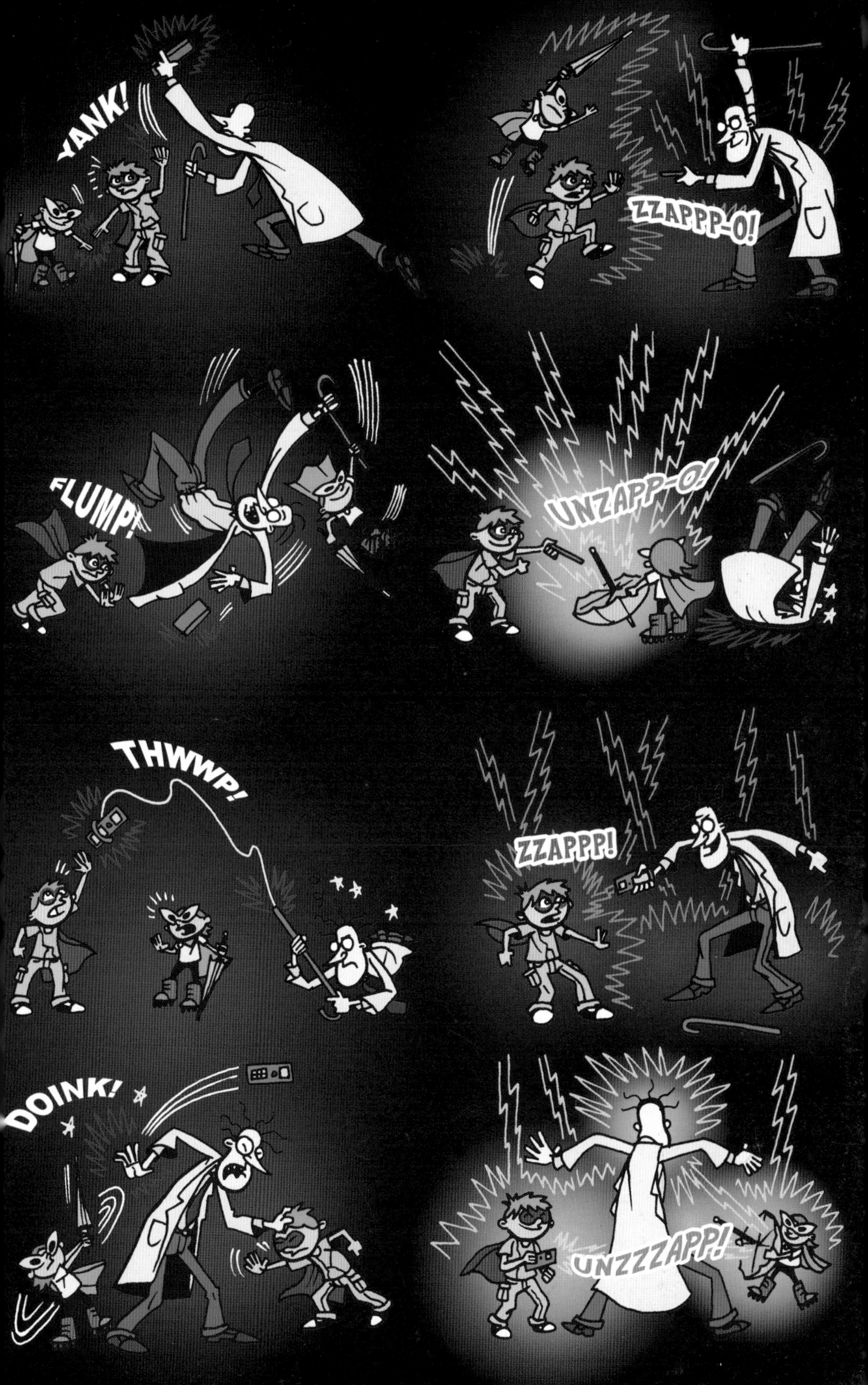
YANK!
ZZAPPP-O!
FLUMP!
UNZAPP-O!
THWWP!
ZZAPPP!
DOINK!
UNZZZAPP!

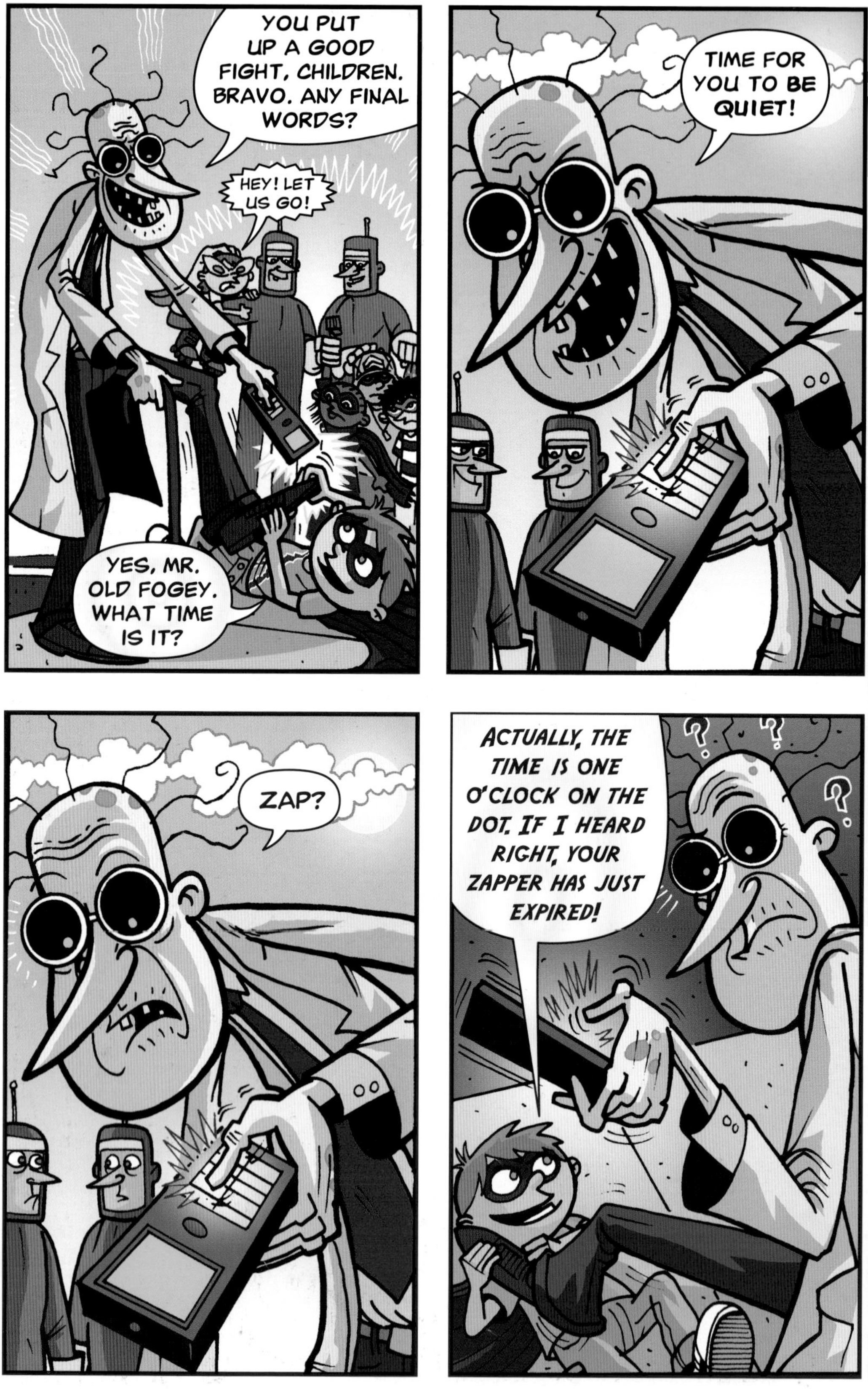
YOU PUT UP A GOOD FIGHT, CHILDREN. BRAVO. ANY FINAL WORDS?
HEY! LET US GO!
YES, MR. OLD FOGEY. WHAT TIME IS IT?
TIME FOR YOU TO BE QUIET!
ZAP?
ACTUALLY, THE TIME IS ONE O'CLOCK ON THE DOT. IF I HEARD RIGHT, YOUR ZAPPER HAS JUST EXPIRED!

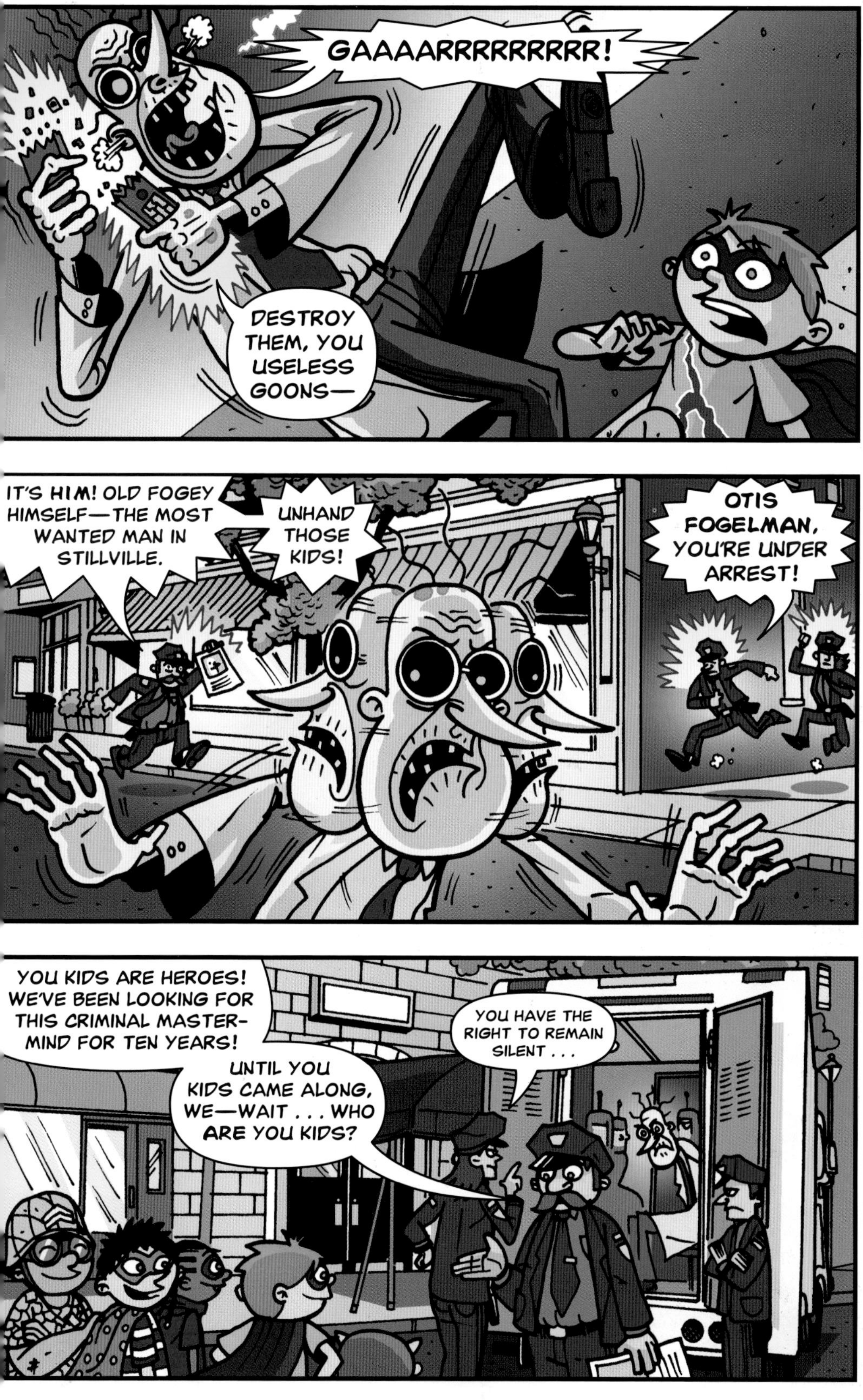
GAAAARRRRRRRR!
DESTROY THEM, YOU USELESS GOONS—
IT'S HIM! OLD FOGEY HIMSELF—THE MOST WANTED MAN IN STILLVILLE.
UNHAND THOSE KIDS!
OTIS FOGELMAN, YOU'RE UNDER ARREST!
YOU KIDS ARE HEROES! WE'VE BEEN LOOKING FOR THIS CRIMINAL MASTER-MIND FOR TEN YEARS!
UNTIL YOU KIDS CAME ALONG, WE—WAIT . . . WHO ARE YOU KIDS?
YOU HAVE THE RIGHT TO REMAIN SILENT . . .

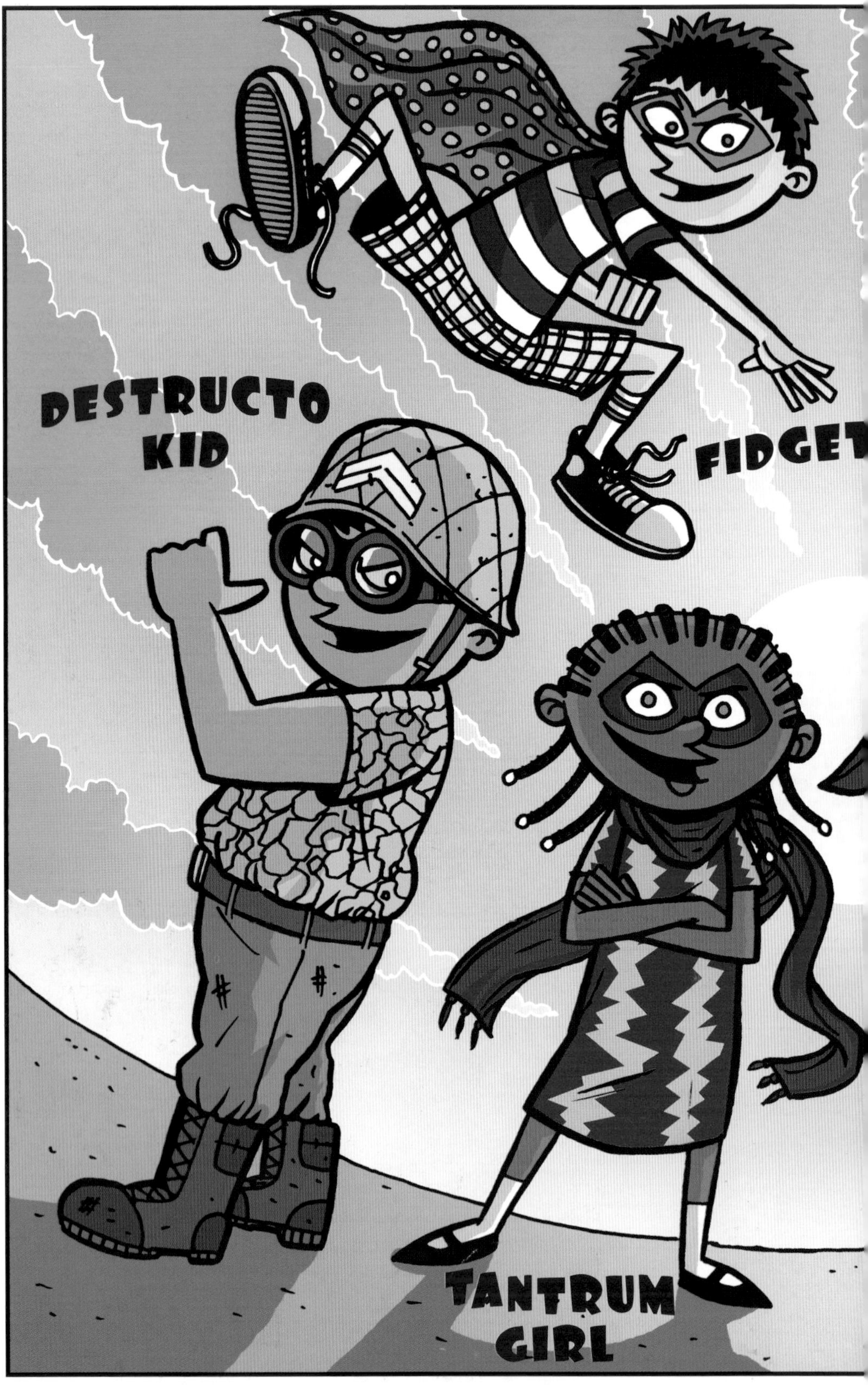
DESTRUCTO KID
FIDGET
TANTRUM GIRL

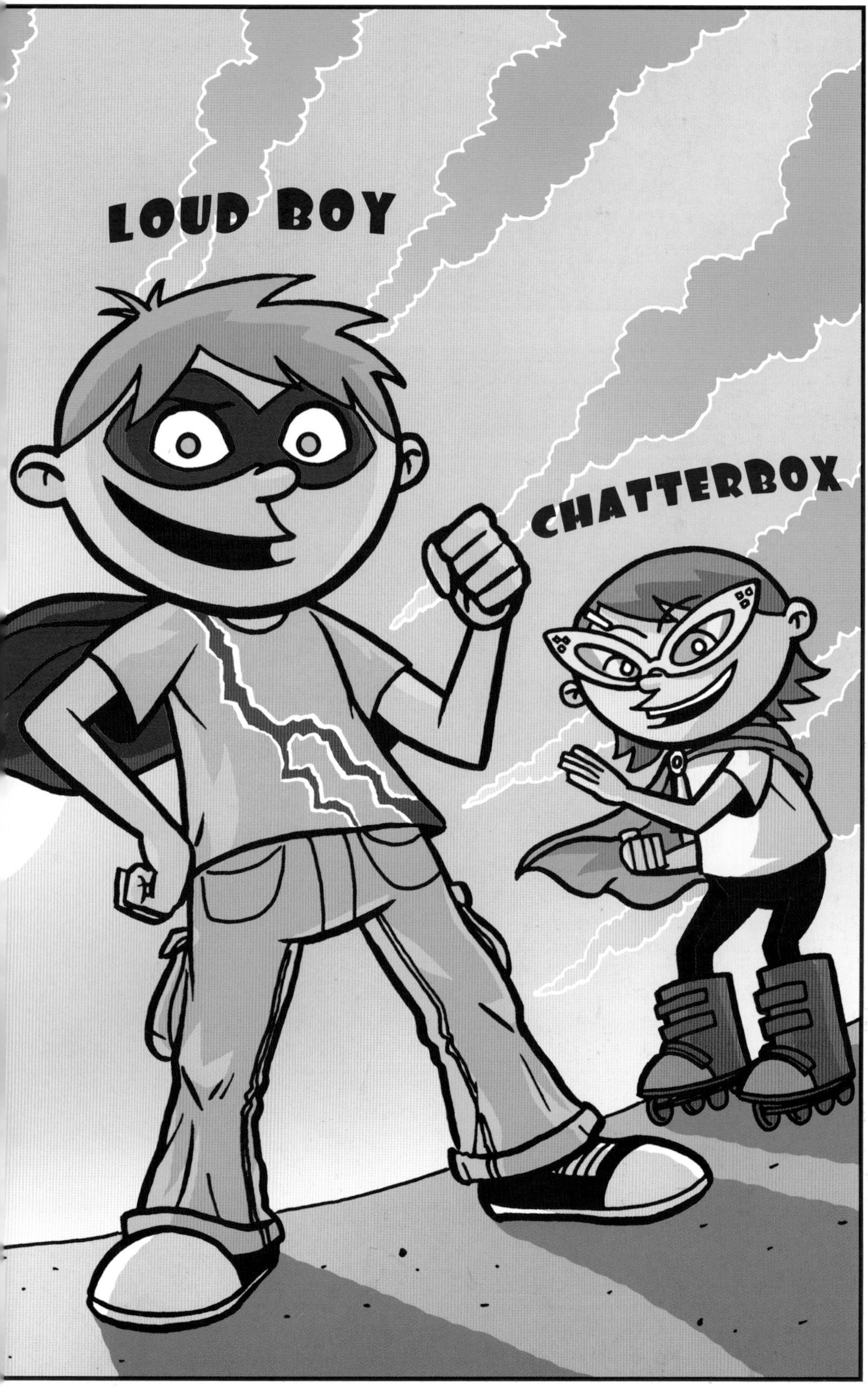
LOUD BOY
CHATTERBOX

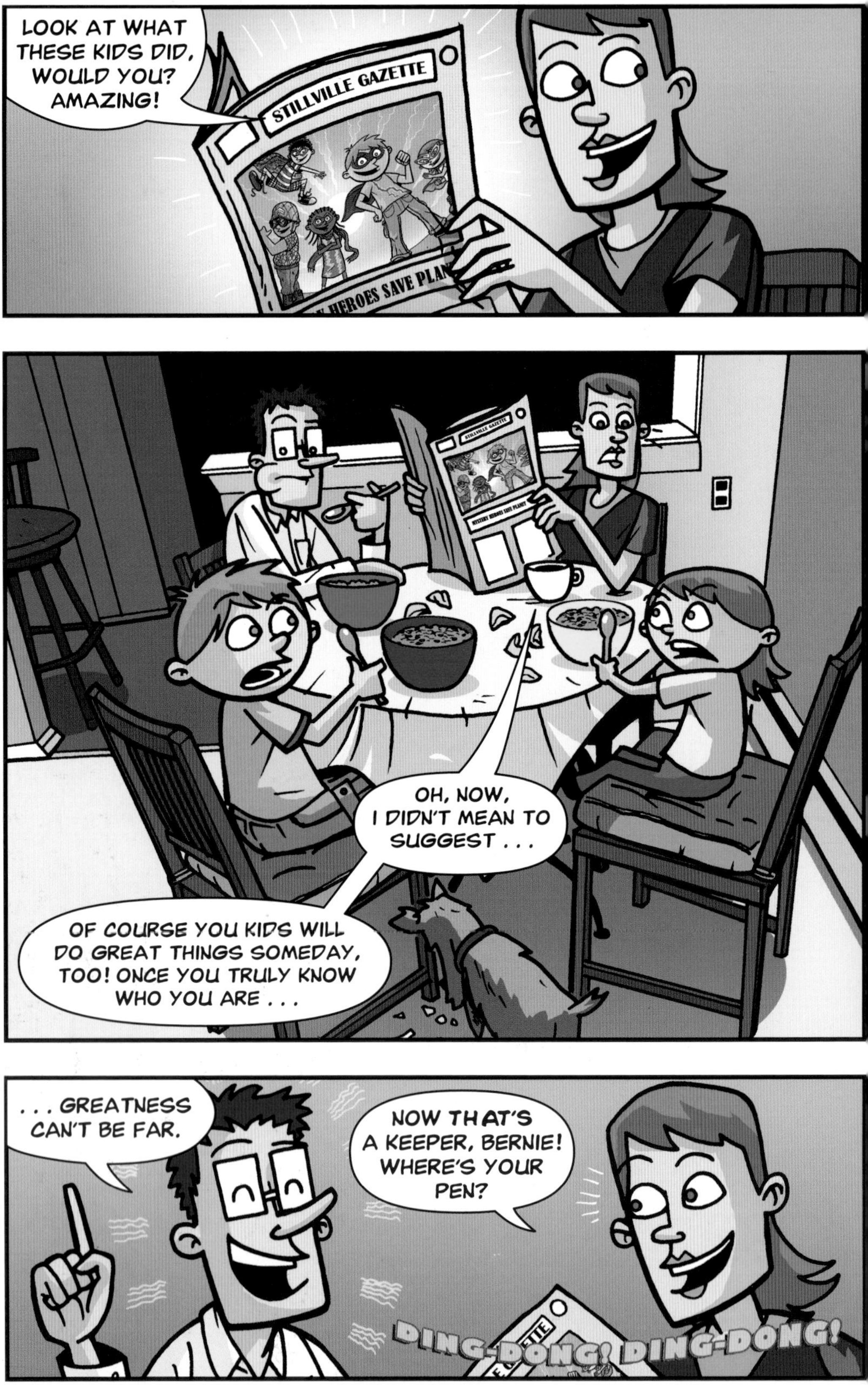
LOOK AT WHAT THESE KIDS DID, WOULD YOU? AMAZING!
STILLVILLE GAZETTE
OH, NOW, I DIDN'T MEAN TO SUGGEST . . .
OF COURSE YOU KIDS WILL DO GREAT THINGS SOMEDAY, TOO! ONCE YOU TRULY KNOW WHO YOU ARE . . .
. . . GREATNESS CAN'T BE FAR.
NOW THAT'S A KEEPER, BERNIE! WHERE'S YOUR PEN?
DING-DONG! DING-DONG!

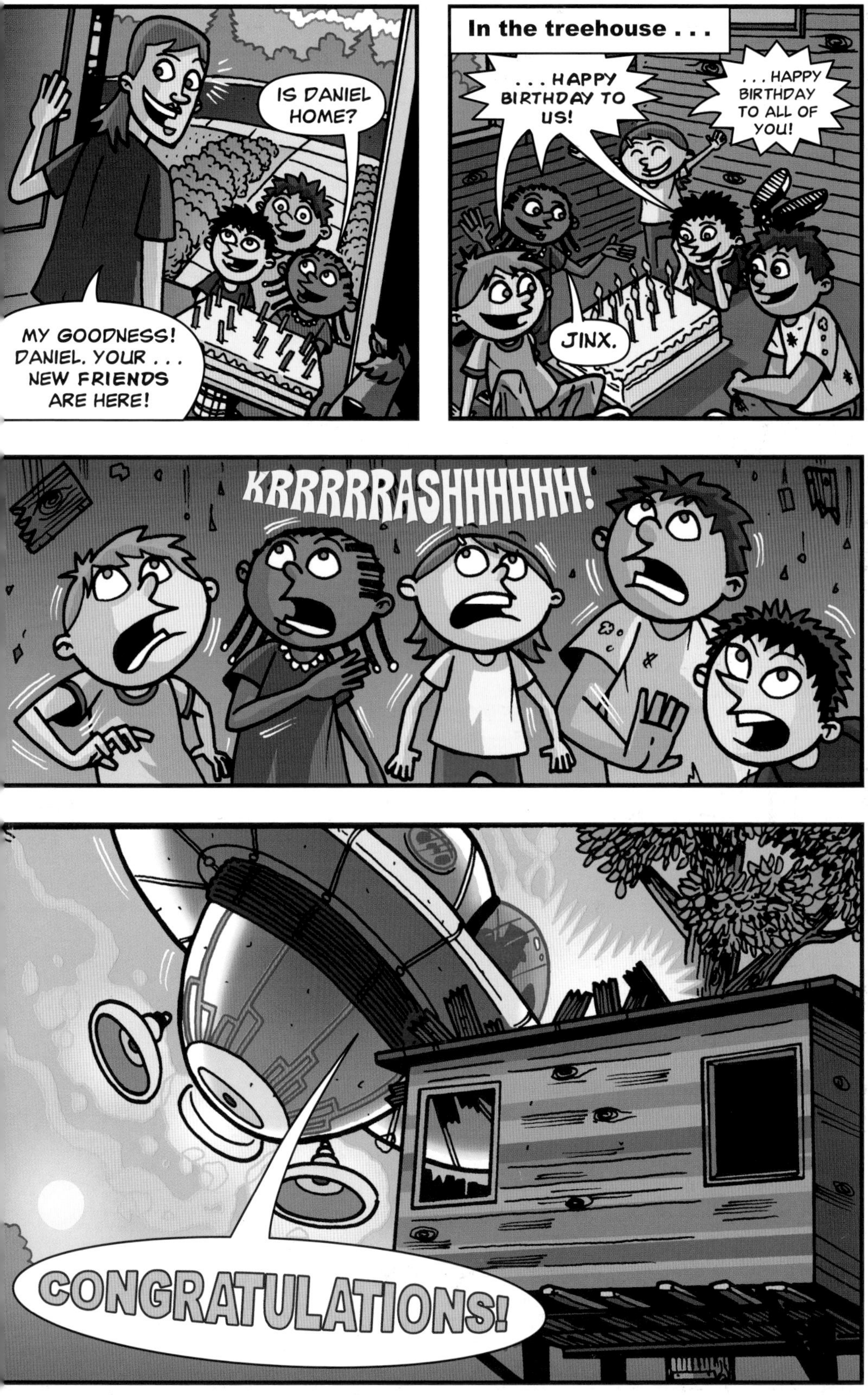
IS DANIEL HOME?
MY GOODNESS! DANIEL, YOUR . . . NEW FRIENDS ARE HERE!
In the treehouse . . .
. . . HAPPY BIRTHDAY TO US!
. . . HAPPY BIRTHDAY TO ALL OF YOU!
JINX.
KRRRRRASHHHHHH!
CONGRATULATIONS!

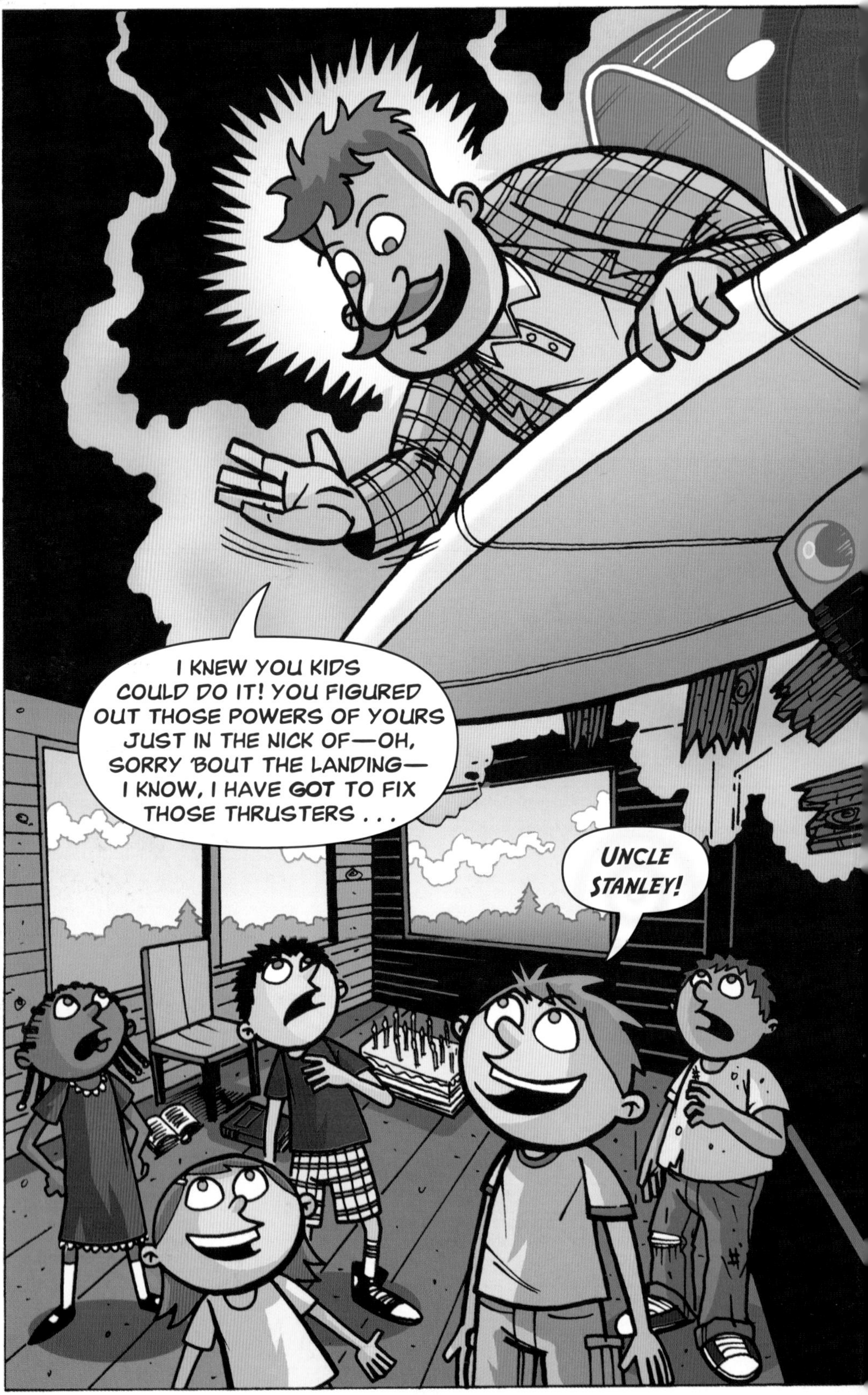
I KNEW YOU KIDS COULD DO IT! YOU FIGURED OUT THOSE POWERS OF YOURS JUST IN THE NICK OF—OH, SORRY 'BOUT THE LANDING—I KNOW, I HAVE GOT TO FIX THOSE THRUSTERS . . .
UNCLE STANLEY!

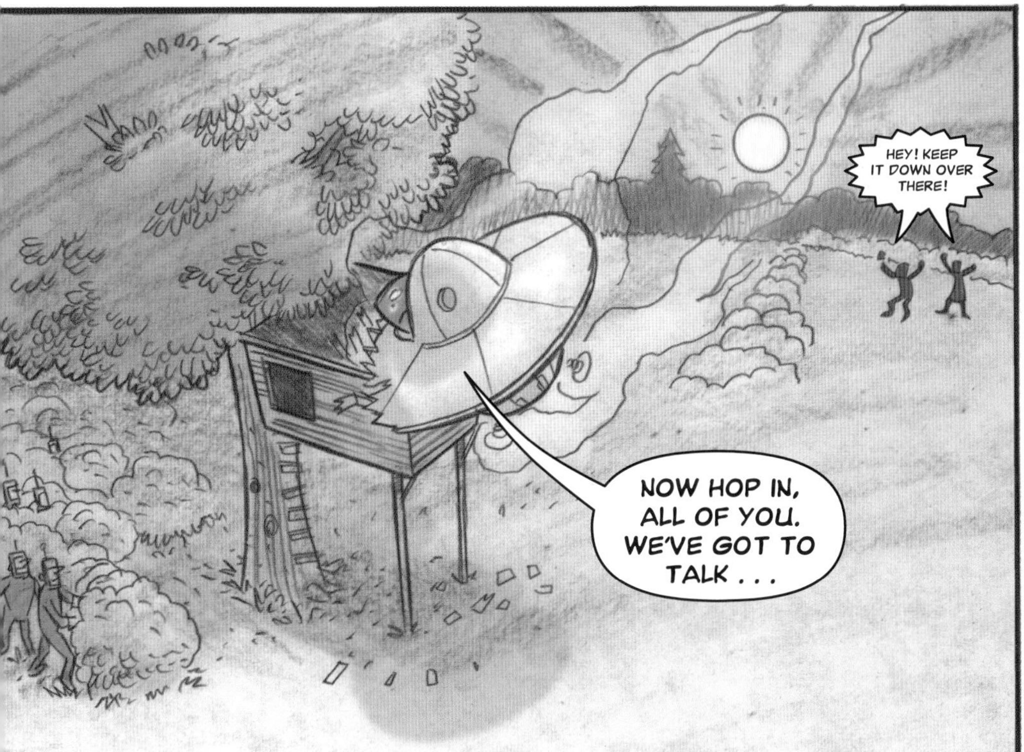
HEY! KEEP IT DOWN OVER THERE!
NOW HOP IN, ALL OF YOU. WE'VE GOT TO TALK . . .

And there you have it—the whole truth about how five everyday kids met, saved the world, and found that their biggest problems turned out to be their greatest strengths. But what you don't know is that their troubles had just begun . . . Will these kids have what it takes to fight back the crotchety forces of evil in the universe again—and still turn in their homework on time?

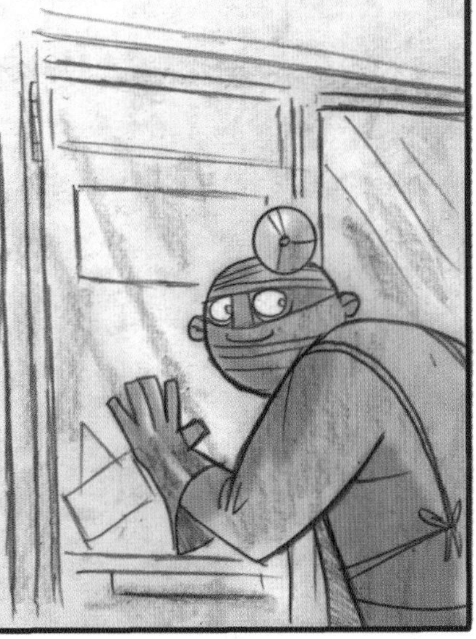

Stay tuned, my friends, stay tuned . . .

—TO BE CONTINUED—

THE ADVENTURES OF
DANIEL BOOM
AKA LOUD BOY

#2
MAC ATTACK!

Old Fogey may be behind bars, but evil Kid-Rid Industries has yet another sinister scheme in the works. And this time, they're teaming up with a new villain who's a little too close for comfort—Stillville Elementary's kid-hating lunch lady. Their unappetizing plot? To add a secret ingredient in the mac and cheese that brainwashes kids into having perfect manners. It's up to Loud Boy and the misfit superkids to save the world again! Because what would it be like if kids were polite all the time? BO-RRRIIING!

Get ready for the next action-packed adventure starring Loud Boy, Chatterbox, Fidget, Tantrum Girl, and Destructo-Kid in the mouthwatering new saga . . . MAC ATTACK!